"Excellent pa[cing]... [not] to be missed by any [reader]..., the dialogue, the characters and their interaction with each other and the wolves all flowed together to make a wonderful read!!!"
- *Reviewed by Gloria, Best Reviews: All Rights Reserved*

Four Stars! "Plenty of explicit sex, mystery, and a unique plot combine for a steamy love story."
- *Kelly Rae Cooper, Romantic Times Book Club*

"A wolf worth waiting for...TANEIKA is a story you won't want to miss."
- *Flora Bell, Paranormal Romance Review*

Mr. Casteel slips some wry humor in the book, which was a welcome change of pace. I look forward to reading more from Mr. Casteel."
- *Robin Taylor, In The Library Reviews*

Ellora's Cave

Discover for yourself why readers can't get enough of the multiple award-winning publisher Ellora's Cave. Whether you prefer e-books or paperbacks, be sure to visit EC on the web at www.ellorascave.com for an erotic reading experience that will leave you breathless.

www.ellorascave.com

TANEIKA: DAUGHTER OF THE WOLF
An Ellora's Cave Publication, May 2004

Ellora's Cave Publishing, Inc.
PO Box 787
Hudson, OH 44236-0787

ISBN #1843609339

ISBN MS Reader (LIT) ISBN # 1-84360-201-6
Other available formats (no ISBNs are assigned):
Adobe (PDF), Rocketbook (RB), Mobipocket (PRC) & HTML

Taneika: Daughter of the Wolf © 2002 R. Casteel

ALL RIGHTS RESERVED. This book may not be reproduced in whole or in part without permission.

This book is a work of fiction and any resemblance to persons, living or dead, or places, events or locales is purely coincidental. They are productions of the authors' imagination and used fictitiously.

Edited by Martha Punches
Cover art by Darrell King

Taneika:
Daughter of the Wolf

R. Casteel

Dedication:

I would like to express my deepest appreciation to some wonderful people for their encouragement and support while creating Taneika: Daughter of the Wolf.

First and foremost is my wife for her willingness to put up with my passion for writing, the long hours spent on the computer and my forgetfulness to take out the trash when my mind and thoughts are absorbed in a story.

To Carol Farrell, who from the start has been an encouragement and believed in my writing. You saw the dim flickering candle of an ability I never knew I possessed.

Where would an author be without someone to point out the missing commas, incorrect words and the frequent sentences left dangling in air like the last rays of the sun before it disappears from view? A very special thanks to my critique partners, Laura Shinn and Nancy Ebinger for their invaluable assistance and comments.

To Scott Carpenter of Carpenter Design, www.carpenterdesign.envy.nu for the excellent artwork on the digital cover.

To my friend and fellow writer, Cindy and the wonderful group of people I met through her. Your encouragement to try something new, to broaden my writing into the paranormal, planted the seed; your friendship was the water that nourished it and caused it to grow.

Prologue

High in the Rocky Mountains, the fresh prints in the new-fallen snow showed the way. The hunter bent a knee to the ground and studied them. They were the same.

He was still on the trail of the killer, a rogue, driven by hunger out of the hills. Remembering the carnage left behind, he stood and pressed on. Topping a ridge, he pulled the high-powered glasses from his bag and searched the other side of the ravine. Movement caught his eye, black fur going behind the large boulder halfway up the slope. Careful not to make any noise, he crept down the steep rocks. Directly across from the boulder where his prey had disappeared, he sat down to wait. An hour later, his patience was rewarded. He slowly drew the rifle to his shoulder. Finding his target in the crosshairs of his scope, he fired.

The wolf lay partially hidden within the rocks, unmoving, silent. The hunter studied the great beast with a heavy heart. He did not enjoy the killing although it was necessary. The wolf had gorged itself from his herd of sheep until it dragged off one of the small lambs. Only severe hunger would have driven the wolf to the valley. They were smart, calculating and cunning creatures, knowing well the dangers that awaited them from the ranchers.

Reaching the downed wolf, he started to drag it from the den when he froze.

Seeing the wolf was a bitch, the sound of pups didn't surprise him. The whimper coming from the den wasn't from a wolf pup. He pulled the dead animal from the entrance of her den and flashed a light from his pack into the darkness. There were two pups curled up in the back of the den, their eyes shining green in the light. A pup moved and he saw the cream-colored skin of a human foot. He was so startled that he hit his head on the roof of the den. A face soon joined the foot, eyes black as coal stared back at him, soft black hair covered the head. He backed out of the den and sat looking at the dead wolf and back to the den. Hoping that whatever he had seen was just his imagination, he stuck his head back inside the den. The wolf pups had gone back to sleep, curled around the child like a living blanket.

John Swift Eagle squatted on the ground next to the dead wolf. Picking up a handful of dirt, he said a prayer for the spirit of the animal. Scattering the dirt to the four winds he finished his prayer and began removing the wolf's still-warm pelt. As he worked, he asked his spirit guide, the eagle, to watch over him and the child. His hands shook as the spirit moved over him. Swift Eagle lifted up bloody hands and cried out. Never before in all his years of searching the spirit world had he felt such as this. He finished the task before him and fashioned a crude but serviceable pouch to carry the infant home. It was a hard day's journey to the ranch at the base of the mountains. He looked at the sleeping child. In order to provide heat to keep it alive, the pups would have to be taken too. This was insane, a sheep rancher taking home not one but two wolf pups. But was there any sanity in finding a baby in a wolf den? Separating the sleeping forms, his wonder grew when he noticed that the child was a girl. Placing her inside his pouch, he placed the wolf pups with her.

Instantly they curled up, covering her as if protecting her.

Daylight was just breaking over the land when Swift Eagle opened the door. His wife, Mary Songbird, was in the kitchen preparing breakfast for the family. Her welcome smile turned to confusion as a cry of hunger emerged from the wolf pelt that he lay on the table. "John, that sounded like a baby!"

"It is, and a hungry one. Get the bottles we use for the lambs and warm some milk."

Taneika: Daughter of the Wolf

Mary started to turn away when she stopped. John lifted first one wolf pup and then another out of the gathered skin of the wolf and set them on the table.

"John, what are...?" She was speechless as John lifted out the baby.

"Mary, the bottles and milk, please. They haven't eaten since yesterday late. Bring a blanket."

Returning with the bottles and a blanket, she set the milk on to heat and took the baby from his arms. "Where did you find her?"

"In the wolf den." John tested the milk and filled three bottles. Attaching the nipples, he handed one to Mary and gave the pups the other two. Within moments the only sound from the kitchen was the slurping sound of contented sucking. "What are we going to do with her?" Mary asked.

John looked from his wife's face to the baby and then to the pups. This was going to change their lives, his spirit guide had showed him that much. "We keep her."

"We what!" Her cry startled the baby and she started crying. As Mary soothed the child, she berated her husband. "We don't know anything about this baby. You just can't go around claiming babies as your own to raise. What about the mother? The tribal police will have to be notified."

"I agree. You take care of her while I go and talk with the authorities."

Several days later, John Swift Eagle stood before the tribal council waiting for their judgment. They had been in a closed session for the past two days, ever since he had related and retold the story of finding the child. Now, they waited. Mary sat in the corner feeding the baby. John knew that she had become attached to the child in the short time they had had her. Although she had delivered two strong sons, she had always wanted a daughter.

The council returned and John stood before them. Chief He Who Stands Tall spoke for the council. "We have decided that the things which have been spoken here shall not be revealed outside the council. This that you speak of is a matter of the spirit world and we cannot interfere. The world will not understand these things. You, Swift Eagle and Songbird, are the chosen ones to care for and protect the life of this girl-child. Have you chosen a name?"

John looked at the beaming face of his wife. "We have named her Taneika." The chief looked at the other council members and nodded. "You have chosen wisely, Swift Eagle. *Itano'mahkapi'si*, Daughter of the Wolf, will be known as Taneika."

Chapter 1
October 1999
Yellowstone National Park

Taneika stroked the head of the wolf sitting beside her. Finding a place allowing pets was easy. Finding one that would allow a full-grown wolf was another.

She had finally found this place, thirty miles from the college in Cody, Wyoming, and had immediately fallen in love with it. There was room for Lobo and her to run with the wind. The game was plentiful and Lobo was an excellent hunter. An offspring of the female she had grown up with, Lobo was a link to a past she didn't understand, a link her parents, John and Mary Swift Eagle, wouldn't explain. The fact she was adopted was never in question. One look and the differences between them were obvious. She wasn't sure where she came from but there was no Blackfoot blood flowing in her veins.

As a child, she had been an outcast, even among the Southern Peigan tribe. Her ability to control the mighty pair of wolves always by her side amazed people while at the same time made them leery around her.

Lobo whined and looked up.

"You hungry, girl?" she asked. "So am I." Taneika opened the door and Lobo bounded into the night. Turning out the light, she followed Lobo's scent across the field.

Reaching the cover of the trees, she stripped off her clothes. If she were spotted returning with them, torn and ruined, it would raise questions impossible for her to answer.

A howl split the night and the chase was on.

Acting on an instinct from within, she turned to the left as her feet carried her swiftly across the forest floor. A yearling doe appeared to her right, blindly running from death following at her heels. Taneika turned and sprang, her weight taking the deer to the ground.

Lobo closed in, her fangs finding the jugular vein, sending a spray of hot blood into the air. Within minutes, the skin was ripped open and they shared the kill. Taneika sat back, blood covering her face, arms and breasts. Lobo came to her and lay down with her massive head nestled between Taneika's thighs. "Good girl," Taneika said. "Let's go down to the lake and clean up."

Lobo jumped to her feet and headed deeper into the woods. She stopped and turned her head back, whimpered then yelped.

"I'm coming. You go ahead and make sure it's safe."

Lobo disappeared through the trees. Taneika, satisfied from her feast, moved cautiously towards the lake. Even though it was night, she was taking no chances. She heard Lobo's short howl and knew the area was free of other people. Coming to the water's edge, she waded in and washed away the blood. Lobo splashed along the shore, sending water droplets several feet into the air. Taneika swam a few yards out which set Lobo into a frenzy of growls and barks. "I'm fine, Lobo. I promise I won't go far. Soon as I come in we can go home."

Lobo lay down and waited.

* * * * *

Taren Carpenter sat on the back porch of his cottage, waiting. An hour ago, while doing some reports due on his boss's desk in the morning, he had seen his neighbor and her pet wolf slip out of the house and disappear into the night.

She was a quiet girl, friendly, yet reserved. Her relationship with the wolf intrigued him. They were, as far as he could tell, inseparable.

Taren thought back to the day he had spoken to her. She had been in the backyard playing with the wolf. At first, he thought she was being attacked and had rushed over to save her. He ended up being the one needing saving. The beast turned, snarling with teeth bared, and charged at him.

"Down," she commanded. The wolf stopped the attack in mid-jump and turned away.

"In the future, you might consider not running towards us like you did. I assure you, I am quite unharmed. We were just playing."

She got off the ground and extended her hand. "I'm Taneika, and this is Lobo." Lobo sat and raised a paw.

Taren shook her hand and, still a bit shaken from the near brush with the wolf's fangs, shook the wolf's paw.

"Now that she knows you, you shouldn't have any problem."

"I'm Taren. I'm sorry, but from where I stood, it looked like she was attacking you." She was a beautiful girl with long black hair, her eyes a deep dark chocolate. The dark tan indicated many hours spent in the sun.

Taneika was a woman with kissable lips.

"We have always played rough." She laughed. "Mother used to get so upset with us, especially when my clothes would get ripped."

His musings were interrupted, when a movement caught his eye. Taneika and Lobo stepped out of the shadows. Lobo growled, low and menacing.

"Good evening, Taren." She heard his chuckle. "Let me guess...Lobo told you I was out here?"

"Yes." His easy laughter sent a flash of warmth to her face. She bent down and petted Lobo, shielding the blush from his searching eyes.

"You and Lobo are quite a team. I don't think I have ever seen a wolf respond to a human as she does to you. What's your secret?" Taren stood and stepped to the porch railing.

"She grew up with me. As long as I can remember, there has been a wolf by my side. I had two when I was small. The male found some poison set out by ranchers and Lobo's mother died a couple of years ago."

Taneika stood just below him. Her hair was damp, as if she had just been swimming. The thought was ridiculous; the water in the lake was fed from the mountains. This time of year it was cold, damn near freezing.

"I have class in the morning and it's late. Goodnight, Taren."

"'Night, Taneika." He stood watching as she walked away. She had been gone for two hours, in the woods with no flashlight and she looked fresh. Clean clothes, neat, no tears, snags or any evidence to show where she had been. He was missing something.

Shoes...she wasn't wearing any. No, that wasn't it. It was everything combined causing his curious nature to perk up and notice. With a body like hers, he was envious of the wolf.

The next morning, Taren watched as Lobo headed for the woods and Taneika drove away. Following the wolf in the general direction she had gone, he crept cautiously through the woods. Making sure to stay downwind, he spotted Lobo at the carcass of a small deer. If he didn't know better he would swear this was a wild wolf. He waited, unwilling to chance the animal's reaction without Taneika to control her.

Lobo ate and ran into the woods.

Approaching the dead deer, Taren studied the ground around it, unwilling to believe his first thoughts. He bent down on one knee. Wolf prints and human, each superimposed over one another. They'd both been here, and at the same time.

Studying the flesh of the deer, his mind reeled in shock. "What the hell?" Taking his pocketknife out, he cut away a portion of the meat. "Son-of-a-bitch." He didn't need a lab report to identify these teeth marks.

Still reeling in shock, he made his way home. The scene from the woods was imprinted like a branding iron on his mind. He had the evidence in his pocket, but logic told him it couldn't be. Placing the chunk of venison on the table, he examined it again. Logic be damned. He was staring at the fact, the actuality, that those bite marks were human!

The ringing of the phone finally caught his attention.

"Hello."

"You had better have a damn good excuse for not having that report on my desk this morning."

Taren looked at the time and groaned.

"I need the report for a meeting this morning, and I would have liked to at least looked at it beforehand and discussed any questions with you."

"I'm leaving right now. I, ah, got tied up this morning and wasn't watching the time," Taren explained. "Sorry."

"Well, move your sorry ass. I'm waiting."

Taren hung up the phone and put the venison in the fridge. He didn't like having his butt chewed before he had breakfast and this could get him out of hot water.

But he was reluctant to report this just yet. Grabbing the report from his desk, he ran to his truck and headed to the park's main office.

Harold Fallings was waiting somewhat impatiently at the door when Taren walked in. The glare he received indicated the chewing he had over the phone wasn't finished.

"Of all the damn times to be late, you would have to pick today. With the brass from Washington here and the budget for next year in question, this report is crucial. Tell me, what was so important this morning you couldn't get this to me earlier?"

"I found a dead deer and was checking it out," Taren stated.

"Poachers?"

"No," he paused. "Wolves."

"You almost blow this meeting over a damn wolf kill. Shit!" Taren watched his boss head to his office.

"Get your ass in here. If I have any questions, I don't have time to chase you down."

Taren sat in the plush leather chair, confident there would be no questions. This was just Harold's way of reminding him who was who in the office. As if he needed any. Harold was a royal pain. The stress level in the office was always hovering around the boiling point. Thanks to his being late, it had boiled over. Now was not the time to mention his discovery. He found it and he would check it out. Maybe there was a plausible explanation.

"Taren?"

Any normal person ate raw meat. What could be so weird about that?

"Taren! Quit your damn daydreaming and get the hell out of here. We're not paying you to sit on your ass all day."

He walked out the door and felt like slamming it. He would have, except Harold was right behind him on his way to the luncheon meeting with the brass.

Checking his schedule, he noticed he had to be in court after lunch. A suspect had been caught spotlighting and shooting deer out of season. So, what was Taneika, suspect or accomplice?

Taneika: Daughter of the Wolf

* * * * *

Pulling into his driveway, he saw the object of his thoughts in her backyard. She was wearing a halter-top and shorts that rode high on the cheeks of a very well-shaped ass. The muscles in her arms flexed as she pulled the recurve bow and sent an arrow into a target with deadly accuracy. October in Montana was coat weather, and yet there she stood, placing arrow after arrow into a target without a sign of discomfort.

As good as she was with a bow, she could very easily have the top spot on the college archery team. He had seen her running with the wolf and knew she was fast, yet according to his friend on staff, she wasn't signed up for any of their athletic programs. In a day already filled with sudden turns, his friend had given him another. Taneika Swift Eagle was listed as a Native American from the Blackfoot Nation. The old adage of things aren't always as they seem could have been coined for Taneika.

Taren got out and slowly crossed the yard. He didn't want a repeat of his last encounter with Lobo. The closer he got, the better she looked. Tan lines were absent from what he could see, which was plenty. Somehow, she didn't seem like a thong panty type of woman, which meant she wasn't wearing anything under those worn cutoffs. He could already feel the heat building deep inside. She was a walking, talking, come-to-life Playboy centerfold.

Lobo sat, watching, vigilant as he drew closer.

"Don't worry. She remembers you." Another arrow flew and found the center of the target. "You shoot?" Without waiting for a reply, she fitted another arrow and drew back the bowstring. Only then did she turn her head and flash him a smile. The bow never shook, the arrow pointing toward the target some forty yards away never wavered. Almost as soon as she looked back to the target, the arrow was in flight.

"Where did you learn to shoot?"

"My father taught me. I spent so many hours in the woods he said if I wasn't going to learn the ways of a woman, I should at least provide food for the table. At first my brothers laughed at me, until I started bringing home more food than they did."

"May I?" Taren took the bow and ran his hand over the smooth polished grain of the wood. "This is a beautiful bow." He looked for the manufacture's name. "What brand is it?"

"Brand?"

"Who made it? I don't see any markings on it."

She laughed, the sound sending warmth through him, diverting his attention from the bow to her.

"I made it."

He heard the pride in her voice.

"I'm impressed." *What would you do if I kissed you?* "You have any other hidden talents?"

The change was almost imperceptible, but it was there. The smile thinned, the eyes became veiled as if she were afraid he could see inside her soul.

"No, none you would be interested in." Reaching for the bow, she called to Lobo. "Sorry, I was just going in. Nice to see you again."

Taren stood watching as they walked away. Her movements were fluid and graceful, matching the stride of the wolf. Or was the wolf matching hers? The picture of the two running after a fleeting deer came to his mind. For some reason it didn't seem as absurd as it had this morning. Funny what a few hours had done to change his way of thinking. The decision not to tell the department supervisor felt good for the first time.

But there was still his job to consider. He couldn't have her killing animals out of season and a bow was a silent killer. If only there had been enough left of the yearling to find the entry of her arrow. Taren turned and walked slowly to his porch.

*****

What was Taren doing and why? She was used to the curious stares on the reservation, the whispers behind her back. Being able to hear them only made them worse, the taunts and snickers of her never finding a man if she didn't know how to be a woman. Maybe she's deformed, a boy without a penis. The boys resented her skills in the woods, her bow and her wolves. Taren's friendship, although enjoyed, would turn out like so many others, shattered on the rocks of cruelty.

She watched as Taren entered his back door. Being attracted to him caused conflicting emotions to spring up from within. Taren was several inches taller than her own five-foot-seven inches. Working so much outdoors had given him a tan almost as dark as her own, giving rise to the speculation of how much of his lean body was golden brown.

He was curious of Lobo, as were others, but she sensed it went deeper. It was a feeling of acceptance, respect. What his feelings for her were, she couldn't tell. Just once, she would like to be accepted for herself, not having to hide the little things that caused her to be an outcast, a freak, even among the people she grew up with.

Lobo came and nuzzled her hand and she turned away from the window. "Sorry, girl. I won't be running with you tonight. You go and have fun."

Taneika was engrossed in her biology book when she heard the scratching at the door; Lobo's announcement she was back.

Lobo sat at the door, a chunk of venison clamped within her teeth.

"What is it, girl?" She smelled the venison and her mouth started to water. "You brought this back for me, did you?" Taking the offered meat from Lobo, Taneika was startled when the wolf started growling and barking.

Looking at the meat more closely, she noticed it had been cut. The smooth edges were a clear warning someone had found last night's meal. "Do you know who it was?"

Lobo's short yelp sent her heart into despair and troubled her mind. "Are you sure?"

Lobo whined, then turned and left the house.

"Lobo, I'm sorry. I didn't mean it that way. Of course I believed you the first time." She picked up the meat and began pacing the floor. What did this mean? Is this what Taren had been referring to earlier when he'd questioned her about hidden talents? Did he know, or just suspect? Unable to resist the aroma, she bit off a piece of meat and began chewing. The sensation was almost intimate, knowing he had handled the meat she was eating.

Once the meat was gone, she went into the bathroom and stripped off her clothes. Troubled over the realization that Taren had found their kill and her thoughts on the complications this could cause in her life, she forgot to close the blinds.

He sat at the window, nursing a double scotch and watching the night. In the graying twilight, he had seen the wolf return and then leave again. Would she leave too, following Lobo into the woods? If she did, what should he do?

A light came on and his eyes turned automatically to the window. He felt like a Peeping Tom as she removed her clothes. Her breasts were full, her waist slim. Just as he'd imagined, there were no tan lines. Knowing he should turn away and being unable to do so, he felt himself grow hard as she slipped the cutoffs down her legs. Expecting to see a mound covered in a thatch of black hair between her legs, he drew in a ragged breath when smooth skin was revealed.

Taneika, the essence of his passionate dreams and exotic fantasies, stepped into the shower and pulled the curtain. Taren moved away from the window and headed for a shower of his own. The cold water did little to chill his heated blood as it coursed its way through his body.

Taneika: Daughter of the Wolf

* * * * *

Taren sat at his desk, looking at the tickets for the conservation banquet held at the park each fall. This was a political dinner with a dance afterward. Senators, Representatives and the Governor would be the featured guests. He stared at the note from the park superintendent for the tenth time.

"No excuses this year. *Be There.*"

"Damn." He slammed his fist on the table. Not only was he being ordered to go, the second ticket meant he was supposed to bring a date. Going over the eligible women in the office, he cringed. The list wasn't very promising. A vision of Taneika stepping into the shower swam before his eyes.

"Taren!" The radio dispatcher yelled. "We have an emergency at the lake. A woman being chased by a wolf was spotted in the water at Willow Cove. When the fishermen approached, the woman ran into the woods with the wolf right on her heels. You are the only person available. Go check it out and report back."

He grabbed his jacket and ran out the door. Trying to explain this to the dispatcher without having gone through the motions of checking on the report would only render him another ass chewing. Picking up the handheld, he keyed the mike. "Five-two-three en route to Willow Cove."

Unlocking the gate, he drove down the overgrown path. This area of the park was a wildlife refuge. It was left as natural as possible while still giving access to hikers and seasoned bike riders. The only motorized vehicles allowed were those driven by park employees with prior authorization. Taren sighed; it was great to get out of the office.

When he finished making a cursory inspection of Willow Cove, he would stop by Taneika's place and have a chat with her. There was no doubt in his mind it was Taneika and Lobo the fishermen had seen at the cove.

Keying the radio mike, he checked in. "Five-two-three...Base, arrived at Willow Cove."

"Ten-four, Five-two-three, keep advised."

Taren stepped through the trees and spotted the fishermen.

"Officer, she was right over here when we seen her. She ran out of the water and I swear she was buck-ass naked. Took off right through those trees and the damn wolf was right on her heels. Damnedest thing I ever saw. She's probably dead by now. Real shame too, a nice piece getting chewed up by a wolf."

Taren took their names. "Thanks, I may need to get back with you and get a written statement." He squatted down and dipped his hand in the water, his eyes going to the footprints in the sand. Just the thought of her running naked on this secluded beach heated his blood.

Returning to his truck, he headed back the way he had come. "Five-two-three to Base, I have met with the fishermen. I didn't find anyone else around, suspect it was a biker with a large dog."

"Ten-four, Five-two-three. Are you returning to station?"

"Negative, I will be ten-seven at my residence."

"Ten-four, have a good night."

Taren knocked on the door and Lobo greeted him with a fierce growl from the other side. A curtain moved and he smiled. The door opened and he was almost knocked down by a blur of gray and white.

Soft laughter floated like jasmine on a spring breeze from the door.

"Sorry, Lobo was a little upset with me. I came in sooner than she wanted to. Sometimes she still acts like a pup instead of an adult."

"The reason you came in early wouldn't be because of a couple of fishermen at Willow Cove, would it?"

Her face turned red and she looked away.

"How...how did you find out?" She composed herself and turned back to Taren.

"They reported you were being attacked by a wolf," Taren grinned. "I suspected you had been swimming the other night but I couldn't bring myself to believe anyone would jump willingly into the frigid water this time of year."

"I don't normally swim in the daytime but I got home early and Lobo wanted to run. We ended up at the cove and I couldn't resist. As to the water temperature, it's difficult to explain. I don't feel the cold, never have. I'm sorry if I caused any trouble."

"It's no problem. The next time you decide to swim in the daytime, maybe you ought to wear a suit of some kind. I'm sure it's one fishing trip those two will remember the rest of their lives."

Taneika felt the heat flush her face. She knew she was beet red. "I will try to remember. What are you going to report to your boss?"

"The fishermen must have seen a biker with a large dog."

"Thank you, I owe you one."

Seeing his opening, he jumped in with both feet. "Well...you can repay me by going to the banquet and dance at the park's Eagle Pavilion on Saturday night."

She felt like a rabbit must feel when cornered by Lobo. "You want me to go with you. Why?"

"I have to go and it was *strongly* suggested I bring a date."

"It still doesn't answer my question. Why me?"

He felt like he was sinking. "Because you are the only woman I would want to go with. If you don't go with me, then I will go by myself."

Taneika had a sixth sense about animals, sometimes towards humans as well. It was telling her he was telling the truth. He would rather incur the displeasure of his boss than take anyone else. There was just one problem.

"I have heard about the banquet. It's a formal affair. I don't have anything fancy to wear. I'm truly sorry." She saw the disappointment in his face. "Unless you count a Blackfoot ceremonial dress adequate."

"May I see it, please?"

"Come in and I will get it."

Taren stood breathless at the beauty of the white gown. Only in pictures or museums had he ever seen anything so intricately made. The doeskin was soft as silk. The stitching was so tiny it was almost invisible. The beading and artwork was of the highest quality he had ever seen.

"My mother made this for me. I was the daughter she could never have and she treated me like her own."

"Taneika, I would be honored to have you wear this to the banquet."

The little voice inside said his words were true; her doubt came from years of conditioning. "I was just kidding. This would look tacky alongside the evening gowns, the diamonds and pearls."

"No it wouldn't. What better way to display the need to preserve the future of our land than to be reminded of our past? Your people were here first and should, by this fact alone, have a say in how it should be kept. You will be the queen of the ball."

"The laughing stock and a punch line for poor Indian jokes is more like it."

"Don't let the cruelty of the past ruin your future, Taneika."

"What would you know of cruelty and ridicule?"

"My great-grandmother was a full-blooded Pawnee. I grew up playing on the old ruins of Pawnee Rock outside of Great Bend, Kansas."

"All right, I'll go."

"Thank you, Taneika. I will pick you up at seven on Saturday."

Closing the door, she wondered what she had gotten herself into.

* * * * *

Taren sat in the same chair, watching the same balding head. This was becoming a habit he would love to break. Harold raised his beady eyes. His face scrunched to the point where his bushy eyebrows were touching. With the pen he held, he tapped out a rhythm that sounded like a death march.

"This is bullshit."

Harold slammed the pen on the desk and held his report up.

"Pure bullshit. I know those fishermen. They know the difference between a wolf and damn dog. I want to know what the hell you did out there. Did you even look? If some hiker finds the remains of a woman, this department is going to look damn incompetent. Do you understand me, Taren?"

"Yes, sir."

"Well, you had damn well better. 'Cause if this department is perceived as incompetent it means I'm incompetent. And if that happens, your ass will be freezing in Alaska before you can take your next piss."

"Yes, sir."

"I want some answers and I want them now."

"I talked with the young woman. She was in no danger from the wolf." Taren waited.

"How the hell do you know if she was in no danger? I suppose you talked to the wolf and it told you this."

"Well, not exactly, but sort of." His guts were tied in a knot. Not an unusual feeling when faced with Harold's displeasure.

"Taren, I am losing my patience."

"The wolf is her pet, sort of. She has had it since it was a pup."

"Owning a wolf is a violation of law, Taren."

"From what I can tell, the wolf is free to come and go. She stays with the woman of her own choice."

"You know this for a fact."

"Yes, sir." Taren felt the noose tighten around his neck.

"How long have you know about this woman and her wolf?"

Harold was a prime candidate for a heart attack. Overweight, smoked, drank too much and if the veins popping out on his forehead were any indication, he was experiencing high blood pressure as well. "A little over a month. She is a student at Cody Community College."

"A month! A whole mother-fucking month and I am just now learning about it. Anything else I should know about this before I kick your ass out of here?"

"No, sir." Taren swallowed the suggestion of what Harold could do to himself. It would be physically impossible anyway.

Chapter 2

She sat on the back porch. Not wanting to take the chance of being seen, she waited until the lights in Taren's house went out. Lobo sat beside her; she could feel the tension radiating from the wolf. "Easy, girl. Wait 'til Taren goes to bed." Lobo yelped. "Quiet. We don't want him to hear us."

The lights went out and Lobo stood. "Okay, go on. I will be there in a few minutes."

He watched, hidden from view in the dark shadows of his room, as Lobo sped across the clearing. Would Taneika follow tonight? And if she did, could he follow without being caught? Would whatever he found ruin any relationship with her? Tomorrow was Saturday.

Movement caught his eye. She moved into the night as swiftly and quietly as the wolf. Finding out more about her pushed the scales of doubt. He realized his best bet on finding her was Willow Cove.

Arriving at the cove, Taren's lungs burned as he breathed heavily. Knowing how fast Taneika could run he had pushed himself to get here before she did. Finding a hiding spot, he sat down to wait.

Taren was about to give up and go home when Lobo came into the clearing. Taneika was right behind the wolf. Neither seemed out of breath nor tired. The cloudless sky allowed the three-quarters moon to bathe the cove in a dim glow.

Taneika was naked. His mind whirled at the thought. She plunged into the water and started washing herself. The wind shifted ever so slightly. Lobo stopped running along the shore and turned toward him.

Busted, with nowhere to hide.

"Taren." She crouched down, the water covering her breasts. "I know it's you."

Slowly, he stood, wishing he had stayed at home. Silently, he damned his own curiosity and the wind for carrying his scent to the wolf.

"What are you doing here?"

"Waiting for you. I got to wondering how you could spend two hours in the woods and still look fresh. When I saw Lobo leave, I waited."

"Go home, Taren. Please."

"Where are your clothes?"

"Hidden inside the tree line, behind the house."

"Taneika, you may not believe this, but I am sorry."

She laughed. "Sorry you got caught or sorry you saw me naked?"

"Yes to the first, no to the second. And I'm sorry for invading your privacy. Taneika, you are a beautiful woman. I hope deep down you will forgive me and this won't change your mind about going tomorrow night. I have been looking forward to dancing the night away with you in my arms. If you change your mind, I will understand. Goodnight." He turned and walked away.

"Taren." He stopped and looked back.

"You're forgiven. I'll be ready by seven."

* * * * *

The soft doeskin cradled her breasts, caressing them softly, the way she thought a lover might. No one had ever been allowed close enough to be a friend, much less a lover. She had always hoped somewhere there was a man who would accept her. A man who wouldn't shy away because of the little oddities that made her different from other women.

The chime of the doorbell returned her to reality. Opening the door, she found Taren dressed in formal attire. His smile showed his eagerness for the night and his eyes were lit with joy as they slowly traveled from her head to her feet and back again.

The heat she felt in her face at his approving smile traveled downward with his eyes. It was a lover's caress. Her breasts tingled and butterflies fluttered excitedly in the hollow of her stomach. Drifting on the current of the night air came the distinct scent of a male on the prowl. This time it didn't disgust her but triggered a primal instinct with her.

She turned around and the fringe fluttered. The feathers tied into her braids twirled and danced.

"Taneika, you will be the queen of the ball. You are beautiful." *In or out of that dress.* "Shall we go?"

Taren pulled into the parking lot of the pavilion and sensed her apprehension. He placed his hand on hers and gave it a squeeze. "Relax, everything will be fine. Try to enjoy the evening."

Every eye found her. Conversations ceased and soon the only noise heard came from the kitchen and the heating system. If it wasn't for his hand somehow finding hers, she would have turned and fled into the tranquility of darkness outside. People whispered, unaware she could overhear their comments. Some of them were what she had expected while others surprised her, warming her heart.

Dozens of waiters in white waistcoats moved about the room. Within moments after being seated, one of them stood at her side.

"I will be your server this evening." He poured a glass of wine for her and then for Taren. "We are serving prime rib. How would you like yours prepared?"

"Please," Taren said. "Allow me." At her nod, he continued. "She will have hers very rare and I would like mine medium rare please."

She wasn't sure if this was a test, or if Taren accepted her preference of meat.

"Is rare all right, miss?"

The doubt in the waiter's voice caused a bubble of laughter. "Yes." Her eyes connected with Taren's and she smiled. "Very rare if you have it."

The waiter nodded, bowed slightly and left.

Taren felt a hand on his shoulder and knew the moment he had been dreading had arrived.

"Well, Carpenter," Harold said. "I'm glad to see you could finally lower your standards and grace us with your presence. I see you have even managed to bring a date this evening. A beautiful Indian Princess. Is *she* the one with the *pet* wolf, Taren?"

The way he said pet left no doubt in her mind how he felt about the wolf or her. "Lobo isn't a pet. Although she has been with me since she was born."

She felt the hostility radiating from him. The tension around the table was smothering. She pasted on what she hoped was a winning smile. "But this isn't the time or place to discuss these things. I would be happy to meet with you later and continue this discussion." She turned her attention away from Taren's boss.

"Yes, we shall." Harold's voice dripped with ice. The part of her that was one with the wolf bristled at the evil she sensed radiating from him. She felt a shiver run down her spine.

"You have a wolf? How quaint. Aren't you scared it will turn on you?" asked another woman seated at their table.

"No, I think of Lobo as a friend," Taneika said. "We have a very understanding relationship."

The loud speaker hummed and crackled. The brief ceremony before the dinner was beginning.

Fortunately, the reports of progress at the park and the speech from the Under Secretary of Interior were short. The waiters were soon busy bringing trays of food to the table. Taneika noticed as Taren made eye contact with the Under Secretary, he gave a slight nod of recognition. It happened so quick she might have imagined it.

The food arrived and the waiter placed her plate in front of her.

"The chef assured me this was the rarest cut he had. If it's not what you want, let me know."

Looking at her plate, she noticed the blood-red juice draining from the meat.

"Thank you, this will fine."

The woman who had spoken earlier looked sick. "My dear, you can't be serious. It's barely cooked."

The only person she was concerned about was Taren. He was trying to hide a smile but the light dancing in his eyes gave it away. She had an urge to shock the Washington socialite. "I was raised on the reservation." She popped a forkful of meat into her mouth and moaned in satisfaction. "Meat was always in such short supply, when we had any, we didn't wait for it to cook very long."

The woman gasped.

"Plus eating it like this saved me from receiving the animal's spirit by drinking blood." Taneika watched as she turned pale and fine layer of sweat beaded on her forehead.

"If you will excuse me," the woman said.

The men at the table started smiling and one of them laughed. It was contagious and she joined in.

Senator Kross's wife spoke. "My dear, I congratulate you on a first. No one has ever gotten to the high-and-mighty Mrs. Worthington, and believe me it has been tried. When I tell everyone else in our garden club about this, you will become legendary in Washington."

Taneika thought for a moment. "Maybe it would be best if this was our own little secret. I imagine she has suffered enough without having anything else said."

"Perhaps. I am just glad I was able to be here to see it for myself."

Mrs. Worthington didn't come back to the table and the meal was finished without further incident, for which Taneika was thankful. The small orchestra began playing and several people moved to the dance floor.

"Shall we?" Taren held out his hand.

Her heart raced with anticipation, her palms turned moist as she stood and placed her hand in his. Once she was in his arms she found a soothing magic that calmed her jitters.

"You are as graceful dancing as you are beautiful taking a midnight swim." Taren whispered in her ear.

"Thank you." She could feel his heart pounding where her breast was pressed against him. Sharp electric jolts traveled from the point of intimate contact to the very core of her being. It was suddenly very warm in the room. Her heart beat with his and the air grew heavy.

She moved like the wind blowing through the trees, swaying and turning with each note played. From the moment she'd placed her head on his shoulder, he'd felt on fire. Never had a dance been more hypnotic or sensual. They moved as one body, one spirit. The world around him disappeared. Only the soft melody remained, moving them across the floor and into a world of enchantment.

The music stopped several moments before she realized it. "Would you care for some fresh air?" His breath caressed her ear.

"Please."

He led her out onto an observation deck stretching the length of the building and stepped into the shadows. Her hopes and desires were met when Taren pulled her into his arms and his mouth covered hers. He kissed her tentatively at first, as if unsure of her reaction. The next kiss was full of passion as she opened her mouth to allow him access. The full force of the impact weakened her knees and she sagged against him. Her breath mingled with his while their tongues battled for space. The wine mixed with his unique flavor sent her head whirling. She felt like howling at the moon.

His hands locked behind her back as he held her. Taren looked into her wild eyes. Her breathing was labored and he could feel her heart raging beneath her breasts flattened tight against his chest. Never had he experienced in a single kiss anything compared to what they had just shared. He rested his head against hers for several moments. "I think we should go in. Another kiss and I might not be able to stop."

The alarm bells were going off in her head. Not because of his hardness pressed intimately against her, but because of her own reaction to it. She took a shaky breath and smelled the essence of her own desire. Brazenly she licked a drop of sweat from his face, tasted the desire and need that oozed from every pore.

"I think you're right." She wasn't sure if she could say no to anything further than a kiss or even if she wanted to.

The flow of the next dance was disturbed, much like the surface of the water when a pebble is cast into it. Their kiss on the deck continued to ripple over her. She tried to concentrate on the music and the other dancers, all to no avail. Every fleeting second of the kiss was etched permanently into her soul. Taneika held herself stiffly in his arms, afraid to get close, afraid not to and never experience it again.

Taren felt her withdrawal and blamed himself for it. Their kiss had been too soon, too sudden, and he couldn't let it happen again. At least not tonight.

"Shall we go?" She looked up at him with relief on her face.

"Yes, please."

* * * * *

Lobo was standing guard, her eyes glowing yellow in the headlights. Taren turned the key and the engine died; yet he made no move to get out.

"Thank you." They both spoke at once.

She laughed and continued. "I had a wonderful time. Thank you for asking me."

"Considering the embarrassment I put you through the other night, I figured you might dump a plate in my lap or something. I am glad you enjoyed it although I don't think meeting the boss was very comfortable for you. I will try to keep him at a distance, but right now, it may be impossible."

"The rest of the evening was very memorable."

"Would you like to do it again sometime?" He didn't specify what it was he would like to do again. He let her field the question how she interpreted it.

"Maybe we can…sometime."

He got out and walked her to her door. Lobo met them, falling in slightly behind Taneika. Taren knew a little about wolves. Lobo was treating Taneika as if she were the alpha female in a pack, waiting to be recognized, following and not bounding ahead.

"Good night." He kissed her on the cheek. What he wanted to do was taste the sweetness of her lips, feel the weight of her breasts pressed against him. Taren sensed another kiss like the first would rush their relationship. The gamble was just too great. He might lose the passion the first kiss had promised.

"Good night Taren." She opened the door and felt a conflicting sense of loss and relief. The kiss had been chaste, leaving her again with an option. Almost with regret, she closed the door.

"What am I to do, girl?" she asked while stroking Lobo behind the ear.

Lobo licked her face and whined. *It's time for you to take a mate. He is a good one.*

"So you think I need a mate and he is the one. What makes you so sure?"

Lobo stuck her nose between Taneika's legs. *You smell different.*

"Just because you smell me you think I am in heat." She laughed, grabbed Lobo's head and shook it. "It's more complicated."

Not to me. Lobo sat and scratched an itch.

"I am not a wolf, no matter what you think." Taneika turned toward her room as she slipped the dress past her shoulders and over her breasts. Her sensitive nipples had her thinking that maybe Lobo was right. Maybe she *did* need a mate.

* * * * *

Taren stood beneath the pulsating hot water. Steam shrouded his body while a cloud of worry enveloped his mind. His boss was a vindictive bastard and rumors of his underhanded dealings had filtered all the way to Washington. But rumors weren't facts and Harold had covered his tracks quite successfully.

If Harold's sights were set on Taneika, both she and her wolf could be in danger. Especially Lobo, and it would be his fault. All he had to do was make up some lame excuse for being late to work. But no, dammit, he had to be honest and tell Harold the truth, or at least part of it. He had gotten her into this mess and it was his responsibility to get her out of it.

Thinking of her, his mind replayed the kiss they'd shared on the deck of the pavilion. His body responded to the passion they had experienced.

The doorbell sounded and his thoughts, already heated, ignited with the hope Taneika was at the door. He wrapped a towel around his waist.

Taren opened the front door and all his hopes died.

"Am I interrupting something?" The Under Secretary of Interior stood at his door. The Under Secretary's eyes dropped to the towel and the obvious hard-on standing out like a tent pole underneath. "Or were you expecting me?

"Linda, what a surprise. Won't you come in?"

She entered, looking around.

"I'm alone."

"Oh *really*. I figured you might have that beautiful woman waiting in the shower or between the sheets. Or doesn't she know of your wonderful delights?"

"Whether she does or doesn't is hardly any of your concern, is it, Linda?"

"No, but I haven't found anyone who can light my flame like you did."

"I know you didn't stop by to discuss my love life and if you remember, you were the reason our relationship stopped."

She smiled wistfully. Obviously, he didn't have any difficulty remembering, but that's all that was left. They were just memories, however fond they were.

"Taren, you have been here for what, almost three years? I am getting impatient. Have you found out anything new?"

With Linda, there were no secrets, no regrets and no future, at least not romantically. "Here's my report, look at it while I get dressed."

"When is this shithead going to make a mistake?" She threw the report on the table as he came back. "There's still nothing we can tie around his neck to hang him."

"I know. There is something brewing and it could open everything up, but I don't want to use it."

"Taren." Her voice had gone cold, vibrating with suppressed anger. "Damn you, don't you dare go soft on me now. I have waited too long to see it fall apart now. Whatever you have, use it. That's an order."

A feeling similar to sinking in quicksand ripped through his gut. Obeying the Under Secretary placed Taneika and Lobo in the middle. The flip side was the possibility of losing his job, or at the very least a reprimand in his record, which amounted to the same thing.

"Fine, but I need a favor."

Chapter 3

"I hate Mondays." Taren poured a steaming cup of black coffee from the office pot.

"Talking to the coffeepot again, Taren?" A secretary sat at her desk, a smirk on her face.

"I suppose you just live for the Monday morning meeting." Taren smirked knowingly and glanced towards Harold's office.

She laughed. "Now, don't go putting words in my mouth, Taren Carpenter. I never said I *liked* Monday mornings, but I don't go around complaining to coffeepots. Besides, the walls have ears. *Shh*, they might hear you."

Taren joined her laughter.

Harold came out of his office and there was a mad scramble to be seated in the conference room before he entered.

Taren took a sip of his coffee, hiding a smile behind his cup. Casually walking to the door he allowed Harold to enter first.

Keeping a straight face, he received Harold's frown with pleasure.

"You're late, Carpenter. I don't like to wait on anyone, especially you. If you want a cup of coffee, get here earlier or have one at home.

"All right, down to business. I am glad everyone turned out for the banquet last Friday night. It went off with only a couple of glitches." He turned to Taren with an icy stare. "Next time you bring a date, inform her it is a formal, not a costume party. Also, try to pick one a little more refined and who won't insult a guest. One I might add who is a friend of mine and very influential in Washington circles."

Harold tossed a copy of the department's, *Rules and Regulations for Management of Endangered Animals*. Taren read the title and thought to himself...*I wonder if I should point out to this idiot what the edited by T. Carpenter means*. He cocked an eyebrow.

"Don't play the innocent with me, Carpenter. She is to be arrested for keeping an animal listed on the endangered species list. It's a privilege allotted to zoos, not private citizens. And I want her damn wolf caught and moved to the upper region of the park. And if you can't catch it, kill it. There are too many people in the area. Hikers and bikers don't like finding dead deer when they are out for relaxation and fun."

Taren clenched his jaw, fighting the rage that boiled and threatened to erupt like Old Faithful. The bastard had tried and convicted Taneika without a hearing.

"Pretty extreme measures at this point. Have her come in and talk to her," Taren said. "Try to settle this without the publicity. There are ways to settle this so everyone is happy."

Harold turned red and then smiled. "An excellent idea, Carpenter. Have her come in and bring the wolf with her. When she gets here, we can arrest her and get the wolf at the same time."

"She's already told you, she doesn't own the damn wolf. And besides, the wolf is helping with the deer population around this end of the lake." Taren stared at his boss and allowed a slight grin to form. "You did receive some bad publicity about thinning the herd. The public wasn't very thrilled to find out we were performing, as the media called it, wholesale slaughter.

"The Sierra Club, Natural Resources Defense Council and the Humane Society of the United States are watching the department and this park closely. They're persistent about the wolf population being allowed to grow and their removal from the endangered species list.

"Besides these things, which we already know as fact and should be taken into consideration, if we arrest Taneika, you'll have the Blackfoot Nation down on us like Custer's last stand at the Little Big Horn." Taren saw several hidden grins around the table.

"Blackfoot!" Harold sprayed spit halfway down the table. "She is no more Indian than I am. If you won't arrest her, I have plenty of others around here who will. They know which side of the bread to butter, something you should have learned by now. I am placing you on administrative leave for two weeks, without pay."

Taren had been waiting for this reaction, counting on it. Get Harold so steamed he reacted without thinking. He took another sip from his cup.

"Your leave starts *now*, Carpenter. Get your sorry ass out of here. When you get back, expect a transfer to *bum-fuck* Alaska to be waiting for you."

Languidly Taren stood and gave Harold a mock salute. Leaving the conference room, he placed his hand in his coat pocket and turned off the recorder.

Taren pulled into the college parking lot and headed for the administration office.

"May I help you?" An attractive blonde was sitting behind the counter. The sultry smile she sent him made it clear exactly how she would like to help.

"I need to see the Dean of Women, please." Taren showed an identification badge reserved for emergencies. This might be stretching the definition of emergency, but he couldn't afford to take the chance and wait. Harold was moving faster than even he had allowed.

"Dean Watkins will see you now, Mr. Carpenter." She walked ahead of him, her hips swinging in a pair of jeans two sizes too small. "If there is anything else I can do for you…" Her voice was dripping with innuendoes of passion.

"Thank you for your help."

Taren opened the door and Dean Watkins stood and stretched out her hand. "Good morning. How may I be of assistance?"

Within minutes of explaining the nature of his visit, the Dean was on the computer pulling up Taneika's file.

"I take it, sir, you want this to be handled discreetly. I'll take care of this myself and no one will know whom she left with or why. Where are you parked and I will send Taneika out?"

Taren sat in the cab of his truck, his fingers impatiently tapping on the center console. Looking at his watch for the tenth time is as many minutes, he fumed at the delay.

The door opened and Taneika stood there with worry lines creasing her brow. Her eyes appeared larger than normal. The flare of her nostrils was the only indication she had run from her building to the truck.

"Get in, I'll answer your questions on the way."

He drove as if possessed, edging the above the speed limit.

"What's the emergency?" she asked.

"You are to be arrested and Lobo's life is in danger." Taren pulled around a slower moving car and whipped back into the lane.

"Your boss didn't waste any time." Taneika slumped against the seat. "Where does this put you?"

"Out on a limb until I can get a hold of certain people in Washington. I have papers coming authorizing you to keep Lobo. I'm just not sure when they will arrive."

"What should we do?"

Taren liked the "we" part, as long as it included him. "Send Lobo away from here and be arrested, or pack a bag and let me take the two of you to my cabin in the mountains until the papers come in."

Taren pulled into the post office. "I have to mail this. I won't be long."

He paused as he stepped out of the truck and turned to face her. "Taneika, there's not much time; even now the authorities may be waiting. When I come back, I need your decision. Whatever it is, I will support you in it."

Taren dropped the tape of the morning's meeting in the mail and returned to the truck. He slid behind the wheel and said, "Well?"

"I've got a few things to pack if this is going to be a lengthy stay."

"It's a primitive cabin, no running water or electricity. Miles from nowhere," Taren explained.

She grinned. "Sounds like where I grew up."

The rest of the ride was silent. Nervous tension increased with each bump in the road; the growl of the engine and the hum of the tires bore testimony that they were headed into uncharted waters.

Taren pulled over just before reaching their turnoff. "Circle around through the woods. If they're not here, I'll honk once."

She started to get out. Taren's face was grim as he placed his hand on her arm. "Be careful."

Taneika heard the concern in his voice, felt the warmth of his hand. Leaning over she kissed him hard on the mouth. "You too."

One moment she was kissing him and the next, she was gone. Taren eased his foot on the gas and rolled down the drive. Approaching the house, he saw no sign of life. Getting out, he hit the horn and closed the door.

A wolf's howl sent shivers up his spine. Taneika walked out of the bushes. "You said we were in a hurry, so move. Lobo will be here before we are ready to leave."

He grabbed his backpack and started tossing in clothes for the high country.

Ten minutes later Taren walked down the steps, hoping he had packed everything. Taneika was waiting, her pack stored in the back of the truck.

Taren picked up a tarp. "Will Lobo stay under here for a while?"

Shaking her head in frustration she took the tarp from Taren. "Jump in, girl."

Taren never ceased to be amazed at the control she had. One whispered word and Lobo was allowing herself to be covered with the tarp.

"Ready when you are." Taneika opened the door and hopped in. "You want me to hide, too?"

"Might not be a bad idea." Scrunching down in the seat, Taneika wedged her legs against the dash.

Taren started the truck and pulled down the drive. Making a right turn at the highway, he started to relax. With one last look in the mirror, he realized they had left with only moments to spare. Two cars and a panel van he recognized from the park left the main road, turning in the direction of Taneika's house.

The subtle fragrance of roses wafted in the air. His mind had been so busy he hadn't noticed it until now. It was the springtime freshness after a rain that filled him with longing, a wistfulness easing his fears and relaxing the tension between his shoulders.

"What are you thinking?" Her question surprised him.

"It's probably safe for you to sit up."

"I guess I can let you get by with a little white lie for now." She sat up and looked behind her. Lobo was still covered.

"Can I let her get up? She likes to see where we are going."

Taren pulled onto the shoulder. "Better bring her up here. A wolf riding in the back might cause too much attention."

Taneika opened the door and stepped out.

Lobo was out of the back and in the seat, her feet barely touching the ground.

Taren received his share of wet kisses from the wolf.

Lobo wasn't content to just sit in the middle and look ahead. She stuck her nose first in front of Taneika, then in front of Taren. She licked Taneika's face and whined.

"All right, you win." Taneika scooted over and Lobo pressed her nose to the glass, which fogged over.

Taren laughed at the mournful expression on Lobo's face. He lowered the window from the driver's side controls. It was soon evident that this was the preferred mode of travel as Lobo, head out the window and fur slicked back in the wind, actually looked like she was smiling.

This seating arrangement worked for him too. A seventy-pound wolf takes up a whole seat. Taneika was wedged between Lobo and his thigh. The heat radiated from where their bodies touched and rubbed together. His mind filled with images of Taneika bathing in the lake, water caressing her breasts like a lover's hand.

"Hungry?" he asked.

Lobo twisted her head back into the cab and barked. *Food, did you mention food?*

Taneika grabbed Lobo by the ears and shook her head. "Taren wasn't talking to you, girl. I guess it's unanimous," she turned to Taren and grinned. "We're starved."

"There's a little town up ahead with a small grocery and a deli. We can stock up on a few supplies, get a couple of sandwiches and go on. We have a half-hour more driving and then a two-hour or more hike to the cabin. I don't want to get caught in the dark."

"Why?" she asked.

"A couple places are difficult to get through in the dark."

"No, why are you doing this?"

"Oh." Taren paused, going over the varied reasons and what he should say. How much he should reveal. "I don't like Fallings."

"Give me a little more credit, Taren. A person doesn't put their career on the line for the possibility of getting a piece of ass. Don't look so shocked, I took it into consideration before we left."

Taren ran his fingers through his hair. "You're right, it's complicated as hell. For now, you will just have to trust me."

"Trust you," she fumed. "Did I hear you right? Do you think I would be here now if I didn't trust you? From what I see, we are both in the same boat. It might be easier with two people paddling. Trust is a two-way street, Taren. Otherwise it's no longer trust, but control."

"You're right, I'm sorry. It has been so long since I trusted anyone, it's difficult to start." Taren pulled into a parking space in front of a small grocery. "I'll go in and get the supplies. Anything you want or need? What about Lobo?"

"It doesn't matter for me. Lobo prefers meat."

"No dog food for you, girl?" he teased.

"If she gets hungry enough for commercial dog food, your fingers might be the appetizer when you set the bowl down."

Taren chuckled. "Thanks for the warning."

He returned to the truck a few minutes later. Placing two large bags in the back he climbed in and handed Taneika another. "There is a little roadside park outside of town. Figure we can stop there to eat."

Lobo, unwilling to wait, sniffed the bag and barked. *Where's the beef?*

The smell of fresh meat was making her mouth water. "Just wait, you can eat when we stop." Taneika scratched Lobo's ears and received a wet kiss.

The rest area was empty, for which he was thankful. Taneika opened the door and Lobo leaped out of the truck. Taneika stepped out and stretched. Her shirt pulled tight across her breasts, outlining them like a second skin. He forced his mind off the sensuous image she created and picked up the food.

"Lunch is served." Taren sat at the picnic table and waited.

"This is nice." She sat down next to him. The view of the valley and the mountains on the other side brought back fond memories of her home — happy times, running free with her wolves, tending her father's sheep.

Lobo returned from making her inspection of the area and stood beside Taneika.

He handed Taneika a sandwich and a package of meat. Just as he had expected, Lobo circled the table waiting. How many times had he seen it in the wild? The alpha wolves in the pack started eating first, then the others would be allowed.

Taneika took a couple bites of her food and opened the package of meat. The smell was overpowering. She glanced at the ham and cheese sandwich before her. It was good but, she swallowed the buildup of salvia, nothing compared to fresh meat. She tossed a chunk of meat to Lobo and watched with envy as it disappeared between sharp snapping teeth. Maybe she could get by just licking her fingers.

She turned her eyes back to the table. Taren held a piece of meat inches from her mouth. She licked her lips and swallowed. Hell, she was almost drooling on the table. "Go ahead, toss it to her."

Instead of tossing the meat to Lobo, he kept it there. "This isn't for Lobo."

Her eyes wide, never leaving the meat suspended before her, she opened her mouth. Taking the meat from him, she licked the juice from his fingers.

She heard a seductive groan. Was it from her, or Taren?

Chapter 4

Lobo barked.

Taren absently tossed her a chunk of meat.

He figured by feeding Taneika a piece of meat it would show, even if he didn't understand, he had accepted the bizarre preference she had. All control vanished, self-discipline shattered, as she placed his finger in her mouth and gently sucked the last of the juice.

Rather than be reduced to begging from the alphas who were ignoring her, Lobo set her sights on a rabbit, which had ventured too far out of the protective brush. The chase soon ended with the prey clamped securely between her teeth. She jumped into the back of the truck and ate her fresh kill.

It was difficult to breathe, much less find his voice. "I—I think we…should go."

"Yes." Taneika leaned toward him, their lips met, tongues touched and dueled. She felt his heat, tasted his desire and relished the worship he gave her body. His hand molded to her breast and she arched to give him more. Reluctantly, she broke the contact. Her breathing matched the rapid movement of his broad chest. "We should."

"Lobo! Where are you, girl?" Taneika laughed as Lobo's head rose above the side of the truck. A sharp bark announced she was ready to go.

Even though Lobo was riding in the back, she slid over beside Taren. After what they had just shared, sitting by the window created more space between them than she desired.

Taren started the truck and pulled onto the road. "You ready for some exercise?"

"Depends on what you have in mind."

"A strenuous hike to the camp with full packs, for now."

"I'm ready."

Taren pulled into a drive and stopped. Nestled among the trees was a small, one-car garage. "We'll leave the truck here and go on foot." He got out, opened the garage door and brought back two solid frame mountain packs and two sleeping bags. He split the supplies in half, filling the two packs. Attaching their smaller packs and the sleeping bags to the frame, he had two more items to add. Taren pulled a lever-action Winchester .30-.30 from behind the seat and secured it beside the smaller backpack. Returning to the garage, he hefted the bag of climbing equipment over his shoulder.

Taneika wondered about his grim expression as she cinched the straps tight across her chest. With bow in hand, she followed Taren behind the garage and up the faint trail.

The path gave out to rock and sheer walls on one side and a drop of a hundred feet on the other. The view was breathtaking, but she didn't have any time to stop and admire it. For almost an hour, Taren had pushed on ahead. His stride never faltered and she knew he was carrying considerably more weight than she was.

Carrying the extra weight of the pack was taking its toll. Her breathing in the thin air was becoming labored. She had been out of the mountains too long.

Taren stopped in a wide section of the path. "Take a breather...the rest is downhill."

Taneika leaned against the wall, her breath forming clouds in the cold air. "Is this the only way in?"

"No, it's the shortest, unless you use a chopper. The other way takes two days of hiking from the closest road, unless you're on a four-wheeler. This time of year, though, better have a snowmobile handy. Snow can come early up here."

She saw the worry on his face as he scanned the way ahead. "We aren't going to make it before dark are we?"

He took the binoculars from his eyes and looked at the darkening sky. "No."

"Can we make it?"

"Maybe. It depends." Taren sat down beside her.

"On what?" He turned and looked deep into her eyes. "On how well you actually see in the dark. With this cloud cover, there will be no moon tonight, and the flashlight batteries are dead."

"The only problem we will have," she teased, "is if you fall off the mountain."

Taren snorted, adjusted the straps of his pack and stood. "Hell, falling is a possibility you live with even in the daytime. Anyone but you and I wouldn't even attempt this trip. You ready?"

A wolf howled, the sound echoed through the mountains. Lobo lifted her head and answered the call. As the two communicated across the distance, Taneika laughed.

"What's so funny?" Taren asked.

"It seems we will have a visitor waiting when we get off the mountain. The other wolf is a young male on the prowl and he is coming to check out the new arrival to the valley."

"Take the top rope out of the bottom bag and attach it to the pack harness. You lead the way. There won't be room on the trail to change places."

The trail narrowed considerably. She heard his muffled grunts of pain as he bumped into jutting fingers of sharp rock. His trust in her ability left her feeling appreciative, flattered and flustered, all in the same breath. He knew more about her than anyone outside her family and even they had a hard time accepting her enhanced abilities.

The words of John Swift Eagle came back to her. "Your mother and I do not understand the things you are able to do, but we love you just the same. Keep these things to yourself or you will become like a rat in one of the white man's laboratories.

They will not understand the spirit world of the Blackfoot. One day you will understand what even the shaman cannot explain."

Lobo's barking from down the trail brought her back to the present. "We have a problem ahead. The trail has vanished."

Taren absorbed the information with dread. Landslides were a constant threat.

None had ever taken the trail out so completely that he couldn't get through. If Lobo said it had vanished...

Taneika stood at the ledge. Loose rock chips lay between them and the remainder of the trail.

He stood behind her, waiting. For the last half hour he had been holding onto the pack she wore. In the enshrouding darkness, he was virtually blind. So close to the cabin and yet so damn far away. The wind whipped at his coat, slipping in and sending chills up his spine. On the wind was the clean freshness of snow. It looked like they were stuck there for the night.

"How wide is the gap?"

"Ten feet, maybe more," she answered.

"Shit."

"No, it's loose shale." She couldn't help the laughter that bubbled up. "I don't smell any shit."

"You're a comedian, too."

"Lighten up. We're not going to let a few loose rocks stop us." She turned around to face him. "You have any climbing equipment with you?"

"Yes."

"Good. Drive an anchor into the rock and pass the rope through it."

"What are you going to do?" Standing on tiptoe, she kissed him. "You trusted me to lead in the dark, trust me in this too."

Taneika took off her pack and waited until Taren had driven the anchor into a crack in the rock.

She told Lobo to go across the gap.

Lobo reached the other side, sending a small trickle of stones rolling down the mountain.

Taking the end of the rope and another anchor from him, she crouched on the ledge. Before he could stop her, Taneika leaped into the night. He held his breath in fear. What was she thinking? It was suicide!

"Relax," she said. "Give me a minute to set the anchor and you can send the packs over."

Taren slumped against the rock face of the mountain. The sudden fear for her life and the realization she was safe left him shaken.

With both packs now on the other ledge it was his turn. He thought of crossing himself but he wasn't a Catholic. His childhood prayers didn't seem appropriate 'cause he wasn't going to bed. Besides, it had been a long time since he had prayed.

Placing his hands on the taut rope, he stepped onto the slide. His feet sank into the loose shale. Rock started to move down the slope. Hand over hand he moved across. With each step, the noise continued to build as more rock joined the moving mass of rubble. A hand reached out in the night and pulled him to safety.

Taren grabbed her and wrapped his arms around her. "Going across the way you did was the craziest stunt I've ever seen. You could have been killed!"

"I told you to trust me. If I had explained what I was going to do, would you have agreed?"

"No."

"And we would still be on the other side arguing about it." She picked up her pack and cinched the straps.

"Probably, but we made it across, thanks to you." He slung his over his shoulder. "Let's go."

The trail widened and leveled out. "We have company," she said. "Off to the right."

She reached out into the shadows with her mind. *We mean you no harm. You have nothing to fear.*

Who are you?

Itano'mahkapi'si.

Daughter Of The Wolf, welcome. I will travel with you in your journey.

"Where is the wolf?" Taren asked.

"Walking beside me."

"You're serious. It's here, now?"

"You are forgetting, Taren, Lobo is also wild. You've fed her and she's kissed your face. Don't be alarmed."

He walked along in meditative silence. Her control over Lobo he could accept, if not understand. She had raised the wolf. But what was it that caused this creature, which put fear into the heart of man with a simple howl in the night, to walk beside her?

"There is a cabin ahead. Yours?" she asked.

"Yes."

It was several minutes before he could make out the dark shadows of the building in front of him.

Taren opened the door and struck a match. The orange tongue of flame flickered and caught on the wick of an oil lamp, driving the darkness into the far corners of the room.

The logs were old. The chinking showed signs of recent work being done to stop the bitter cold from intruding. Sections of the roof were new as was the door and window. An old pitcher pump sat on a corner shelf. Taneika walked over to the stone fireplace. It was already laid, ready to bring life and heat back into the house.

"Catch." Taren tossed her a box of matches. Deftly, she snatched the box out of the air. Striking a match on the hearth, she touched the flame to the dry tinder. The flames grew, spreading over the wood.

"Like I said, it's primitive." Taren began emptying the packs.

"I like it." She stood and walked over to the table. "Need any help?"

"Sure. Find an empty spot on the shelves for this stuff."

Taneika carried several items to the open shelves and began putting them away. "How did you find this place so far from civilization?"

"I was with another Ranger and flew over it. We set down in a clearing and came back to check it out. I found out who owned it and leased it."

Taneika heard the wolves outside and went to the door. They each had a rabbit in their jaws. "Thank you for the food. Now go, run with the wind and find your own."

"I'll clean them, Taren, and cook yours over the fire."

"Thanks." He stared at the closed door in a state of utter confusion. "I'll be dammed. If I hadn't seen it with my own eyes, I'd call someone a liar." The realization came. *Exactly what someone would call me!*

Things were beginning to fall into place, her reluctance to socialize, the absence of sports in her curriculum at the college. Were her abilities known, she would become a scientific study in a lab somewhere. Her peaceful life would be over, sacrificed to the supposed good of mankind. The impact of the trust she had placed in him was staggering.

The door opened and Taneika carried the skinned rabbits in. Skewering one with a stick, she held it over the fire. "This will be ready in a few." She wondered if he would feed her again. If he did, she knew where it would lead. Probably end up there anyway. If the roadside park had been more secluded…

"Unless you are going to share your rabbit, you might want to turn the stick." Taren snorted at the flustered look on her face. "Daydreaming?"

"No, just thinking." The juice from the rabbit sizzled and crackled as it hit the hot coals.

"What about?" Taren leaned back against the table and crossed his legs.

"Oh, nothing really." She heard his soft chuckle and the scraping of his feet on the floor.

"Liar," he accused. "You were thinking about the last meal we shared, and how erotic it was to feed each other. I can still taste your last kiss, feel the heat of your breast against my hand."

Taking his rabbit from the fire, she carried both to the table. Taren's eyes radiated molten heat with the intensity of his desire.

She handed him the uncooked meat. "Feed me."

Chapter 5

Taneika sat beside him. She watched his hands tremble as he tore the rabbit apart. Blood oozed out, covering them and dripping onto the table.

The pungent smell of the freshly killed rabbit triggered the animal spirit residing deep within her. She had managed with sheer willpower to keep control when she had cleaned them, but no longer. Her breathing and heart rate increased until it became a pounding in her chest. He held the meat, dripping in blood before her. Opening her mouth, she allowed him to place the meat in her mouth. Biting down she severed the leg bone and began chewing.

Taren stared at what was left in his hand. She had chewed the bones and all. She captured his hand in hers and licked the blood from his hand. He knew he should feel repulsed, but it was just the opposite. The feeling was overpoweringly erotic. The tightness in his jeans was uncomfortable.

He opened his mouth when she touched the meat to his lips. Lost in a sensuous fog of desire he ate, mechanically chewing and swallowing the food. When his tongue licked the juice from her fingers she moaned and swayed toward him. Taking her mouth with his, the food was forgotten.

His hands were in her hair, on her face, and when the heat curved around her breast, her body arched, wanting more of this sweet torture. Hot kisses trailed down her throat and over the material of her shirt. His hands trailed down her side. Fingers frantically pulled the shirt from the waistband of her jeans. Delirious from pleasure, she gasped when his lips surrounded and sucked on a nipple.

Taren picked her up and carried her to the bearskin rug in front of the fireplace. Her hands had found their way to the front of his shirt, and fingers hurriedly worked at the buttons. Her arms snaked around him as he knelt to the floor. Lying beside her, Taren cupped her heat through her jeans. She moaned against his mouth, digging her nails into his back. Releasing the snap, he slid his hand inside, his fingers massaging the folds of slick velvety flesh.

Taneika writhed against his hand, wanting more. Raising her hips off the floor, she pulled the jeans down and kicked them off. She was flying, soaring. She thought she couldn't get any higher. His mouth moved from her breast and left a trail of fire down her stomach. She was wrong. Her body pulsed with each stroke of his tongue. Bursts of light exploded behind tightly closed eyelids. Taneika lay panting, gasping for breath as he moved slowly up her body, branding her with his kisses.

She felt his hardness enter and then searing, tearing pain.

Her body tensed, pain replaced the passion on her face. Taren lay still, waiting for the pain to subside, allowing her to get used to him being inside of her. He hated to cause her pain, but this was unavoidable. In a few minutes, she would forget it as though it never happened. His mouth sought hers with tender caresses meant to reassure and comfort.

The pain lessened and she was filled with his heat. It surrounded her, rekindling the flame of passionate desire. She returned his kisses and wrapped her arms around him. Relishing the feel of him deep inside her, she became bold. Shoving on his shoulder, she rolled him over and sat astride, taking his full length. His hands found her breasts as she rocked against him. She moved faster, chasing after the elusive lightning that flashed across the sky. The explosion rocked her, sent her spiraling out of control. Arching her body, she raised her head and howled in ecstasy.

From out in the woods, answering jubilant howls split the silence of the night.

She collapsed on his chest, her head resting on his shoulder. His heart pounded against her breast, the aftershocks of their mating racked his body. Never had she imagined it would be this fierce, this shattering. Her body still vibrated from the intensity of it.

Taren was content just to lie there with her in his arms. Nothing had ever come close to what he had just experienced. He realized nothing ever would again. Taneika, a woman of unbelievable abilities, surrounded by mystery, was the only woman who had ever satisfied him, and yet left him yearning for more. Satisfaction took on a new meaning. She had set a new standard for the word. There could only be one person he could reach it with or even want too.

Taneika.

She whimpered when he rolled her onto the rug. Such an amazingly beautiful woman, the spirit within was wild, free and full of life. His fingers idly stroked her damp flesh. Blood covered her inner thigh. He hadn't known and by the time he'd found out, it was too late. Leaning down he kissed her.

"Is it...always like this?" She returned his kiss.

"The pain?" Taren fingered a lock of hair, slowly twisting the strands of black silk around his finger.

"No...the end, the middle, everything we felt."

"I have a feeling with you it will be." He kissed her and whispered against her mouth. "I just hope you let me stay around long enough to find out." Taren trailed the back of his finger slowly down her face. "You didn't bother to mention you were a virgin."

"Would it have mattered?" Her body was languid; she felt more complete. Taneika hoped he had no regrets.

"Probably. Yes."

"Then I for one am glad I didn't mention it." Fingers splayed across firm cords of muscle as she moved her arm around him. Closer she edged. Her breast touched his chest sending tingling sparks of excitement to her very core. "Does the pump work?"

Her question confused him at first. "It does now. I had to rebuild it."

Gracefully she rose from the floor. Filling a basin with water, she cleaned herself. She appeared totally unconcerned about her lack of clothing or that he was watching her bathe. A picture of her washing in the lake flashed through his mind. With unwavering certainty, he knew she had been washing blood from her body. She hadn't just eaten. The bite marks on the venison, her footprints and the wolf's, interspersed around the carcass...the grisly scene played out before him.

Taren's eyes were locked on her. The color drained from his face. He looked like he was going into shock. Taneika rushed to his side, touching him. "Taren, what's the matter?"

Moving away from her touch, he tried to reason it out in his mind.

"Taren?"

"How long have you joined in the hunt and the kill?"

"You're just now putting all the pieces together? I thought after finding the deer you would have understood. I'm sorry."

"How long?"

She flinched at the tone of his voice. "I can remember riding on the back of a wolf, fingers clenched in her fur, the wind blowing through my hair as we ran through the trees. I was so young they tore chunks of meat and gave me little pieces to chew. The first time I came back with blood all over my clothes, my mother screamed and carried on. She thought I was hurt. I started taking them off once we got away from other people."

Taren dropped his head in his hands. "I just can't fathom it. It's beyond reasoning. What about your other...abilities?"

"The same. I kept them hidden, except from my family. Like you, they never understood. But they learned to accept them. After I got big enough to help my father, he never lost another sheep or lamb to wolves."

"They obeyed you, even at an early age?"

"Yes."

"What about your friends? The other children on the reservation."

She laughed; a tear trickled slowly down her cheek.

"What friends? Do I look like a Blackfoot Indian? I have white skin like you. I couldn't bathe with the rest of the girls. Why? Because they made fun of me for not having any hair between my legs like they did. My skin wasn't dark like theirs. I had an Indian name, raised by an Indian family. Spoke their tongue and attended their school, but I was…different."

Years of frustration, bitterness and hurt leaked out of her heart and soul. Tears flowed, unstoppable as the rain, down her cheeks.

Taren sat beside her, gathered her in his arms and kissed the tears away. "Shh, it's all right." She laid her head on his shoulder. Rocking her gently, the sobs tapered off and stopped. Soon, even the occasional sniffle ceased and she was asleep.

Taren carried her to the rug and covered her with a sleeping bag. He stirred the coals, banking the fire for the night.

His communication with the outside world was limited to the battery pack for his computer and his cell-phone. Still unsure after three years of investigation as to Harold's network of information, he was hesitant about using either. Harold Fallings had money. Where it had come from, he had his ideas. Finding proof was next to impossible. He had power and influence in Washington. To the best of his knowledge, Harold's money didn't control his two bosses, the Secretary and Under Secretary of Interior. Anyone else was suspect to greed.

Opening his laptop, Taren checked his messages. A top-priority message waited, flashing on the screen.

Where the Hell are you? Fallings is pissed. Filed obstruction of justice charges. Contact ASAP. Linda.

Taren began typing. "Safe. Tape in mail. Contact Santa if needed. Need discussed papers ASAP." He sent the message and turned the power off.

* * * * *

The phone rang.

"Hello!"

"Mr. Fal..."

"Shut the fuck up, you idiot! How many times do I have to tell you? No names."

"I got a couple of short transmission bursts. Not long enough to get an accurate fix."

"Well, can you give me an inaccurate fix?"

"Yes, sir. They came from somewhere inside the park, sir."

"Inside the park. Do you know how many acres are inside this fucking park? I need something more to go on."

"Sorry, sir. It's all I've got. I'll keep watching."

"I'm not paying you to watch, find the son-of-a-bitch."

For the second time in his career, Harold felt threatened. He had eliminated the first threat without being caught, and he would do the same to Taren Carpenter, when he found him. He had built a large network of informants on both sides of the fence. His shipments would have to be delayed. It would cost him dearly but in the end, Taren Carpenter and whoever placed him here would be the ones to pay.

* * * * *

Taneika woke with an arm curled warm and sensuous around her middle. Memories of last night came back with a rush: the heat, the passion and the pain of her confession. Her last thoughts were of being held within his arms, cradled safely against his solid chest. His breath tickled her ear, blowing a strand of hair gently against her face.

"Morning, Little Wolf," he whispered softly against her ear.

"Morning." She turned her face away to hide the tears that came unbidden to her eyes. "Little Wolf...is what my Father called me."

"Called?" He heard the catch in her voice.

"Yes. He went to be with the Ancients a year ago. A bear came down from the mountains and attacked the sheep. Father tried to drive it off. By the time I got to him, he was dead."

"I'm sorry."

"His death was avenged. I tracked the bear back into the mountains. It died by my father's bow. My mother's knife skinned it."

"And what of Little Wolf? How did she avenge?"

"Little Wolf cut out the heart of the bear, while it was still beating and ate it before he died." Taren tucked a strand of hair behind her ear.

"Little Wolf was very brave."

"Bravery had nothing to do with it. Little Wolf was pissed!"

A bark sounded outside. She got up and opened the door.

Lobo bounded in and stuck her nose between Taneika's legs. Taren laughed. Lobo dove under the covers and put her cold nose between his legs. "Damn!" He jumped out from under the covers. "What's gotten into her?"

Taneika laughed at Taren, standing there with his hands cupped protectively around his manhood, and at Lobo, still under the covers with only her wagging tail exposed. "Out, now."

Lobo stuck her head out and barked.

"Not another word, you hear me? *Outside!*"

In a whirlwind of feet and flashing tail, Lobo bounded for the door. Taneika grabbed the sleeping bag before it could be dragged out. Once outside, Lobo began barking and chasing her tail with such speed she became a blur of gray against the newly fallen snow.

"Mind telling me what that was all about?" Taren padded over to the pump and drew water for his morning coffee.

"You wouldn't understand. It's strictly a wolf thing."

Taren threw a log on the fire and set the pot close by. "Your smirky little smile tells me it's something else."

His sudden move surprised her. She flung open the door and tripped over Lobo. In a tangle of arms, legs and gray fur, they landed in the snow.

Lobo bounded away, unsure as to what was going on. This was the alpha's fight and she wanted nothing to do with it.

Taneika lay on her back. Snowflakes speckled her golden skin like sugar on creamy chocolate. He licked the snow from her cheek and her nose, and kissed them from her eyes. Their lips touched and sealed in a kiss. As it deepened, passion and desire swept through them. She wrapped her hand around him, guiding him into her inner core. Lying in the snow, nestled between her legs, he experienced a world of fire and ice. The wolves gathered close, sniffing, watching and circling. Taneika arched beneath him in release. Muscles of steel clamped around him, locking him deep inside. Taren slumped against her, his strength drained from his body. Lobo crept forward, licked the melted snow from his face, turned and ran into the woods.

* * * * *

With his finger poised to turn the connection off, he glared at the message displayed across the screen.

Sit tight. Needed papers misplaced, suspected inside mole being questioned. This may not be related, but three strong arms of mob drug lord left Chicago this morning, on westbound puddle jumper. Present location, unknown. Repeat, sit tight. Santa is standing by with sleigh if needed. Linda

His eyes glared like black diamonds. Steel cords stood out in his neck. The knuckles of his clenched fist turned white. Taneika placed her hand on his shoulder, the muscles quivered with unreleased energy. Reading the message, her confusion grew.

"This isn't just about a wolf, is it? And what about Santa standing by with his sleigh?" After three years of watching and waiting, the realization he had placed an innocent life at risk made the victory bittersweet. "No, this isn't just about your wolf. Santa is a nickname for my partner, Nick Strange. The sleigh is the helicopter he flies."

Taren took his identification out and handed it to her.

Special Investigator, Department of Justice, United States of America. "I thought you worked for the Interior."

"I do. I was a game warden and had just transferred to the Justice Department when a senior warden was killed here at Yellowstone. I was sent back before the ink had dried on the first transfer papers. The Under Secretary and I had just quietly broken up from a short affair. To make my transfer out here seem more believable, we made the breakup appear scandalous and fed it to the press.

"Harold Fallings likes his world neat and tidy, sort of like looking into the mirror image of calm water. Having his image distorted in anyway upsets him greatly.

"After three years of waiting for him to screw up we decided we had to go on the offensive. We started with little things. Reports written so they would have to be redone, showing up late with lame excuses."

"And then I showed up with Lobo. And your attempt to protect me further enraged him."

"When I invited you to the banquet, I never dreamed he would come after you personally. Considering who was at the table, I should have seen it coming. I'm sorry."

"What if these thugs are coming here?" she asked.

"First they have to find us." Taren turned off the computer. "Well, for now the problem with Lobo may be solved." She walked over to the window. "Those two are curled up under a young pine tree. Figuratively speaking, I may be a great aunt in a few months."

He heard the sadness in her voice. "Hon, I'm sorry. I know how attached you are to her. But as you said, she is a wild animal."

"I know...I should be happy for her."

He saw her lip tremble, the twitch at the corner of her eye. A large, sparkling diamond-like tear formed and trickled down her face.

"Come here." He turned and placed her in his lap, surrounding her in the security of his arms.

Chapter 6

Harold Fallings sat in a rundown bar. The blaring rock music and the smoky haze was perfect cover for the meeting. The stripper presently on the runway was good and all eyes were on her. Later he would stick several dollars in her G-string to have her shake her big tits in his face and even a lap-dance in the private Champaign lounge.

The lap-dances here went beyond the normal. For an extra fifty he could get a blowjob, something his prissy little wife refused to do, even when he got violent. But that was okay. He liked to see the fear in her eyes whenever he slapped her around.

A man sat down at the table next to him. "I think Chicago is colder."

"Not if you have a wolf-skin coat."

Harold looked across the table at the man from Chicago. Even in the dimly lighted bar he wore dark sunglasses. "You made good time. I want this problem removed. Here's their location." Harold slid a pack of cigarettes across the scarred, glass ring-stained table and raised his voice. "Keep 'em...I'm trying to quit."

A few minutes later, the man got up and walked out. Harold sat back with his feet stretched out in front of him. Catching the attention of the dancer, he shifted his erection so that the bulging outline it created in his pants would be more visible.

Hidden from view of the other patrons and the bouncer, he slowly unzipped his pants, exposing himself to the dancer.

Chapter 7

Taren closed the door against the blowing snow. Taneika stood by the sink. Her body sparkled like jewels from the firelight reflecting off her wet skin. He openly admired her beauty, the fullness of her breasts, the sleek, gracefully body that was surprisingly and deceptively strong. Placing the wood he had brought in by the fireplace, he continued to feast upon her with his eyes.

"You look at me like you have never seen me before." She washed between her legs and heard his breathing deepen.

"I enjoy watching you." Walking over to her, Taren slid a finger slowly from the side of her face, down her neck and over a golden breast. "And touching you."

His finger left a trail of warmth on her skin. The aroma of wet, freshly cut wood, newly fallen snow and the smoke from the fireplace mingled with his unique manly scent, drawing her closer. "I like you touching me."

Their lips met. The intimacy of their last mating that clung to his lips was an aphrodisiac to her senses. She dropped the washcloth and moved her hands to his shirt. Trembling fingers worked frantically to free the buttons. With the last one released, Taneika pulled the fabric apart and splayed her fingers across his chest. His heart beat wildly against her palm. She lowered her hand to his waist and released his belt. Her fingers fumbled with the jean snap and lowered the zipper.

Taren gasped as she freed him from the confines of his shorts. Her fingers sent shocks of delight surging through his body. She left a string of kisses and love bites down his chest. His legs shook, threatening to fold beneath him as her tongue snaked out and captured a clear pearl.

The sound of Lobo's warning broke through the fog of sensuous heat. Taneika sprang from the floor and grabbed her bow and quiver. "We have company."

Before Taren could pull up his pants, she was gone, disappearing into the thickening shadows of the late afternoon. With one hand he buttoned his shirt, the other picked up the rifle by the door. Glancing around the door, he was rewarded with a bullet inches above his head.

Taneika saw the gun barrel sticking out from behind the tree. Movement from the other side caused the man to turn and fire. The piercing cry of an injured wolf was joined by he inhuman scream of the killer. Lobo's weight took the man to the ground as her massive jaws clamped around his throat.

She ran to where the two thrashed upon the ground. Blood from a torn jugular filled the air with its hot bittersweet odor and turned the snow into a crimson mat. With one final twist, Lobo ripped the man's throat away. Blood flowed down the man's broken windpipe. She knew that within minutes he would be dead, drowned in his own blood.

Lobo nuzzled her fallen mate, licking his face.

Taneika approached.

Do something, Taneika! Lobo cried.

"There is very little I can do, girl."

She heard the gurgle as the man drew his last agonizing breath. She felt the evil surround her as his spirit departed, only to be met by the angels of death as they carried his soul into the bowels of *hell*.

"Stay with your mate, girl." She softly ran her hand over the injured wolf's head. "You are brave, oh gallant one. I would stay with you but others hunt us. I must go or we will all be lost. I will be back."

He whimpered and licked her hand. *Go, Daughter of the Wolf...protect your mate.*

Taneika crept through the trees, watching and tasting the air for any scent of the killers. Her helplessness about Lobo's mate filled her with a resolve that left no room for mercy. The loud report of a shot from just ahead pinpointed another killer. Fading deeper into the trees, she stalked her prey.

A long mournful howl sounded. Lobo's mate was seriously injured. She wanted to try and stop the bleeding, but right now that would have to wait.

A shadow ahead moved. She notched an arrow and waited. The man stooped over and ran toward another tree. With the skill of a practiced warrior, she pulled the bow and loosed an arrow. A surprised gasp of shock and pain erupted as the arrow struck him low in the side.

The man looked up as she lifted the rifle from the ground. Surprise mingled with the pain as he held the arrow shaft with his hands, trying to pull it out.

"There's a broad-head on the end of that shaft. Every time you move it, razor sharp blades are slicing more of your insides, cutting your guts apart."

"What can I do?" She looked around and then riveted her eyes on the man. His eyes were wide with fear and there was panic in his voice. He had stopped trying to remove the arrow, but the damage had already been done.

"Out here?" she smiled. "Die."

Taneika turned her back and left.

"Larry, I'm hit! The bitch shot me with an arrow! I need to get to the hospital!"

"You fucking moron, there's no hospital around here!"

Taren laughed as the two men yelled back and forth across the clearing.

"You gotta do something, Larry, I'm gonna die!"

"So shut the fuck up and die!"

"Hey! Larry!" Taren called out. "Ask him how it feels to be dying."

"Why should I do that, pig?"

"Because you're next...just figured I'd give you something to think about."

The doorjamb splintered as a dozen copper-plated lead bullets from a machine pistol tried to chew their way through the thick logs. The window shattered, a sack of flour exploded from the impact of a round. Taren dove for the woodpile just outside the door, praying that with the angle the shooter was from the house he hadn't been seen.

Spotting the man hiding behind a fallen tree, he fired and ran. Halfway across the clearing, the ground erupted around him. A searing pain raced up his leg. His leg, hit by a round, folded and he crashed to the ground.

The shooter stood and stepped into the clearing, the Mac-10 held at his side. "Well, pig...any last words before you die?"

Taneika watched the scene unfold before her. She saw Taren on the ground. Rage filled her heart and tears filled her eyes. She pulled the bowstring to her cheek.

Taren rolled, aimed and fired. "Yeah, you first."

The power of the deer rifle and the impact of the arrow turned the man around. She watched the shock register on the man's face as he fell into a lifeless heap.

Dropping the bow, she ran to Taren. "I saw you fall. I thought you were dead. Where are you hit?"

Taren pointed to his leg. There was a hole in his pants between his knee and hip. The material was turning red.

"It looks like a flesh wound. Need to get you inside where I can look at it."

With her help, he was able to stand and make it to the house. "There is a first aid kit in my pack."

Taneika put some water near the fire and began looking for the first aid kit.

Taren sat at the table and started to take off his boots. The heel of one was missing. "There's the reason I fell." He tossed the boot to Taneika. "Makes walking out of here difficult. The heel must have come off when I went down."

"Another inch higher and you wouldn't be walking." She carried a bowl of hot water and the first aid kit over to the table. "Shuck those pants so I can take care of that wound."

The burning in his leg was turning into a painful throb. Taren unsnapped his jeans and Taneika helped slide them off. An ugly gash of torn flesh was a stark reminder of how close he had been to death.

She washed the blood off and removed pieces of material and loose flesh. She glanced up. Beads of sweat formed on his brow, eyes glazed with pain were riveted on her. "That is going to be painful but should do 'til we can get you to a hospital." Taneika applied some antiseptic and a bandage.

Taren shifted in the seat. His side felt like he had been kicked. Pulling back the shirt, he could see a bruise was already visible.

"How did you get that?" She ran her fingers gingerly over the discolored flesh.

"I don't know." Taren checked his coat pocket. A small round hole in the fabric caught his attention. Inside, his cell phone was useless. A round had destroyed it, saving his life.

"This is a good example why people should carry these things in the woods."

"Well," she said. "We still have the laptop."

Taren looked at the table and his heart sank. Hopes of a quick ride out of here were crushed. The monitor was fragmented into a thousand shards of glass and electronic parts.

"When those boys don't show up or contact Chicago in a few days, their bosses are going to send someone else searching. We can't call in reinforcements or get help out of here. We'll have to manage on our own."

"You walking out of here right now is out of the question. I could go for help but that would leave you here alone. I don't think that's a good idea."

Taren dreaded asking the next question. But he had to know. "Lobo?"

Lobo isn't hurt, physically; her mate was shot. I don't know if he'll make it. He needs medical attention."

Although he felt bad for Lobo, he wasn't quite sure how to convey that feeling into words. "Damn, sorry."

She nodded and a sad smile formed.

"What shall we do with the bodies...leave them?"

He ran his hand through his hair searching for the right answer. "For now, remove any identification and bury them. Keep the animals from destroying the bodies. See if you can find out how they arrived. Somehow I just don't see them walking here. My thoughts are horseback."

"I'll have Lobo look around. If there're horses out there, she'll find them. I'll be back in a little while."

"Don't you think you might want to get dressed?" He smiled in spite of the pain in his leg.

"It's easier to wash the dirt from me than my clothes. That reminds me. One of the thugs was still alive when I left him."

"Any chance of him getting out of here alive? He could be the key to closing these sordid dealings and put Fallings where he belongs, behind bars."

"Sorry, none, the ride would only hasten the inevitable."

Taneika found Lobo with her head lying across the shoulder of her mate.

Lobo raised her head. "I know." She sat cross-legged on the ground. Her hand stroked her friend and companion. "Taren has been hurt. See if you can find how these men got here."

With one last look at her fallen mate, Lobo left.

She took the first aid kit and slowed the bleeding in the wolf's side. "Sorry, boy, that's the best I can do. Rest, I will be back as soon as I can."

Taneika dragged the first body to a small depression, covering him with a shallow layer of dirt and rock. For the man in the clearing, she dug a grave deep enough to hold the body. She retrieved her arrow and the extra rounds for the pistol and rolled the man in. The last man, in an attempt to either remove the arrow or to quicken the end had shoved the broad head into his chest cavity. Whatever the reason, the result was the same. He was in no more pain.

Lobo came back as she finished covering the last body.

"What did you find, girl?"

There are three horses downstream, Lobo barked.

"Good girl." Taneika dropped to her knees and gave Lobo an affectionate hug. "Show me where they are." Lobo turned and ran into the woods. Taneika followed a couple of steps behind.

Taren fussed and rearranged the log in the fireplace for the umpteenth time. He had always prided himself on his patience. But right now, that virtue was on short supply. His leg throbbed and burned where he had been hit.

Forced to lie in front of the fireplace, he couldn't even help with the things outside. The gut feeling he had told him that she wouldn't spend much effort in burying those three. In all honesty, he couldn't blame her. Who really cared if the wolves and bears tore up the bodies? She was probably right, let the buzzards have them.

"Taneika!...Lobo!...Damn it!" Linda had said there were three men. There could have been more. Her length of time gone now fueled new fear for her life.

Taren threw back the covers and reached for his pants. Getting them on was relatively easy—standing was another matter. He broke out in a sweat. Pain shot up his leg as torn muscles stretched and pulled. Grabbing the back of a chair, he closed his eyes against the dizziness that sent the room reeling around him.

"You can do this, just take it nice and slow." Keeping his weight on the chair, he pushed it ahead of him. He moved the injured leg forward and then lifted the other foot.

Each step was slow, making progress in inches instead of feet. The chair leg hit an uneven seam in the floor and twisted. Reacting automatically, he placed his weight on the wrong leg. He gasped as his world erupted in breath-stopping pain. His eyes closed, shutting out the white-hot flashes burning in his mind.

* * * * *

She found the horses tied to some small trees. With Lobo nearby, they became skittish. Eyes wide with fear, they jerked at the secured reins. "Lobo, go back to the cabin." Her soothing voice soon calmed them so that she could approach. Taking the reins of the two horses, she mounted the third and headed back to the cabin.

"Taren!" She ran to where he lay on the floor. His pant leg again was soaked in blood. She placed her hand on his forehead. "Damn you. You just couldn't lie there and rest."

His eyes opened into thin slits. "I was worried about you."

"I can take care of myself." She began changing the ruined dressing. "I don't need you to play nursemaid."

Taren closed his eyes and sighed. "I know. You don't need anyone, do you?"

The tone of voice, the words he spoke, cut through her heart like a knife. Just a few weeks ago, they would have been true. But not now.

* * * * *

Early the next morning, Taneika helped Taren outside and onto one of the horses. With their packs lashed to the other horse, she mounted and headed down the valley.

Taren glanced back at Lobo. A long pole was tied to each side with a makeshift harness. Taneika had used a sleeping bag as a hammock for the injured wolf. Somehow, he had managed to hold on through the night.

The throbbing pain had eased some. He didn't feel as feverish. They had been lucky, this time.

Going back now was sure to do two things. Surprise Fallings, causing him to hopefully make more mistakes, and make the big boss in Chicago really pissed. Working undercover was dangerous but with his cover blown, it was suicidal. It was time to call for help.

Late that afternoon they came upon a rest area inside the park. There was a vehicle with a horse trailer hooked up to it.

Taneika took the keys she had found on one of the bodies and unlocked the door. Lying on the seat was a cell phone. Taren took the phone, started to dial and then changed his mind. He hit the redial button.

"Larry, this had better be good news."

He tried to remember Larry's voice. "Yeah, job's done."

"You been drinking again, Larry? You know the boss don't like you drinking on the job."

Taren put more slur into his voice "Screw him, the job's done and it's fucking freezing up here." Without waiting for a reply, he turned off the phone.

"Get these horses loaded and find a phone that can't be traced as easily."

Taren sat sprawled across the passenger seat with his leg up and tried to get comfortable. With all the hard riding they had done, his leg throbbed and burned.

Lobo rode in the back with her injured mate.

"You handle this trailer like an old hand." Sweat beaded on his brow as the truck hit a pothole and took a hard bounce.

"I ought to." She spared him a brief smile. "Father had one the same size that we used for hauling horses and sheep."

"There's a first aid station in that town where we stopped for our supplies. I can call from there."

"What about a vet for the wolf?" Taneika slowed down for a sharp curve.

"On the right, as you enter town. He's retired from the city but still has a small office open here."

Taren sat in the cab and waited while she talked with the vet and took the wolf inside. The grim expression on her face when she returned wasn't very encouraging.

"What did he say?"

"Doc doesn't give much hope, but he will do what he can."

She pulled into a double space on the side of the street and helped Taren out of the truck.

With his arm over her shoulder, he limped slowly into the first aid station.

The receptionist's smile turned to concern. "Taren, what happened?"

"I got shot."

Her face turned pale. "Jeanie!"

"I have told you not to yell. It disturbs the patients." A voice came from down the hall.

A nurse wearing a maroon blouse and pant uniform came around the corner. "Hi, Taren. What's all the commotion out here?" Her collar-length auburn bounced with each step. She was tall, approximately five-foot-ten inches. Laugh lines were visible despite the slight frown she displayed at the moment. Although no longer having an hourglass figure, she was still a very beautiful woman.

The receptionist, normally a calm, collected girl, was agitated. Taren, despite the pain in his leg, chuckled.

"Taren's been shot."

"Shot?" Taren watched the transformation in her face. "Where? When?" She was already in motion, circling around the counter. Her trained eyes gave him a quick assessment. "Damn you, Taren. I knew this would happen."

"Jeanie, I would like you to meet Taneika. Taneika, meet Jeanie, my overbearing older sister who still thinks that because she changed my diapers, she can still tell me what to do."

Jeanie cut away the pant leg and removed the bandage. "Nice to meet you. Did you do the patchwork? Looks good, clean. Brother, looks like you caught a wicked one. This is a wide tear, ricochet by the looks of it. It's going to require some internal sutures."

"So don't just stand there. Start sewing," Taren ordered.

"I can't, you know that. Not anymore. This isn't the military. I could lose my license."

"Listen, Sis. There are three bodies buried up in the mountains. Hospitals have too many rules, miles of red tape, and if someone talked there could be more bodies to bury. With your emergency field training, this is a cakewalk. Just shut up and sew. While you are getting a needle and thread, I need a phone."

* * * * *

Jeanie took off the latex gloves and tossed them on the table. "That's it. The rest is up to you. Stay off the leg for a few days. Give it a chance to heal or run the risk of ripping it open and going to the hospital."

"Thanks, Sis. I have one more favor."

"You need a place to stay?"

"Just 'til I'm back on my feet."

"Sure. It's time to lock up here anyway. Bill will be by any minute to pick me up. You can follow us over."

The front door opened. "You ready, Jeanie?" Taren had to laugh every time he heard Bill's voice. Soft spoken, meek and high-pitched, the assumption one made without seeing him was effeminate. Those that still had that idea after seeing him were fools.

"Well, what have we here? Hello, Taren. Jeanie still patching up little brother?"

"Taneika, this is Bill Yates, the local sheriff. Bill, this is Taneika Swift Eagle."

Bill towered above her, broad shouldered, narrow waist, his grip, when he shook her hand, was solid. A warm friendly smile greeted her.

"Glad to meet you, Miss." He turned to Taren. "Taren, what kind of trouble are you in and how can I help?"

"You have a deputy that you would trust with Jeanie's life?"

Chapter 8

Late that night Taren sat on his sister's couch with his leg propped up on a pillow. His hands were busy reassembling the Mac-10 that Taneika had taken from their attackers.

Taneika sat on the floor, comforting a grieving Lobo. Her hand lovingly stroked the wolf's head.

The door opened and Bill came in. "The truck and trailer are hidden and the horses are tucked away in a safe location." Hanging up his coat, he walked in and sat in a chair across from Taren. "With the hardware those men had with them, you two are lucky to be alive."

"Bill," he looked up knowingly. "They weren't expecting to be outnumbered. Otherwise," he laid the Mac-10 on the table, "the outcome would have been different."

"You're welcome to stay here as long as need be. Our fall festival will be in a couple of days. If you are feeling up to it, I think you would enjoy it."

"We appreciate the place to stay," Taren said. "My concern right now is Lobo. Keeping a wolf in the backyard might cause some comment from your neighbors and if your son says anything at school…"

"Josh is spending the night with my parents. We have until he comes home from school tomorrow to figure something out."

"Lobo can go into the hills. She won't want to be too far from her mate," Taneika said.

Hearing her name mentioned, Lobo sat up.

"It's not safe for you here, girl. I told the doc you would probably be by to visit your mate. Just be careful and go in the early morning."

Lobo barked.

She gave Lobo a kiss. "I will miss you too. Okay, avoid any people. I'll be going home as soon as I can. Lobo, if he doesn't make it, it's not the doc's fault. He will do everything he can to help."

Taneika opened the kitchen door and with a final look towards Taren, Lobo left.

"Taren," Bill said. "If you're not too tired, could you answer some questions? Jeanie has a fresh pot on. Let's go into my office." He picked up Taren's coffee mug.

You're not leaving much choice. He got the crutches and followed Bill through the house.

Bill leaned against his desk. "How well do you know this girl? And I'm not talking in the biblical sense."

"Well enough to know she's a woman with some amazing abilities." Taren sipped his coffee and hoped that answer would suffice.

"Do you trust her?"

"Yes."

"I know you are protecting her. Something else is bugging me. She and the wolf, they...understand one another?"

He took a long sip of coffee and looked at Bill over the rim of his cup. "Do you realize what would happen to her if it became public knowledge?"

"Yeah, I see your point." Bill sat at his desk, thoughtfully running a pencil through his fingers. "Maybe it's better I don't know anything else about her."

Bill got up and stood staring out the window for several minutes. "I'm worried about all this, Taren. What are you going to do when the Mob comes after you again?"

The same worry had plagued him ever since they had survived the first attack. "I'll have to deal with it."

"Damn it, Taren!" Bill roared. "Just how in the hell are you going to deal with a single hit man or a full crew of hired killers?"

"I called in extra help. They'll be here in a couple days." Taren sat the empty cup on Bill's desk.

"I'm a small town sheriff. What you're into up to your neck is way over my head." He walked over and placed his hand on Taren's shoulder. "I hope to God you know what you're doing.

"It's late and you've had a long day. I'll see you tomorrow."

Taren opened the door to the guest room and all thoughts of sleep evaporated from his mind like the morning fog over the lake. She was invitingly stretched across the bed; her nude body revealed to his hungry gaze. The wanton, smoldering heat from her eyes caused his loins to stir.

He crossed the room, his palms sweaty on the rungs of the crutches.

"I thought you were going to talk all night. Did Bill give you the third degree? I see you still have all your fingernails."

"He was...curious."

"And?"

He sat on the bed's edge and dropped the crutches to the floor. "I told him you were an amazing woman with a unique way with animals and that you wanted to live your life as quietly and unobtrusively as possible. He respected that."

She sat up and swung a leg across his lap being careful not to touch the wound. "Thank you."

Her lips met his as she snuggled closer, bringing the center of her velvet core against him. Taneika gently pushed against his shoulders and he fell back on the bed. She ran her fingers teasingly down the side of his neck to the first button of his shirt.

With each one released, more of his skin was revealed to her hot searching touch. Her tongue left a wet, electrifying trail across his chest and circled each nipple before gently nibbling on them. He felt ready to explode. His fingers wound themselves through her black tresses as she slowly slid down his body. A strong tug at his belt, and his pants were being unzipped.

Taneika's mouth covered the wet spot that had formed on his shorts and sucked greedily. Pulling the waistband down, she freed his shaft. Barely kissing the tip, she took him 'til the mat of hair tickled her face. Taren arched his back and she felt his body tremble. With her tongue, she stroked him. The pulsating power of his body enflamed hers, driving her faster.

Unable to wait any longer, she climbed back on the bed and straddled his waist. Taking his length fully inside her, she rocked against him. His hands massaged her breasts, squeezing them, but it wasn't enough. She leaned forward placing a breast against his mouth.

His teeth grazed her nipple, jolting her body.

"Bite me. Oh, yes. Harder!"

She locked her legs tightly around his hips as wave after wave of blinding light exploded behind her closed eyelids.

Taneika's head rocked back on her shoulders. The mating call of the wolf that filled the room was joined by his own cry of release.

The door bounced off the wall as Bill rushed into the room with his service revolver drawn. Jeanie stood behind him peeking over one shoulder, her face pale and her eyes wide with fear. Taren pulled Taneika to his chest and flipped the bedspread over them. Jeanie's fear quickly dissolved and she placed her hand over her mouth. She ducked out of the room and Taren heard her laughter from down the hall.

"Sorry. I, ah, thought…" Red-faced, Bill lowered the revolver and backed out of the room, closing the door.

Taneika's body shook, her laughter hot against his neck. "Jeanie didn't seem too surprised or shocked, but Bill didn't know quite what to do or say…or where to look."

"Well, Jeanie is a nurse and a very liberated woman. I think Bill led a more sheltered life growing up. Sis said he was a virgin when she met him."

"I'm glad you weren't."

"Weren't what?"

"A virgin." She rolled over to lie beside him. "Where did you learn how to please a woman?"

"I don't think that is something you should be, ah, concerned with."

"No secrets, now. Not after all we have been through and all you know about me.

"Are you afraid that I will get up and leave after finding out about your past lovers? I suspected your involvement with Linda before you told me. She wasn't the first."

"No. After high school, I spent the summer working at the college where Jeanie attended. The girls in her dorm decided that they needed more study in human anatomy and I became the object of their studies."

"Jeanie knew this was going on?" Taneika smothered her laughter with her hand.

"Like I said, she is a very liberated woman." Taren thought back to the times when Jeanie had walked into a friend's dorm room and had found him in bed with one of her classmates. Or going into the bathroom and having naked girls going to and from the shower, giving him a friendly smile and a playful shake of their tits. It wasn't long before the nudity in Jeanie's dorm became, if not totally unnoticed, certainly less noteworthy.

"Well, I don't know about their grades, but I give you an A plus." She kissed him, got out of bed and went into the bathroom.

Taneika was different. She drew him. Whether she was clothed or nude, his eyes followed her. He couldn't get enough of her. The vivacity she had towards life carried over into their lovemaking.

The aroma of frying bacon and fresh coffee woke him the next morning. Slipping on a borrowed robe, he went to the kitchen.

"Morning, Sis. That sure smells good. Bill gone?"

"Good morning. He just left. After last night, I don't think he wanted to be here when you woke up. I have never seen him so flustered or so turned on. Thanks."

"Sis, could Bill's parents keep Josh while we are here? The chance of him telling one of his schoolmates about us being here is too great. It could place everyone in danger. These people are ruthless. They wouldn't think twice about using a child as leverage to get to me."

"I'll call and find out." Jeanie dialed the numbers and, when Bill's mother answered, briefly voiced Taren's concern.

"She says not to worry. Josh can stay there as long as needed."

Taneika walked down the hall. "Good morning. So, Bill didn't want to face us. Sorry if we embarrassed you last night, but at least you got some enjoyment out of it." She smiled coyly.

"You heard us?" Jeanie asked.

Taren chuckled, "Her abilities are rather complicated to explain. That is another reason that Josh should stay with Grandma."

Taneika stopped beside him and gave Taren a kiss. "Morning."

"I'm off for work. Make yourselves at home," Jeanie invited. "Taren, take it easy on that leg. Call if you need anything."

Taren hated the inactivity, but the only thing his jailer would let him do was go to the bathroom. Taneika propped his foot up and waited on him like he was some kind of invalid. It was okay for a while, but it got old quick. He wasn't into game shows and the news was the same old story. The world was going to end when all the computers crashed on New Year's Eve with the coming of the new millennium. He scoffed at all the alarmists with their dire predictions about the future.

They reminded him of the carnival fortunetellers. Normal housewives and mothers who would put on gypsy garb, and for a couple of dollars look at your hand or gaze into a glass ball and tell all. He always had a good laugh at their acting ability, their mumbling of incoherent words. They were good at giving the people what they wanted to hear, painting rosy pictures of good health, a prosperous future and a long life of love and happiness.

Deception and lies. As long as a person remembered that it was just for fun.

Chapter 9

After three days of confinement, Taren was glad to get out of the house. The fight with his sister had been worth it. He was free of the crutches and on a cane, which left one hand free to use his Glock nine-millimeter, if need be. With it safely tucked in a shoulder harness, he felt more secure.

There had been no word from Linda or the Justice Department. It was as if they had forgotten about him and the dead goons now buried under a couple feet of snow. He knew that once the hit men failed to report back, shockwaves of revenge and anger would be felt all the way back to Fallings and himself.

The town of Red Rock, Montana was bustling with people. Although the ski slope had been open for almost a week, today was the official start of the skiing season. It also marked the opening of the Winter Festival that drew moderate crowds from the surrounding communities. The mood was festive and contagious. Snowballs whizzed through the air, children darted in and out of the adults, and hot chocolate was the favorite drink in the twenty-degree weather. Local craftsmen displayed their work while the contest entries of pies, cakes and jellies were all laid out for the judges. With Halloween just two days away, the haunted house was the center of attraction for the young and young at heart.

They walked along, hand in hand, looking at the exhibits.

"Shall we?" Taneika asked.

An old trailer was set up on the far edge of the grounds. A faded mural of an Indian woman covered the side with the words "Medicine Woman, seer and fortuneteller." Taren knocked on the door.

When she came to the door, he stood transfixed, staring at the woman. It was impossible to determine her age. The lines of time were etched into her face. Her long, silver-white hair flowed like snow over her shoulders and fell to her waist. Her eyes danced with vitality and life. Looking into them, Taren had the strangest feeling that she was peering into the depths of his soul.

"Come, come, children. This cold is hard on an old woman's bones."

She stepped back for them to enter.

"I am She Who Walks Ahead. Please have a seat. Which one of you would like to know the path before you?"

"I would," Taneika said.

They sat at a small round table. Incense burned in a small earthen bowl, its tendril of smoke spiraled slowly toward the ceiling. Dream catchers hung suspended in each corner of the room. Prisms sent beams of multicolored light bouncing off the walls.

"Give me your hand, dear, and allow me to walk in your mind."

She took Taneika's hand and closed her eyes. The smoke from the incense encircled their heads. She Who Walks Ahead began to tremble. Her eyes opened, transfixed on Taneika as if looking through her.

Damn, she's good, Taren thought.

The old woman spoke quietly. "You are no longer a virgin. Your destiny is intertwined with an ancient legend, which has all but been forgotten. Its surety is signed in your maiden's blood and sealed in the heavens. Your life will be changed forever in the near future. Be careful of those you put your trust in. None will understand this change and there are those who, if they found out, would destroy your life. There is evil stalking you. You must act quickly and decisively when confronted with it or face life alone."

"What is this change you speak of, oh wise women?" Taneika asked.

She shook her head. "I regret that I am fearful of telling you. Knowing about it now will not change the results. You can't run or hide from it. And knowing what it is beforehand will only bring stress to your soul. You must remember that when it happens, you must remain calm and relaxed. Accept this change...for if you fight it, it could end your life."

"Will you tell me, She Who Walks Ahead? This change, which you speak of, when is it going to happen?"

It appeared that the woman wasn't going to answer.

Taneika added, "Please."

"When Jupiter pulls the rings of Saturn into alignment with Orion's Belt and sets the hunter free. When the moon is full and at its peak; before its ride down the mountain to the sea. Then the change will come. This, *my child*, your destiny shall be."

The woman let go of her hand and closed her eyes as if asleep. Taneika sat with a bewildered look on her face. "That's it? That's all you will tell me?"

The old woman opened her eyes, which now appeared as smoked glass. "Yes." She bowed her head and folded her hands in her lap.

Taren heard the emotional and physical exhaustion in the seer's voice. Their time was up.

He laid the money down and touched Taneika's arm. "Let's go."

* * * * *

She continued to think about the words of the old Indian woman. All her life she had wanted answers and no one could give them. Here was someone who knew the answers and wouldn't tell her.

Taren stroked her body with his hands, caressed it with his mouth, but tonight she was obsessed with what She Who Walks Ahead had spoken of. *What is my destiny? What is this change that I'm supposed to blindly accept? And why?*

Taren had hoped that he could, with a little tender passion, bring Taneika out of her sullen mood. Giving up, he drew her head onto his chest and wrapped his arm around her. His hand slowly stroked her black tresses. *Damn that cantankerous, meddling old woman! Tomorrow she is going to give me some answers or confess that she made it up.*

He arrived at the fair grounds bright and early the next morning. The workers and craftsmen were just setting up the booths for the day's events. Taren looked for the old woman. The trailer was gone; he threw his arms up in frustration.

Taren found a worker collecting trash left from the day before. "Excuse me. Did you notice what time that trailer that was parked here left?"

"Wasn't a trailer parked there," he answered.

"It was parked there yesterday." He pointed to an empty parking spot. "An old Airstream with a faded mural of an Indian woman on its side. She was the fortuneteller with the festival."

"Sorry." He shook his head and leaned on a broom handle. "You must be mistaken. I was here all day yesterday. I know all the vehicles belonging to the people working here. Besides, she wouldn't have been parked there. Anyway, we don't have a fortuneteller here. Had one several years ago but she died. Come to think on it, you described her trailer to a tee. Excuse me, I have work to do."

Taren walked back to his rental and started back to Bill's house. The impact of what he had been told struck so suddenly that he slammed on the brakes, sending the car sliding sideways in the street. The car came to a jolting stop against the curb.

This...this isn't possible. I was there, we both were. She held Taneika's hand. We both heard her speak.

He became aware of someone shaking him, repeatedly saying his name. He drifted out of the fog and focused on Bill's face.

"Taren, come on. Speak to me." Bill's voice began to register.

"What happened?" Taren asked, seeing the concern written on Bill's features.

"I was hoping you could tell me. Someone in the cafe saw you slam into the curb and almost flip the car. You've been sitting here for half an hour with your engine racing and your doors locked. I finally got one of them open and turned off the engine."

"I don't... remember any of it."

"Well, you look like shit. When I got here, you were shaking like a leaf. What did you see, a ghost?" Bill laughed.

"Yeah." Wearily he laid his head against the back of the seat. "I...think I did."

"Taren, you're not making any sense. I'm confused." Bill knelt in the snow. Concern for his brother-in-law etched on his brow.

In bewilderment, he turned his head and stared at Bill. "I know the feeling."

"Come on, we'll get a cup of coffee and you can tell me about it, from the beginning." Bill helped him out and back to the squad car.

"I should be getting back to the house. Taneika will be wondering what's taking me so long."

"You won't be taking your rental." Bill handed him a steaming cup. "You blew out both tires when you hit the curb. I'll call the wrecker and give you a lift."

He had lost an hour in some mind-numbing never-never land. He laid his head against the back of the seat and closed his eyes. "Shit." *How am I going to explain something like this? What the hell am I going to tell Taneika?*

"I got in contact with the rental company. They'll send a wrecker."

"Thanks."

Taren sat waiting for Bill to pull the police cruiser out into traffic. The warmth of the cup crept into his cold hands.

"Taren, I have known you for several years now. You want to explain what this ghost crap is all about?" He stared out the passenger window.

"Not really. I'm not sure I can."

"Try."

Bill's tone left no room for argument. Taren took a swallow and scalded his tongue on the hot liquid. "It happened at the festival yesterday ..."

* * * * *

"That's what the man said. Honest." Taren pleaded for Bill's understanding even though he didn't.

Bill stared in disbelief at him for several minutes and then left the curb, heading out of town. Taren wondered where they were going when Bill pulled into a junkyard. He drove slowly between rusting piles of wrecked cars and trucks.

Taren saw it, an old silver Airstream that was crushed on one side. Visible, though distorted by the damage, was a faded mural of an Indian princess.

"Over twenty years it's been sitting right there." Bill's voice broke the silence. "Her truck and trailer went off a cliff during a snowstorm, but they never found her body.

"What are you going to tell Taneika?" Bill put the car in gear and headed for the entrance.

"Christ, Bill, I don't understand it myself! You want to try and explain that the trailer she sat in yesterday has been in the junk yard for twenty years and the woman she spoke to, in all probability, is dead?"

"No." He felt Taren's frustration and understood his aggressive attitude. Backing up, he turned around and headed home.

Taren finished his coffee and slowly crushed the disposable cup and tossed it in the floorboard. *If only I could solve my problems by crumpling them up and throwing them away.*

Bill pulled into his drive and parked beside a Ford F150 pickup. "Friend of yours, I hope."

"Yeah, my partner Nick. Wonder what brings him up here?"

"Let's go find out."

Once inside, Taren and Nick shook hands.

"Looks like you met Jeanie and Taneika. This is Sheriff Bill Yates. Bill, Officer Nick Strange, Department of Interior."

He watched as the two shook hands, sizing each other up.

"What brings you up this way?" Taren sat carefully on a kitchen chair. "Fallings can you, too?"

Nick pulled out a chair, flipped it around and straddled the seat. "Last couple of days he has been happy as a brown bear with a tree full of honey. Fallings went on the warpath as of this morning demanding that I take him up in the chopper and find you. I told him the bird was down for parts, and that I was going to get them. No one knows what set him off, but I figured that you should know."

"Take him up and get him to tell you where to go. That will prove that he gave the location to the mob when they sent their goons after us. Maybe we can get him for conspiracy to commit murder, and he will squeal on the Chicago boys for a reduced plea. I am convinced that he is running drugs from somewhere within the park. We may not get him for the murder of Agent Majors, no matter how much we, or his daughter, are convinced he is guilty."

"Majors," Taneika said. "Isn't that the Under Secretary's name?"

"Yes, Agent Majors was her dad. He had been stationed here his whole career and was soon to retire. He knew Yellowstone like the back of his hand. Some hunters found his body in a ravine. He had been shot, close range in the back of the head."

"If I am going to take him flying tomorrow," Nick stood, and with a quick turn of the wrist placed the chair under the table, "I need to be going. I called in an order this morning for a part, just to be safe in case Fallings checks up on me."

Taren eased up and walked outside with him. "Watch your back, friend."

"You too. When you coming back?"

"Couple days, just enough time to let him see the cabin and the blood everywhere. When I show up in the office, it may be just the surprise we need."

"Let me know if you need anything." Nick got in his truck and drove away.

The sound of the back door closing caught his attention. Taren turned and Bill came over to where he was standing. "I have to get back to work. Jeanie asked why I was home, told her you slid and hit a curb. We don't have any secrets, Taren…it helps her understand the pressures of the job. If Taneika hadn't been standing there, I'd have told her everything, as bizarre as it is."

They were waiting when Taren went in. He glanced from Jeanie—who had been a substitute mother, a big sister and friend; to Taneika—who had quickly become a part of him. It was a new experience, this feeling he had towards her. Was it love? If it was, he hoped it would last.

"Where did you go so early this morning?" Jeanie asked.

"Out to the festival grounds." He took a sip of his coffee and grimaced at the cool bitter taste.

"Why?" Taneika asked.

"Shit." Taren got up, hopped to the counter and poured a cup of coffee.

"Quit stalling, Brother."

"I wanted to talk to the fortuneteller."

"Why?" Taneika drilled him with a stern look of determination.

"I wanted to get more information from her about our visit yesterday, find out more about these strange predictions she made. But she wasn't there."

"Maybe she'll be back later," Jeanie offered.

"I know this is going to sound strange, but she was never there."

Taneika's eyes opened wider.

"Apparently no one but us saw her or talked to her."

"Brother, you realize what you're saying is a *little* hard to believe?"

"It doesn't end there. Bill took me out to the junkyard on the edge of town. The trailer we sat in yesterday has been there for twenty years. Same Airstream, same mural on the side. The truck and trailer went over a cliff, and her body was never found."

Chapter 10

Taren watched as her eyes glistened, the muscles and tendons in her arms tightened. She stood slowly, turned and walked over to the fireplace. In an almost distracted manner, she undressed and sat Indian fashion on the stone hearth. He started to rise and go to her, but his sister's hand on his arm stopped him.

"This is something she has to work out. We don't understand this, she does. She was raised among the Indians. Not much is known about certain Native American rituals. Don't interfere."

Taren sat back in his chair. Knowing Jeanie was right didn't make it any easier. He felt out of control, unable to do anything, and that fueled the frustration that was building within him.

Taneika sat so close to the fire that he was sure she would get burned. Beads of sweat formed on her face and breasts. She raised her hands as if praying. The sound of her low chanting came to him, drifting in the air. It was a mysterious sound. The soft musical notes surrounded Taren, invading his mind and soul. His eyes closed, he seemed to be floating with the music, suspended above the table.

A cold breeze swept by, kissing him on the cheek. His eyes snapped open, riveted on the center of the room. A semi-transparent, cloud-like apparition stood behind Taneika.

Taren tried to call out and warn her, but he couldn't speak.

It swirled around her, enveloping her in a misty shroud.

He looked at his sister. She was standing at the kitchen counter, a warm smile spread across her face, her hands busy preparing a meal. Jeanie wasn't aware of what was going on. The door opened and he turned around. Bill walked through the door and stopped, confusion written across his face like the headline news. Taren glanced down and saw himself, sitting at the table. *What the...*

A heavy weight settled on Taren. The sounds around him began to filter in and register.

"...been that way since this morning," Jeanie said.

Taren shifted his eyes to the window and saw that the sky was dark. The clock on the wall showed six o'clock. *Where had the day gone?*

"She's been sitting there all day...like *that*," Bill said, his eyes drawn to Taneika's nude body.

"They both have." Jeanie shrugged her shoulders and smiled sheepishly. A low rumble from the hollow pit of his gut attested to the fact that he hadn't eaten. A strong demanding urge to piss overcame him. Taren shifted the chair, his legs felt heavy, awkward. Still trying to grasp what Jeanie had said, he made his way to the bathroom.

Bill followed and stood leaning in the doorway. "Mind telling me what the hell is going on?"

"Wish I could, Bill, but... I honestly don't know. Taneika started this Indian chant and the next think I know you're home."

"Taren, you saw something here today you aren't telling me. Did she have another visit from the fortuneteller?"

He shook himself and zipped his pants. "She had a visitor...who or what it was, I don't know. Not sure I want to."

"I'm not sure you should stay here." Bill heaved a heavy sigh. "I have my family to think of, and this is well beyond my thinking."

"I understand." He walked past Bill and into the living room. Taneika was dressed and helping in the kitchen. There was a calm serenity about her. He wished he felt the same. Jeanie didn't seem concerned or alarmed over the events that happened in her living room.

"Taren, where are your crutches?" Jeanie glared across the room. "You shouldn't be walking without them."

"It doesn't hurt anymore." He flexed his leg, surprised he didn't feel any pain or stretching. "In fact, it feels good as new."

"Shuck those pants, Brother. I want to look at it."

He recognized the no nonsense tone of the nurse authority in her voice, dropped his jeans and sat on the couch.

Jeanie knelt on the floor and began taking off the bandage.

"I see it, but I don't believe it." She stared in awe at the stitches as her hands expertly felt the flesh of his calf. "It's healed, completely. The stitches need to come out tonight."

"That's impossible, Jeanie," Bill scoffed. "Bullet wounds don't heal overnight."

"Bill, I have never told you how to be a sheriff. Don't start telling me how to be a nurse."

"But…"

"I don't pretend to know how." Jeanie interrupted. "I do know that there is no evidence of a wound, not even a scar. If you don't believe me, look for yourself."

Taren remembered the cold kiss of whatever had been in the house. "As soon as you get the stitches out and we eat, I think we need to leave. Bill, if you can run us up to my truck I would appreciate it."

"That's not necessary, Brother." Jeanie sat her medical bag on the table and started removing the stitches.

"Sis." He put just enough rebuke in his voice that quieted her argument.

"Okay." She held up her hands in defeat. "Obviously this is a guy thing, already decided on while you were hanging out in the bathroom. There, I'm finished. As you are in such an all-fired hurry to leave, we had better eat."

* * * * *

The lights from the oncoming traffic flashed across the cab, illuminating Taren's face. Lips pursed together, brow wrinkled, he reminded her of *The Thinker* statue at the college library. The miles stretched on with only the sound of the tires on the road and the whine of the heater keeping them company.

"Don't shut me out, Taren. You haven't said two words since we left your sister's place."

"Nice weather tonight, clear—going to get cold."

"Cut the crap," she said angrily. "Neither one of us cares about the weather nor how cold it is. We were both affected by what happened today, whether we understand it or not. There's not even a damn scar on your leg where that bullet ripped it apart. I can't explain that any more than you can."

"What about the...visitor that came while you were doing your chanting? What was it or probably more correct, who was it?"

"You saw the spirit or are you just guessing?"

"I not only saw it, but felt it, almost like a kiss."

"It was the spirit of She Who Walks Ahead. It would seem that she is also a healer as well a mystic. My father sent her to me as a spirit guide because the way ahead is difficult. If we had not made love, her visit would not have been necessary. That is what she meant when she said my own blood sealed my destiny."

"And that is?" Taren asked.

"She wouldn't tell me."

"All this seems normal to you, spirits showing up in bodies or floating in the air and healing bullet wounds?"

"No, but I can accept it. Because of my abilities, an elder of the council took me under his wing. He taught me the ancient rituals and customs. Taren, let's put it behind us for now. Make love to me." She pulled her shirt over her head and unsnapped her jeans. "Please." She wiggled out of her jeans, leaving her body bare to his gaze.

"You want me to just pull over on the side of the road and make love to you?"

She reached over and ran her fingers up Taren's thigh, grasping his hardening penis. "I want you to fuck me," she whispered. "I want to feel you explode deep inside me." She let go long enough to undo his jeans and lower the zipper. Her hand found his swollen length as she rubbed her fingers over the velvet tip.

Taren pulled over on the shoulder of the highway, turned the engine off and took her mouth in a savage kiss. He scooted clear of the steering wheel so she could straddle his legs. Placing the head of his penis inside her, she thrust her hips down on his. Almost in desperation, she ground her hips against him, wanting him deeper. She leaned back against the dash. His mouth found a nipple and sucked, sending out shockwaves of pleasure that swelled within her. The first wave of ecstasy rolled over her as she locked her body around his. Taneika gasped for breath as the next wave built in intensity. The beast within was released and a long sensuous howl filled the confines of the truck. She collapsed against Taren's chest.

"Wow, that was awesome."

"It was pretty amazing." The rumble of laughter came from deep inside him.

Taneika slid off his lap and knelt on the floor. "Need to clean you up." She lowered her head. The strong musk scent filled her senses, reigniting the flames of her own desire. Using her tongue, Taneika licked away the residue of their mating. He grew hard against her face and she took his length, stroking him with her mouth. Taren's low moan drove her, excited her. His body trembled and arched beneath her.

The hot flow of his release filled her mouth and she drank greedily from his well. Taren laid his head back. His languid body slumped in the seat. Taneika climbed into his lap and laid her head on his shoulder, her breasts flattened against his chest. Tenderly she kissed his neck. Slowly, his breathing returned to normal.

It was several minutes before he noticed the cooling temperature of the cab.

Taneika, wearing a satisfied smile, leaned back against the dash.

"If you can drive, I think we can go home now."

"If you...insist." Taren refastened his jeans and lethargically slid across the seat.

* * * * *

Taren stood in his living room and felt the rage boiling up inside him. Nothing had been left untouched. Every book, every picture had been purposely destroyed. His computer lay smashed on the floor, disks broken and crumbled beyond use. His furniture cut, the foam padding scattered wantonly about the room. He walked through the house surveying the damage. From the carpets on the floor to the mattress on the bed, even the dishes in the kitchen, all had suffered the same fate.

"Someone," he growled, "has gone to a hell of a lot of trouble." Taren ground his jaw in anger and frustration. With fists clenched tightly at his side, he stared at the debris.

"Fallings?" Taneika said.

"I have no doubt he ordered it. I can't see him getting his hands dirty with this; too far beneath him to get personally involved."

He was startled at Taneika's movement. "What are you doing?"

Taneika moved around the house, stopping and sniffing. A coffee cup—unbroken on the kitchen counter, a computer floppy that had received a little more attention than the others, the potted plant that now lay dying—its root system exposed to the harsh dry winter heat of the furnace.

"It wasn't the men who came after us. One man was here and did this."

"A single person." The meticulous destruction by one person would have taken time, probably hours. "Who?"

Her shoulders sagged and she hung her head. "Taneika, I have to know. Who did this?"

"You introduced me to him a couple of days ago."

"Bill, my brother-in-law? That's crazy. No way would he be involved."

"Wasn't Bill." She looked up, her eyes narrowed into pinpoint daggers.

"It was your partner, *Nick*!" she spat with a vengeance.

The almost physical blow of what she said staggered him. Taren began to put all the pieces together. For the first time in three years, the puzzle took shape. The reason they hadn't gotten any closer to Fallings was the misinformation and redirection he and the department had been receiving over the years.

"*Son-of-a-bitch!*" He slammed his fist into the cupboard door, splintering it.

Getting proof would be difficult. If Linda's dad had surprised them in a drug deal, then Nick could also be guilty of murder, or at the very least, an accessory.

"Any chance of finding prints?" she asked.

"No! Nick might be dumb enough to get caught up in the drug dealing, but I doubt he would leave any evidence behind. Without your sense of smell, we wouldn't have known he did this."

"What now?" She picked up a heavy winter jacket with the lining ripped and the pockets torn off.

"See if there is anything that is salvageable and then check your place. Maybe he missed it."

Taren found a few clothes that weren't ruined, threw those in a bag and left.

They entered Taneika's back door and surveyed the house. Everything seemed to be in order.

"Well, he has been here," she said. "I can smell him."

"Anything missing?"

She went from room to room, searching. "Nothing that I notice offhand."

"Well, at least he didn't trash your place. We might as well get some sleep. Later we can decide what to do."

"Go ahead and get a shower if you want one." She stripped off her clothes and started for the door.

"Where are you going at three in the morning?"

"After seeing your place and knowing that bastard was here, going through my things, I have this desperate urge to kill something. Besides, I'm hungry."

"I know the cove is always free of ice, but please, don't go there tonight."

"Taren, I am out of *fresh* meat." She took a knife from her pack and strapped it around her waist, tying it snug against her leg with a leather thong. "I'll come straight back if you want me to, just to make you happy. Please don't wait up for me."

He watched through the window as a silent shadow slipped into the woods. *I wish Lobo were here, and then she wouldn't be alone.* Knowing her abilities, he knew he shouldn't be worried, but he was.

He sat down to wait. The minutes seemed to drag by slowly. His fingers drummed an unsteady beat on the arm of the chair. The desire to go find her was squelched by the knowledge that he would be lost at night in the woods. She would be the one finding *him*.

The back door opened and he stared. Her hair was matted and tangled, her body smeared with drying blood. Bits of leaves and refuse from the forest floor clung to her. Two long strips of meat dangled from her hands.

Instead of the repulsion he knew he should feel at what he saw, he grew hard.

"Damn you! Taren, I asked you not to wait up. I didn't want you to see me like this." She stomped across the kitchen floor.

Standing in the doorway, he leaned against the frame. She stood at the kitchen sink washing the meat free of hair.

"What? You want to take another look before you leave?" A sob broke her voice. She turned towards him. A tear rolled down her cheek.

"Who said anything about me leaving?" Taren's smile broadened. "I was just going to offer to help you clean up in the shower."

She ran her fingers through her matted hair and looked down at the blood that covered her breasts. "You don't find this repulsive?"

"I admit the smell is a little strong, but a shower will take care of that."

She turned back to the kitchen sink. "That's not what I meant."

"Then why don't you tell me?"

She lowered her head and took a ragged breath. "This is who I am. This is what I look like after I eat. Taren, I can't change who I am. I try to be careful but there is always the chance of being seen, just like at the lake. You were at the banquet. You saw the shocked look on everyone's face, and that meat was partially cooked."

"Your point?"

"My point? All the blood flow must be below your waist if you can't see it. I'm not normal. I will live forever on the fringe of society. God forbid my abilities, as you call them, ever come before the media and scientific world. I have never been sick or seen a doctor that I didn't have to lie to. My medical record is full of childhood illnesses that I never had." She turned back towards him. "Look at me, go on and take a good look. Is this normal? I'm a freak of nature, Taren. How long will you want to be around me? How long will this fascination with me continue?"

"What brought on this nonsense?"

"It won't work. Maybe, if we lived in your cabin year round it would, but not here. I think you had better leave. You have your job to do and a criminal to catch. After that, you will be moving on. I would feel like a caged animal in the city. This is for the best."

All the wind was knocked out of him. She had blindsided him with this and she expected him to casually walk away. *The hell I will.*

Walking over to her, he grabbed her shoulders and kissed her. The kiss, filled with hurt and frustration, was brutal and hard.

"This isn't over. Too much has happened between us just to walk away. I'll be next door when you reconsider."

Taren walked into his house and kicked a broken lamp across the room. The destruction of his place matched the mood he was in. Something had happened in the woods. He wasn't sure what, but Taneika was a different person when she came back. It wasn't because he had been waiting up for her, or that he had seen her after a kill.

Repulsive, far from it. He had been ready to take her on the kitchen floor.

She was right about one thing. He had a job to do. Close down a drug ring and put a bad agent behind bars.

Taren cleared the bed of debris and stretched out. Thumbing off the safety of his pistol, he placed it under the covers and closed his eyes.

* * * * *

Taneika sank slowly to the floor. Silent sobs racked her body as scalding tears flowed down her face. She hated the lie, and at that moment, she hated herself for telling it. Taren was hers and she had sent him away.

She felt a cold hand on her shoulder. "Rest, child, for the way before you is hard."

"Go away." Taneika shrugged off the hand. "Leave me alone. Haven't you done enough?"

Chapter 11

Taren walked into the office the next morning and found Nick flirting with the receptionist. *Could she be involved too?*

"Morning, Taren." Nick smiled and gave a wink. "You're back sooner than expected. Boss isn't going to like that any."

The son-of-a-bitch acts like he's glad to see me! "I got bored sitting around the house with nothing to do." He felt like wiping the silly grin off of Nick's face. Realizing his hands were clenched into tight fists, he forced them to relax.

Harold came out of his office and stopped short, his face turning ashen. "What the hell are you doing here? Your leave of absence isn't up yet."

"Just wanted to get a couple things out of my office. Gee! No, 'nice to see you Taren, how've you been'?"

"You don't have an office here anymore. I sent a request for your transfer in the day you left. I also took the liberty of having all your things packed and put in storage."

"Find anything of interest while you were packing my things, Harold?" Taren sat nonchalantly on the edge of the desk.

"What the hell is that supposed to mean?"

"Someone went to a lot of trouble ransacking my place while I was gone. I just figured it was you."

"You accusing me of doing it?" Harold puffed up his chest like a bantam rooster.

Touchy this morning aren't we, you fat little prick. "Oh, not you personally. But I have no doubt that you had it done."

Harold bristled and turned red. "You can't prove anything. Get the fuck out of this office!"

He swiveled his body around. "How 'bout you, Nick ol' pal? Any ideas on who could've trashed my place?"

"*Me?*" Nick sputtered. "How the hell did I get involved in this?"

"Did I say you were involved?" Taren gave him a sly, knowing grin. "I asked if you had any ideas, that's all."

"Did you hear what I said, Carpenter? Get your personal things and get out," Harold ordered.

Taren came back carrying a small box. "Where's the rest of it?"

Harold stood there with a self-satisfied beaming smile. "The rest is department property and doesn't leave the building. By the way, I want all the access codes to your files."

I just bet you do. "The access codes are my personal property." Taren turned and headed for the door.

"Carpenter! Dammit, I want those codes. *That's an order!*"

Taren chuckled and looked over his shoulder. "Make up your mind, Harold. You can't order me around if I don't work here. So, until the transfer request comes back denied, I guess you will just have to wait. Later."

With a mock salute and what he hoped was an infuriating, button-pushing grin of disdain, he opened the door and left.

* * * * *

Harold closed the door to the phone booth and dialed. The voice on the other end barely answered before he began to angrily talk.

"I thought you said that problem was taken care of. The bastard walked into the office today without a scratch on him."

Harold slammed his fist against the glass wall. "This is your problem. I can't move the stuff tomorrow with him around.

"I don't have those types of people working for me. You want your shipment, you take care of the problem or I will find another buyer who will. Until then, nothing moves."

Taren watched from down the street as Harold got back into his car and drove away. A self-satisfied little smile played at the corners of his lips. *Did I mess up your plans, Harold?*

He stepped into the phone booth that Harold had just left and dialed.

"Linda..."

* * * * *

Taneika sat in the darkened room and watched Taren get out of his truck. He stood there for several minutes looking toward her place, his fist clenched at his side. He turned and walked slowly to his back door. With one last woeful look at her door, he turned and disappeared from view.

If only she could go to him, explain why she had sent him away. *I miss you too.* Dressed in skin-tight buckskins, she grabbed her bow and slipped out into the night. She looked up at Taren's window. *Sleep tight, my love.*

In the graying haze of predawn, she heard a car turn off the highway. It pulled up in front of Taren's house. Two men got out and approached the front door. Taneika notched an arrow and stood poised, the deadly tip centered unwavering on a man's side.

The porch light came and the door opened. With Taren's smile of recognition and extended hand, she slowly lowered the bow.

"Charlie, Steve, sorry to drag you out here on such short notice. Come in."

Taneika crept to the window.

"*Damn*, this place is a fucking mess."

"Steve, you should have seen it before I spent half the night cleaning. I bought a new coffeepot and cups today. I'll put the pot on."

"Any idea who did this?" Charlie asked.

"You haven't been briefed?"

"Wasn't time. All we were told is that Nick had turned and you were in trouble."

Taneika crept back to the woods and waited.

An hour later, Charlie and Steve stepped out the door and shook hands with Taren. "That's the way it stands, boys. This could get real messy."

"We came prepared. We got some things for you in the trunk. "

Taren followed them to the car.

"We brought you some hardware but it looks like you have enough. How you standing on rounds?"

"Only what I took off the guy that was shooting at me."

Charlie reached into the trunk and pulled out a small bag. "There's a thousand rounds and a vest. I would suggest you sleep with it."

"Thanks. Might not be a bad idea."

"There's a radio in the bag," Charlie closed the trunk. "Give us a call before the party starts."

Taren stood there, the snow that had started falling speckled his hair. He watched as his new partners drove away, and then turned and looked toward her house.

I know, Taren, but don't go there. Don't make this any harder than it already is.

He started across the yard and stopped, looking at the ground. Taren walked over to the side of his house and slipped behind a bush. Moments later he came out carrying an arrow. *Shit.*

She knew she was hidden from view but she crouched further when he scanned the woods looking for her. Twirling the smooth wooden shaft in his fingers, he watched the deadly blades spin in the early morning sun. Slowly he made his way back to his porch. With one hand still clutching the arrow, he picked up the vest and sack of shells. Giving the woods one last searching sweep, he opened the door and stepped inside.

Berating herself for losing the arrow, she made her way through the woods to the back of her house. Once inside she stripped and took a quick shower. Knowing Taren's life was in danger didn't make it easy to sleep, but even she needed a few hours to keep going.

* * * * *

Taren finished loading the spare magazines for the automatic and checked his pistol. He didn't know when Harold's call would bring the Chicago thugs to find him, but he had no doubt they would. He had to be ready at all times.

The one factor that he hadn't counted on was Taneika. Finding her arrow outside the window meant she was still in the picture. *What are you up to, sweetheart? Why were you outside my window with your bow?* The possibilities were few. The implications and the danger she was placing herself in were too staggering to think about. No doubt, if Charlie or Steve had a weapon drawn this morning, one or both would be dead. There was just so much one person could do. Even a person with her talents was limited.

He put on the vest, slung the Mac-10 over his shoulder and put on his coat. He didn't like leaving Taneika alone out here, especially with Lobo not around. He had to draw the coming danger away from her. *How? That's the question.* What was the one element that Harold depended on to move his drugs? In a flash, all the pieces of the puzzle fell in place.

He threw the remainder of the ammo in the bag and ran out the door. If he hurried, he might just be able to make it.

Taren pulled into the driveway and got out. Nick's Ford was running. He reached in and turned off the key.

The back door opened. "What's up, bud? I've got to leave. You know how Harold is when a person is late. I seem to recall," he chuckled, "you getting your ass reamed many a time."

"Nick, we need to talk."

"Not this morning, partner. I'm supposed to have a flight this morning."

"Flight's been cancelled."

"I just talked to the boss, he said it was on. Besides, you don't work there any more."

Taren pulled his pistol from his shoulder harness. "Sorry it had to come to this, Nick. I *cancelled* the flight. You won't be running any more drugs."

He saw the cornered, scared look in Nick's eyes, the shifting of weight from one foot to the other.

"Nick. Please, don't make me use this. I will if I have to. Just drop the belt on the ground and we'll go back in the house."

"Taren, I don't understand. What the hell has gotten into you? I'm your partner, for Christ's sake!"

"Drop the belt, Nick. It's over. I know all about how you're using the chopper to move the drugs. About your supplying both sides with just enough information to keep them apart. You have been walking a dangerously fine line for years.

"We found your bank account, Nick. Afraid you won't be using it. Inside."

Nick's shoulders dropped in defeat as he undid the belt and dropped his revolver in the snow.

"You have the right to…"

"I know my fucking rights!"

"Turn around, Nick, and don't try anything. After what you did to my place it would give me great satisfaction if you resisted." Taren placed the cuffs on Nick, making sure they were tight around his wrists.

"What about your place? I didn't do that."

"Stop the bullshit, Nick. I may not be able to prove it in court but I know you were there. What were you looking for?"

Nick glared at Taren and went through the door. Taren picked up the phone. "You want to talk to him or do you want me to?"

"Go to *hell*," Nick spat.

Taren shrugged and dialed.

"Hello."

"Hello, Harold."

"Carpenter, why the hell are you calling here? Don't tell me. You're calling to apologize and beg for your old job."

"No. I'm calling to tell you that it's over. I'm sitting over at Nick's place and we're having a very interesting conversion. Seems he won't be making your pick up today. He doesn't like small places so he is singing a real sweet song. Course, he won't get to spend any of that hundred grand you've paid him, but at least he will be free. Oh, by the way, tell your boss in Chicago that his boys won't be coming home. They're buried in shallow graves up in the mountains. One of them didn't die right away. Can you imagine it? He thought I was a priest," Taren laughed. "Anyway, it must have been a long time since his last confession."

"You don't know who you are dealing with. You're a dead man Carpenter. You hear me, you're fucking *dead*!"

Taren was left holding a disconnected line. He smiled in satisfaction and hung up.

"You just signed both our death warrants. These boys don't play games."

Taren took off his jacket, the Mac-10 hung by his side. "Who said I was playing?"

Chapter 12

The ringing of the phone pulled Taneika out of a deep but troubled sleep.

Blindly, she reached for the offending noise.

"Hello."

"Hon, it's me. Get out, now. I just forced Harold's hand this morning and he may come after you."

"I'll be ready for them."

"No! They will probably be park game wardens or security. He may even get the local police to come for you. That's why you must leave immediately."

"All right, Taren. I'll go, but I won't be far away. Don't worry about me, just take care of yourself."

"Hon, when this is over, we need to talk."

"I know, Taren." Her voice softened and nearly faded away. "I know. Bye." She gently hung up the phone and got out of bed.

Taneika pulled on her buckskins. Taking an empty backpack, she placed the meat from the fridge inside. Taneika slipped the straps over her shoulders and with her bow and quiver in hand, headed for the safety of the woods.

Her safety was dependent on the weather. If it snowed before Harold sent someone to find her, she was safe. Otherwise, her footprints would lead them straight to her. She circled around cutting across the path, doubled back and retraced her steps. Climbing a young tree, she used her weight to bend the tree over to another. Repeating this, she was able to put considerable distance between her meandering, overlapping tracks and where she came back to the ground. Hopefully it would be enough to keep someone from following.

With the deep snow, she was forced to slow her pace. Three hours after leaving, she crossed her first wolf sign. Taneika lifted her head and howled a greeting. She sat against a tree to wait.

With their heads low to the ground and lips pulled back in a snarl, the pack came in from downwind and stood nervously watching her. Their long, razor-sharp canines flashed deadly white against their dark fur.

Come, I mean you no harm.

* * * * *

"How long are you going to wait?"

Taren glanced over to where Nick sat handcuffed to the kitchen table. "Why, you got somewhere you have to be?"

"You can't keep me chained here. I know my rights. This isn't legal."

"Neither is being a pack mule for drug dealers, Nick, but that doesn't seem to bother you. Look at it this way, *partner*, if I'm wrong, you have nothing to worry about. If I'm right and they send another crew out from the city…"

"Taren! They will shoot both of us on sight. When did you become such a cold bastard?"

"For starters, how about when three thugs showed up at a place only you and I know about."

"Taren, I swear to God. I didn't have anything to do with that. Harold gave me the location of the cabin. I was as surprised as you."

"Then there is my place. Deny that you were responsible for that, and I may shoot you myself."

"Okay, so I did it. I had to. Your leaving left me no other choice."

"You're doing good, Nick, keep talking. Why?"

"I had to find out what you knew and hadn't told me."

Taren gripped the edge of the table. His knuckles turned white with the pressure. "What I hadn't told you? We were fucking partners. I trusted you with my life."

Nick hung his head. "I know. I had to make it look good, in case Harold sent someone else out there."

"What about Agent Majors?" Taren slammed his fist on the table. "Who put the bullet in the back of his head?

"I don't know. He was dead when I found him."

"You found him? The report says a couple of hunters found him."

"False."

"What about the location of the body? Is that false too?"

"Yes. I moved the body away from the pick up location."

"So you admit to picking up the drugs. How long has this been going on?"

"Four years. Just before Majors' death. The investigation was new and we couldn't afford to have it jeopardized." He shook his head in frustration and disgust. "Four years of searching, watching, and waiting, all gone."

Taren sank down slowly in a chair. What Nick was saying finally began to soak through. *Shit!* "DEA?"

Nick nodded. "You have to believe me, Taren. I couldn't trust anyone with the truth, not even you. Sorry. Now, can I have the damn key?"

Taren tossed the key to the handcuffs on the table. "Looks like I really screwed the pooch on this one."

"Yeah," Nick chucked. "But it's not really your fault. I had orders not to bring you in, even after I found I could trust you.

Harold has his fingers in so many pockets I couldn't trust where the information you were sending was going.

"We have most of the route and major players from Harold down. We just can't get a connection to the supplier. I have to call my contact and let him know what has happened."

"How do we play this mess?" Taren watched the street. The weight of what Nick told him settled in his gut.

"I am ready to end this game of cat and mouse. When they show up, they won't be expecting two people. Let's hope that surprise will be enough of a trump card that we can win this hand."

"In the meantime, *partner*." Nick smiled as he rubbed his wrists. "We wait."

* * * * *

The wolf pack had accepted Taneika into their group. After traveling most of the night, they rested at the sight of an early morning kill. They stirred only to gorge themselves and then go back to sleep.

The tranquil quiet of the afternoon was disturbed by the approach of snowmobiles. They were off the normal trail and getting closer.

The wolf pack scattered and hid. Taneika crouched behind a fallen tree and watched as the riders approached. Three snowmobiles came into view. Each one carried two people and towed a tarp-covered sled. At first she thought they were campers, but the automatic weapons that the passengers carried told a different story.

The lead vehicle turned sharply and the sled flipped, scattering its cargo across the snow. The other two snowmobiles pulled up and stopped.

"You stupid asshole! Now look what you've done. I told you to slow the fuck down."

"Up yours. Get off your lazy ass and help reload this shit."

"Fuck you, you flipped it, you reload it."

"Shit! There's a couple packages busted."

"You fucking moron. That's pure uncut coke. When the boss finds out part of the shipment was lost, your ass won't be worth a plug nickel."

Taneika was stunned at what she heard. These were the drug dealers and Taren wasn't here. It was up to her to do something.

"With the pick up cancelled, the boss is already pissed."

She laid two arrows against a tree branch and notched a third onto the bowstring. She took a deep breath to steady herself for the task ahead.

"You think *he's* pissed. I was getting laid when the call came to get this shit out of the woods."

She stepped to the side of the tree, her bow arched. The soft fletching brushed her cheek. "Just leave the drugs where they are and put your weapons down," she ordered.

She heard the metallic click of safeties being released and she fired. Bullets sprayed the ground in front of her.

As the first arrow struck, the second was being released from her fingers.

Shock and panic broke loose as the second arrow found its mark in the chest of another passenger. The third gunman carrying an automatic started running for the cover of a tree. As he turned his weapon in her direction, an arrow pierced his neck. Bullets sprayed the tree inches above her head.

"I said, nobody fucking move! Now, drop your damn weapons!"

The drivers of the snowmobiles carefully lifted pistols from shoulder holsters and dropped them in the snow.

"Back up and kneel. Don't try anything."

When they had done what she ordered, Taneika stood and walked toward them. The three she had shot were dead. Taking a length of rope from the overturned sled, she tied the men's hands. She forced each man onto the righted sled and tied him on with another rope.

Retrieving her pack, she slipped into her buckskins. There was nothing she could do with the other snowmobiles, except leave them for the authorities. Being closer to Red Rock than she was home, she headed the snowmobile in that direction.

Besides, she knew she could trust Sheriff Yates.

* * * * *

Taren kept a close watch on the street as he peeked out from behind the closed curtain.

They had been keeping two-hour watches since yesterday. Nick was asleep on the couch. Taren glanced at the clock on the wall and noticed it was time to wake Nick up.

Movement on the street caught his attention. This van wasn't on the list of normal vehicles that Nick had supplied. The van was a non-descriptive, plain, white panel Ford. As it passed in front of the house, it slowed.

"Nick, wake up. I think we might have something."

Nick was instantly wide-awake and standing beside him, looking after the retreating van. "Could be. Keep a sharp lookout. I'll go to the back and watch the alley."

Taren picked up the radio. "Steve, possible contact. White panel Ford van."

"Got it. Turned the corner just in front of me. It circled the block. Here it comes again. Two men in the front. They don't look like repairmen."

"Heads up, Charlie. They're headed back your way."

"I see them. They turned at the next corner."

Taren shifted the safety off of his pistol and double-checked the Mac-10 that hung from the strap around his neck.

The radio microphone at his ear crackled. "They pulled into the alley and stopped." He heard the tension in Charlie's voice.

"They may be waiting for another vehicle so stay alert." Taren kept shifting his eyes up and down the street.

"Nick, heads up. The van just pulled into the alley." Nick wiped the sweat from his hands. "Talk to me, Charlie."

"They're just sitting there, haven't gotten out."

"Where the *hell* did they come from?" Steve's voice crackled from the radio.

"Who, Steve?" He felt the adrenaline kick in as his heartbeat pounded in his ears. What do you have?"

"Two guys, dressed in black pants, long heavy black coats, headed your way."

"Two people just left the van, heading towards the back of the house." Charlie said. "Driver's still with the van."

"Charlie, take the van. Could be more than the driver still there. Steve, keep your eyes open. Those two on foot might have friends close by.

"Nick!" Taren yelled loud enough for him to hear. "Show time. Two on foot in the alley, two on the street out front and at least one in the van."

"Okay, boys," Taren keyed the microphone, "Let's do this by the book."

Taren watched the men approach. They glanced around quickly and walked towards the front door. As they reached the door, they unzipped their coats. Both men were heavily armed; one carried an Uzi and the other a sawed-off shotgun complete with pistol grip and extended magazine.

He felt with a cold certainty that he wasn't going to get out of this unscathed. There would be no spirit this time to heal his wounds. *At least I have a vest.*

Taren stood to the side of the door, the Mac-10 braced against his side. As he turned the doorknob, the door fragmented under the barrage of bullets from outside. He felt a burning fire race across his leg as the gunman raked the door from side to side.

The air buzzed like hornets as the bullets passed just inches from his head. The wall on the other side of the room began to crumble as they pounded relentlessly into sheetrock and wood.

Taren was aware of continuous sound of gunfire in the back room and the alley.

The front door, what there was left of it, was kicked open and the man with the shotgun entered.

Taren fired, catching the man in a sweeping line from his hip to his shoulder.

With the sledgehammer force of an impact against his chest, Taren staggered. His right arm was suddenly useless, hanging limp at his side. Losing his grip on the Mac-10, it fell useless to the floor. Another blow slammed him in the chest, knocking him backward, driving him to his knees.

The second gunman stepped through the door. Taren pulled his pistol from its holster with his left hand and fired through the pale bluish-gray cloud of burnt cordite.

Chapter 13

Taneika sat at the kitchen table with Bill and Jeanie. She ate without really tasting what she and Jeanie had fixed earlier. The food was good, as was the company, but she felt this growing apprehension...something was wrong. The feeling had come over her in the early morning and wouldn't go away. She had tried calling Taren, first at his house and then at hers.

The phone rang and Bill answered.

"Sheriff Yates."

"Bill, Nick Strange..."

Taneika heard Nick's voice. Apprehension turned to fear.

"I wanted to let you know that there was an attempt on Taren's life this afternoon. He's been shot, nothing serious. He's in the Cody General Hospital."

"Thanks, we will be there as soon as we can." Bill hung up the phone. Taneika was pale; her hands trembled.

"You heard."

She nodded.

"Jeanie, Taren is in the hospital. He's been shot."

"When? How bad?"

"Calm down, he'll be fine. I'll call the hospital and then the office. Throw some things in a suitcase and we'll be ready to leave."

Jeanie headed toward the bedroom. "Call and leave a message on the clinic's answering machine."

The trip to Cody was quiet. Fear, the unwelcome brother to worry, rode beside Taneika. *Could I have prevented this?*

The words of She Who Walks Ahead came back to her. *His life is in danger. If he is worried about protecting you, keeping you from harm, then you will lose him forever. If you love him, then send him away.*

The tires seemed to pick up the taunting chant. *Send him away. Send him away. Send him away.*

* * * * *

Nick met them in the lobby of the hospital. Taneika wanted to rip his heart out.

This was his fault. His betrayal had caused this. She sat in the lobby with Jeanie as Bill and Nick walked down the hall. Resentment ate at her with the fierceness of a hungry wolf pack. *Why had Taren been shot and not Nick?*

Jeanie took her hand in a warm friendly grasp. "Relax…Taren will be fine."

"I know that. This is all so unfair. I keep thinking…if I had been here, he might not have been hurt."

"Taneika, you could have both been wounded, or worse. Just be thankful it wasn't serious."

"I am. It's just…"

"I know." Jeanie put her arm around Taneika. "I live with this fear every day Bill goes to work. Every time the phone rings, I wonder if this is the call telling me he is in the hospital or…that he has been taken from me. It never gets any easier."

Taneika sat there with Jeanie's arm around her, waiting for word of Taren, to see him and verify with her own eyes that he was going to live. She also waited for the chance to have a few minutes alone with Nick Strange.

Bill came back to the lobby. The smile he wore gave her a much-needed boost.

"I got in to see Taren. He's doing fine. The worst of the injuries is his right arm. A round nicked a bone and he will be in a cast for several weeks."

Taneika sat on the edge of the cushion. "When can we see him?"

She read the answer in his face before he spoke.

"I'm sorry, Taneika. Only immediate family members can see him. Security is tight right now. They are afraid of another attempt being made. I did tell him about your bringing in the drug runners you caught."

"And?"

"He smiled and said, 'Well I'll be damned.'"

"That's it? That's all Taren said?"

"There was one other thing. 'Tell Taneika to trust Nick. He saved my life.' Not sure what that is about, and Taren didn't elaborate on it."

Taneika was confused. Could she trust Nick? *Maybe, as long as I don't have to turn my back to him.* "Where's Nick? I need some answers to a few questions."

"Gone," Bill answered. "Went out the back door, said something about looking for somebody that he hoped would resist arrest."

"I'm going to go see Taren," Jeanie announced. "Taneika, anything you want me to tell him?"

"Yes..." *send him away* "...tell him that I'm..." *send him away* "...thankful it's nothing serious."

"That's all?"

Jeanie raised her eyes and gave her a disapproving glare. "Or is there something else you would rather have me tell him?"

She shook her head and watched Jeanie go down the hall. Her vision blurred. *Tell Taren...I love you.* Taneika blinked and a tear rolled slowly down her cheek.

Taneika stood at the window, looking out over the city. Its glow of artificial lights dimmed the stars and created a false sense of security in an insecure world. For the first time she was alone. Always before, she had her wolves to keep her company. Now, even Lobo was gone, back to the wild, free life in the mountains.

Maybe she should just chuck the whole college and higher education thing. Find a wolf pack and live in the mountains. But, could she be happy there? Could she be happy living in an atmosphere where family structure was so strong? So much had changed that it frightened her.

She became aware of Bill's presence beside her and was startled to see his reflection in the window.

"Coffee? Not sure how fresh it is." Bill held out a Styrofoam cup.

"Thanks."

For several long minutes, he stood beside her. "It's probably none of my business, but did you and Taren...have a falling out or something?"

Seconds ticked by like hours as she replayed their last time together. The things she had said that had ripped her heart in two. The pain she had caused Taren, the hurt and confusion that had been so evident in his face.

"Yes." Her voice was barely above a whisper, but in the quiet waiting room of the hospital, it echoed down the halls. If not in reality, then in the crushed chambers of her broken heart.

"Do you want to talk about it?"

His voice was soothing, inviting, like her father's would have been had he still been alive. "No. As you said, it really is none of your business."

"Before I married Jeanie, I was rather a quiet shy person. People who knew me were surprised when I ran for sheriff. I don't know who was more shocked that I had actually won the election, me or the people who knew me. Being married to Jeanie, I must have picked up some of her, shall we say, more aggressive attitude. If you don't want to talk about your relationship with Taren, then you can listen while I ramble on.

"Nick told me about the attack. Taren took on two heavily armed men head-on. Nick said...it was almost like he didn't care if he survived or not. That's not like Taren. While never backing off from a fight, he has never gone out deliberately looking for one either."

"Bill..."

"And you, taking on six drug runners with nothing but a bow. I'm not so certain it was an act of courage. Maybe it was like Taren, you didn't care. Deep down inside, you just didn't give a damn about living anymore."

"Enough!" Taneika turned to face him. "I didn't take time to psychoanalyze my actions in the woods. Taren and I were living in a sensuous make-believe world. One of us had to wake up and realize it wouldn't work. We are too different to make it a long-term relationship."

"At least you are right about one thing. You two are different. I could tell that as soon as I met you, and I'm not sure I want to know how different you really are. What is evident, at least to Jeanie and me, is that Taren chose to ignore, or in spite of them, overlook the differences. And you simply shoved him out the door, probably with no warning."

"Bill, there is...there is more to it than that."

"Did you even try to explain that to Taren?

"I couldn't."

"Dammit, Taneika!" Bill ran his hand through his hair. "You can't play with people's emotions like that."

"I'm sorry."

"Sorry, hell! Taren almost..."

"Hey, you two." Jeanie came back into the waiting room. "Bill, I can hear you clear down the hall. This is supposed to be a hospital. You know, quiet."

Bill turned on Jeanie. "Then you try to talk some sense into her."

"Hon, as much as I agree with you, this is something they will have to work out by themselves. I'm hungry, lets go find a place to eat and maybe we will all feel better."

Bill looked at his watch. "Better make it someplace that serves breakfast."

"I don't feel much like eating right now. If you could drop me off at a motel, I'd appreciate it."

"Taneika, are you sure?" Jeanie placed a comforting hand on her arm.

"Yes. I will catch something to eat later."

* * * * *

Taneika stood outside the office door of the *Frontier Inn*, and watched as Bill and Jeanie drove away. She pocketed the money Bill had given her for a room and went inside.

"May I help you?" a small, dark-complexioned man with a heavy accent asked from behind the counter.

"Can you please call me a cab?"

A few minutes later, a City Cab pulled into the drive.

"You the lady needing a cab?"

"Yes. Please take me to the west side of town."

"What's the address?"

She handed him thirty dollars. "There isn't one. Just drive west 'til you use this up and I'll get out."

"Miss, that far out there's not much around. Are you sure you don't have an address?"

"Look, here is an extra ten as a tip. You get me out of the city and it's yours. If you have a problem with that, I'll find another cab."

"Okay, get in. I hope you know what you're doing."

Me, too.

"Pretty cold out tonight and you're not dressed for spending any time outside. Why don't you let me take you to a shelter? You can get a warm bed and a hot meal. I know one that is always open to women."

"Thanks, but I don't need a shelter."

"They don't call the law unless you want them to. All that's required is that you need help."

What is it with this guy? At three a.m., the city streets were like a ghost town. The business had given way to houses and the occasional convenience store. The cab pulled into the Pelican Truck Plaza between Cody and Wapiti, Wyoming.

"Miss. This is the end of your twenty-dollar ride. We're about ten miles out of Cody."

"Thank you." She handed him the fare plus his tip.

"Miss. I am worried about you, out here without a proper coat. Better go in and see if you can find a ride with someone. At least wait 'til daylight if you are hitchhiking."

"Thank you for your concern, but I will be fine." Taneika got out and headed across the parking lot to the door of the truck stop.

As she sat at the counter, she heard the low voices of the truckers.

"I wonder if she's cold. I wouldn't mind warming her up."

"Hell, she looks like more woman than you could handle, better let me warm her up."

The waitress came up. "Coffee?"

"Please. I would like your hungry truckers steak special, rare, and ranch dressing."

"That is a twenty-two ounce steak," the waitress cautioned.

"Yes, I'm not very hungry, so I'll just order one."

The waitress's eyes bugged out and her jaw dropped.

* * * * *

"What the hell do you mean, she never checked into the hotel!" Taren roared.

"We dropped her off and went to eat. When we got back, we found she hadn't checked in. She had the night clerk call a cab and I figured she came back here."

"Give me my clothes. I'm leaving."

"You can't up and walk out of here!"

"Watch me."

"Taren, those guards outside aren't going to let you leave. Your life may still be in danger."

"Then you don't know the half of it. Fallings is missing. His wife hasn't seen him since yesterday when he came home and beat the shit out of her. She's in the hospital in serious condition. He cleared out the bank account and split."

"You think he'll go after Taneika?"

"It's a possibility I can't ignore." Taren pulled on his pants and winced when the material went across his thigh. "Let's hope he goes to Canada. At least we can extradite him from there."

"We better find Taneika," Bill helped Taren with his shirt, "in case Fallings is looking for her."

"Pray we find her before he does." Taren limped to the door. "I want him alive and behind bars."

* * * * *

Taneika sighed and laid the fork down beside the empty plate.

"I can't believe you ate the whole thing." The waitress stood there with her eyes wide open. "I have seen some really big men almost cry when they couldn't finish it. How did you do it? I would die to have a figure like yours. Course, working here doesn't help any. I swear the calories must jump on me when I serve the food."

"I stay active. The steak was delicious. Please give my compliments to the cook." Taneika paid the bill and put on her jacket.

"I noticed you came in a cab. Is someone meeting you here?"

"No, I'm walking."

"It's ten degrees outside," the waitress said with concern. "That coat is so lightweight you will freeze to death. Why don't you let me check with some of the drivers? I know most of them and I will pick you a safe one to ride with."

"Thanks, but I don't have far to go." Taneika headed for the door.

"Hey, doll baby, need a ride?"

She turned to face the men she had heard earlier. "Look, mister, you got nothing I want to ride, and that includes your truck." With a backward glance and a wink at the waitress, she opened the door and stepped out into the cold night.

As she walked across the parking lot, the large lights cast her shadow across the packed snow. She felt the eyes on her back from the people inside the restaurant. Twenty miles, no sweat, be home before the sun comes up.

Once outside curtain of light that surrounded the parking area, Taneika picked up the pace. She wanted to be home before the light of day or an increase in traffic forced her into the woods. With her senses alert for vehicles approaching from behind, she ran easily down the road. She knew that to sustain this speed she had to push her body past the pain barrier. The slower she ran the longer it took to reach her destination, and time was against her.

Sweat began to form on her face; she knew that the edge was close. This time she embraced it, welcomed the pain. She had only broken the barrier once before, when tracking down her father's killer. Then she had been so obsessed with grief and blood lust for revenge that she hadn't cared. The pain increased until she thought her heart would explode, her lungs burned and still she ran. The road blurred and then her vision cleared, the pain dropped away as quickly as it had come.

She was through the barrier.

Lengthening her stride, she increased her speed. At this grueling pace, she wasn't overly concerned about vehicles approaching from behind and any vehicle she met would only see a momentary flash of her in its headlights.

A mile from home, she started slowing down. Climbing the steps to her door, she doubled over in agony. Stumbling through the door, she headed toward the bathroom. Weaving with every step, she bounced off the wall. She had to get her clothes off; they had to come off, had to...

Chapter 14

Taneika opened her eyes and stared into Taren's concerned face. He held a cool washcloth that was pressed against her forehead. She looked down at her clothes that were crimson-stained and sticking to her skin. Attempting to sit up, the room spun; behind her eyes, bright explosions sent shockwaves through her head.

"I thought you were in the hospital." She leaned back against his solid thigh. "How did you get here?"

"Bill and Jeanie brought me."

Very slowly, carefully, she sat up and looked around. The bathroom door was closed. "Where are they?"

"Waiting in the living room, I had to almost manhandle Jeanie to keep her out. I couldn't hide the blood on the floor. What happened?"

"How long have you been here?"

"Not long. Now answer my question."

"I need a shower." Taneika stood on shaky legs and opened the shower door. *Why is this time so much worse than before? My insides feel like they had been ripped out.*

"There was no blood outside, only inside the house. Now what the *hell* happened!"

"Taren..." A knock sounded at the door. "Is everything all right in there?"

"Yes, Sis." He looked from Taneika to the door and ran his hands through his hair, frustration and impatience gnawing at his gut. "If I need you, I'll holler. Go put on a pot of coffee or something."

"I can't explain it." Taneika turned the water on and stepped under its cleansing spray.

"Can you explain whose blood you are covered in?"

"Oh. That's easy...it's mine." She leaned back against the shower wall and began to slowly unbutton her blouse. The water turned red at her feet before swirling down the drain.

"Yours!" His heart was gripped with terror at the thought of her being injured.

"Calm down." Taneika raised a hand to stop him from entering the shower. "I'm not hurt. Only tired and hungry."

She peeled off the blouse and started washing the blood out of it.

"It just happens, that's all I can tell you." Unsnapping her jeans, she let them fall around her ankles. She felt too weak to step out of them.

The water swirling at her feet continued to turn red. He reached in and turned the water off.

"Hey." She reached up to turn the water back on but his touch on her shoulder and arm stopped her.

"My God! You're bleeding from every pore."

"That's why I want the water on." She wiped her arm clean. "See, it's almost stopped now. The cold water helps." In slow motion, she turned the water on. *Food, I have to have food.*

"This...this has happened before." Even as he watched, the water flowing off her body became clearer.

"Once when..." Her legs grew weak and she slid down the wall. Taren's arms were instantly around her.

"What's wrong?"

"I need food to get my strength back. There's," she opened her mouth and let the water quench her ravaging thirst. "...meat...in the fridge."

Taren closed the door behind him and went to the kitchen.

"Is she okay? Should I check on her? Should we call for an ambulance?" Jeanie's rapid questions were fired at him.

"Slow down, Sis. Yes, she is going to be all right." Finding the meat, he headed back to the bathroom.

"What are you doing with that haunch of venison?" Bill asked, puzzled.

"Bill, some things are better left unquestioned. Besides, I'm not sure you would want the answer." He paused, and turned to them. "You two go over to my place and get some sleep. I'm going to make sure Taneika gets into bed and then keep watch for a while. I'm still not convinced that Fallings has left the area."

"Taren." The tone of Bill's voice stopped him. "Do you know what you are getting into? Might be best to walk away while you can."

"Too late, Bill." He turned back towards the bathroom. "I'm already in too deep."

Taneika was still sitting in the shower. With her head slumped forward, her hair hung around her like a black veil. Taren reached in and turned the water off. Ever so slowly, she raised her head, her hollow gaze intensified with purpose and riveted on the meat he held in his hand. Yet, she made no attempt to reach for it.

Taren realized immediately she was too weak and tore off a chunk of meat, placing it in her mouth. With each piece he fed her, she grew stronger and was soon feeding herself, tearing into the venison as if there were no tomorrow. He had handed her between two and three pounds of meat, and within minutes, it was gone.

"Thanks, Taren." She stood quickly and turned the shower on, washing away the blood and juices from the meat that had dripped on her breasts and legs. The increased throbbing in his arm was the first indication that he was responding physically to her. A tightening of his trousers was the next.

This was torture, being this close to her and wanting her. But because of what she had said, he was holding back. As if reading his thoughts, she turned toward him and gave him a hot, sultry, *I need you inside me* pleading grin. Gone were the hollow eyes and lethargic movements.

Stepping out of the shower, she stood in front of Taren, water pooling at her feet.

"What game are you playing, Taneika? A couple days ago, in this very house you sent me away. Now, you're coming on to me like I was fresh road kill."

"I'm sorry, but it was necessary. I can't explain it." She took Taren's own words and threw them back into his face. "I guess you will have to trust me."

Her words chilled his desire. "I'm not some lapdog to come running every time you're in heat. Go to bed, Taneika. If the itch is that strong, scratch it yourself."

Taren turned and left the room.

A short while later as he set the empty but still warm coffee cup on the counter, a wolf howl split the dead quiet of the night. The bathroom door opened and Taneika walked down the hall and into her bedroom, slamming the door behind her.

His shoulder hurt like hell, his leg burned where the bullet had grazed his thigh. The day was bright and clear, yet his soul was troubled, all gray and dim. Taren poured the last of the coffee from the pot into his cup. All he needed to do was rest his eyes for a few minutes. Taking a couple of aspirins for the pain, he carried the cup into the living room and sat on the couch.

One hell of a mess this turned out to be, Taren ol' boy. Fallings is missing and Taneika slammed the door on you. All you had to do was keep your mouth shut and you would have been in there with her, instead of on the couch. Next time yo...

His eyes drifted closed.

No, Harold, let her go. I promise you a fair trial. If you kill her, you're a dead man.

You wouldn't shoot an unarmed man, Taren. Surely not over a piece of ass.

Taren watched helplessly as he pulled Taneika's arm further behind her back. Her face twisted in agony as Harold increased the pressure.

You think I am going to jail. I would rather die, but first I plan on giving you a little hell on earth to remember me by. Every time you go to sleep in an empty bed, you will remember me. Remember that I sent this little creature from hell back to where she belongs. Go find yourself a real woman Taren...and say good-bye to dear little Taneika.

"No!"

Taren bolted up from the couch and the pain shot through him like an explosion. With his head spinning and feeling nauseous, he stumbled to Taneika's door. Without bothering to knock, he barged in.

Her bed was empty. The house was dark.

He had slept through the day. Where was Taneika? What about Bill and Jeanie? They should have been here by now.

On the kitchen table, he found the answer to one of his questions.

Taren. I hated to leave but Bill has an emergency back home. Didn't want to wake you or Taneika, I hope everything can be worked out between you. Take care of the arm. Love, Sis. P.S. Try to keep from getting any more holes in you.

The back door opened and Taren spun in a crouch, his pistol pointed toward Taneika. His arm dropped and he sucked in large gulps of air. Her face had gone pale in his sights. Shaking with the realization that he could have easily shot her, he holstered his weapon. *Thank God, it was only a dream.*

"My God, woman! Knock or say something before you come in."

"This is my house. I'll come and go as I damn well please."

"It may not be safe to go out. We still aren't sure of Fallings' location."

She carried the hindquarter of a young deer in her left hand. Her left side was heavily covered in blood, probably from carrying the deer over her shoulder.

Visions of them making wild passionate love at the cabin filled his thoughts. "Go get cleaned up and put some clothes on. We need to talk."

Taneika put the venison on the counter, sliced off a piece of meat and started eating. "So talk." She said between bites.

"After your shower."

"I'm hungry." She sliced off another chunk of meat and bit into it.

Blood ran from the meat down her face and between her breasts. His eyes locked on the scarlet trail as it slowly made its way past her hips to the silky V of her legs.

"You want me to fry up a couple steaks?"

"I can fry the steaks while you get cleaned up." He wasn't sure how much more of this he could take. The longer she stood there naked in front of him, the less resistance he had.

She could feel the frustration in his voice. She was going to push him into going home or taking her, and she was counting on the taking. It didn't matter where or how. His early morning suggestion that she scratch the itch did nothing but make the hunger for him stronger.

"You seem to have an obsession with my taking a shower. Did watching me shower this morning turn you on? Is that why you keep insisting I get cleaned up? You want to watch?" She walked to the table and stood just across from him. Leaning over, her breast hung within easy reach, inviting his touch. *Come on, Taren, fuck me or go home.*

The passionate pleading in her eyes to be held and touched, drove Taren beyond reasonable thinking.

His hand darted out to capture her thick black tresses. Pulling her across the table, his lips locked onto hers, grinding and punishing. Her tongue warred with his for domination.

He unsnapped his pants and let them drop to the floor. Impatient hands pulled at his shorts and grasped his hardness. Reaching out, he grabbed her leg and spun her on the table, her hot wetness stopping directly in front of him. Her legs on either side of his, she was spread open, ready. Further invitation wasn't needed as he drove home into her creamy depths.

The crossing of her legs behind him locked them together in a frenzy of thrusting and pounding of hips. Leaning forward, he took a taut nipple in his mouth. His teeth grazed her skin and she arched her back, lifting his feet off the floor.

In a screech and splintering of wood, the table leg collapsed under their combined weight.

Taneika ended up on top of Taren. Her mouth again sought his as his hands held her breasts in a firm grip. As his fingers squeezed her nipples, electric impulses were sent out, stimulating her already overloaded senses. With each thrust into her, she was drawn further toward the threshold. The blood roared in her ears as her heart felt ready to burst. His face blurred before her.

Taren's body stiffened and she felt the essence of his power fill her, his hot explosion triggering her own shattering release. Waves of ecstasy shook Taneika and her human cry of passion fulfilled, turned wild and unrestrained.

She lay on his chest gulping air. The tremor she felt filled her with alarm. Relaxing her muscles that held him captive inside her, she got up and hurried to the bathroom.

No! Not again!

"Taneika. What's the matter?"

"Nothing." *What's happening to me?*

Even as he heard the words, her backside was turning a brilliant crimson hue.

He tried to get up and stumbled. Kicking off the pants that were bunched around his feet, he ran to the bathroom and flung open the shower door.

She stood under the full spray, letting the water wash away the blood that oozed from every pore. Eyes wide with fear, she stared at her arms.

"Taneika, what can I do? Tell me how can I help?"

She looked up at him, her eyes large, the pupils dilated 'til there was almost no brown.

"Why is this happening to me?"

This is your fault. You caused this. If you had controlled yourself, she wouldn't be bleeding again. Guilt flooded over him before sound reasoning took over. *Couldn't be my fault, she provoked me.*

"Hold me, please."

Her voice was a whimper, pleading like a child frightened awake by a bad dream. Only, this was no nightmare, it was real and he felt at a loss as how to help.

Taren stepped into the shower and wrapped his arms around her.

"I'm scared, Taren." She cried against the fabric of his shirt. "I'm losing control."

She grew heavy in his arms. Taren carried her to the kitchen and sat her on the counter. "Here, eat." Thrusting the raw, bloody meat into her hands, he waited 'til she had gotten her strength back.

Picking up the phone, he dialed a number he knew by heart...

"Hello, Sis...No, I'm fine. It's Taneika. She had another relapse of what happened this morning. I want to bring her up there and have you to look her over... I can't do that, Sis. She can't afford the questions that would be raised if I took her to a doctor here... You're the only one I can trust... I'll be there in the morning. Bye."

Chapter 15

"Have you ever had blood drawn?" Jeanie wiped her arm with a cotton swab.

"No."

"I'm just going to draw a small vial of blood and do a type check on you."

Taneika sat on the exam table. She was beginning to have second thoughts about the whole process of this checkup. The blood flowing into the syringe could bring the answers to her innermost questions, but it could also be the beginning of what her adopted father had warned her about. Now that she had time to think about it, she wished she hadn't agreed to have Jeanie do all these tests.

The last time hadn't been as bad even though she had started bleeding.

"Jeanie, are you sure the blood test is necessary?" Taneika watched as she pulled the needle out.

"I can't find anything that can tell me why this is happening to you. I want to take an x-ray and have this blood sent off. Don't worry, after what Taren told me about you, I'm not going to make a file or folder on you. We do need to try to find out what is causing this, but more important is to see if your physical health is endangered." Jeanie paused, as if trying to find the right word.

"You said this last time, while you and Taren where having sex, the pain wasn't as sharp and it took you by surprise?"

"Yes."

"I won't be but a moment. Sit here and try to relax."

She tried to, but the apprehension continued to eat away at her. After finding the wondrous joy of sex, was she destined to go the rest of her life without it? Taren had been so concerned and understanding. What would he do if this were to be a normal reaction after every time they mated? Somehow, her life had taken a path that she wasn't sure she wanted to travel, but she saw no way of avoiding it.

The clock on the wall continued to tick off the minutes.

"Sorry it took so long."

Taneika turned toward the sound of Jeanie's voice and was ready to speak when the troubled look on her face stopped her.

"I...I was unable to type check your blood."

"Why's that?" She saw the confused look on Jeanie's face.

"When I did yours, it showed it was type O, but when I did a reverse check it showed it was type AB. It's not the test procedures. I drew some of my blood and the test results were normal."

"I don't understand."

"I don't either, 'cause medically it's not possible. O blood types are considered universal donors while type AB is considered universal recipients. If the test is correct, I'm guessing you are both."

"Could that cause my skin to bleed?"

"I don't think so. Taneika, I'm a nurse practitioner. It would require a complete lab to give a detailed analysis and I wouldn't recommend it."

"Why not?"

"Assuming I'm correct, the scientific world wouldn't rest 'til it found out *everything* about you. Your life would be a living nightmare from then on. I'd be lying if I told you I wasn't curious as hell about it myself. If I had the ability, I'd run the lab tests here."

"So where does that leave us?"

"There are some basic tests that I can run. First let's get some vitals and a chest x-ray. That will give me a starting point."

Jeanie went out to the waiting room. She smiled. Taren was pacing the small room like an expectant father.

"Taren, I'm going to run a stress test on Taneika. She says she gets hungry afterward."

"Hungry isn't the word that describes her appetite. Are you sure this test is safe?"

"Safer with me than a lab somewhere else. Brother, the fewer people that knows about this...the better."

"I'm aware of that, Sis. She had two episodes yesterday. Maybe we should wait a day or two."

"I promise that I will take care of her. She wants to know what is going on. Taren, she's scared."

"Can you help her?"

"Maybe, if what is happening to her can be controlled, I can help her find out how. I need you to get enough meat for her. I have to see the reaction she is having myself. I want to take a series of x-rays. Maybe I can find some answers between them and her vital signs."

"Okay. I'll be back in a few minutes. I think I better be there when you run those tests."

"When you get back, lock the door."

Taren wished he had fresher meat than what the store had in stock. Something with a little more blood in it. Carrying his large grocery bag through the door, he turned and flipped the dead bolt.

"Taren, we're in the back room. Come on back, we're ready to begin."

He walked through the door and Taneika stood naked on a treadmill with wires attached to electrodes on her chest. Several monitors were on and a tube ran from her mouth to one of them.

"I've hooked up about everything we have onto her. It won't be an accurate study but any information we get may be helpful."

Jeanie turned. "Taneika, are you ready?"

She gave a slight nod and started running. Taren watched her blood pressure and her oxygen level. After ten minutes, they were slightly elevated. He looked down at the speed she was running. *Ten miles an hour and she hasn't even broken a sweat.*

"Do you feel okay?" Jeanie asked. "Can you increase your speed any?"

A smile formed around the air tube.

Taren watch the indicator jump to twenty miles an hour and steady out. Her heart rate spiked and then settled down, but higher than before. Jeanie was making notes on a chart when she turned suddenly to Taneika.

"X-ray now!"

Taneika stepped off the treadmill and in front of the unit. A slight buzz was heard and Jeanie motioned her to get back on the treadmill. The indicator climbed steadily and leveled off. Jeanie slid a new plate in place and continued monitoring the readouts.

"Well?" he asked.

"Hush."

Lights flashed and alarms sounded. Taren didn't have a clue as to what he should do. He looked down at the speed indicator and was astonished to see she had doubled her speed without any apparent effort.

"Her heart rhythm changed, and her blood pressure went up drastically." Jeanie looked from the monitor to Taneika.

"How are you doing?"

Taneika gave her a thumbs-up accompanied by a wide smile.

"Are you through this barrier you told me about?"

Again, Taneika gave her a thumb in the air.

"Taren, I see it but I don't understand it," Jeanie stared open-mouthed and wide-eyed at the monitors.

"Taneika, I need to get the x-ray now. Okay, don't move, don't breathe."

Jeanie hit the controls and the machine rumbled.

"Taneika, get back on the treadmill and slow your body down. We have meat and a cold tub of water waiting."

As she got back on and started running, she felt the pain in her chest. Doubling over she held on to the handrails.

"Talk to me, is this like the other times?" Alarm sounded in Jeanie's voice as she tore the hose from Taneika's mouth.

"Yes!" She gulped air into her now heaving chest. Her lungs burned and her heart pounded. "Yes! This...is...like the...last time."

Blood began to ooze from her skin.

Taren picked her up and carried her to the stainless steel tub that was half full of water. Setting her in it, he began to splash water over her face and shoulders, cooling her fevered skin.

"Here, give this to her." Jeanie handed him a large roast. Taneika snatched the meat from his hands and tore into it, trying to appease the ravenous hunger.

"Are you feeling better now?" Jeanie asked. She stuck a syringe in Taneika's arm and drew a vial of blood. Taking a swab, she collected another sample of the blood that was flowing from her skin.

"I'm still hungry, but yes, I'm better."

Jeanie handed her another roast, smaller than the one before and marked down its weight. She examined Taneika's skin, her eyes, listened to her heart and lungs.

"Everything sounds and appears normal, now. I have to process the x-rays." She took the plates in to another room and closed the door.

"Taneika, you don't have to do this. I don't like to see you suffer." He brushed his hand though her hair and softly stroked her cheek.

"Yes, I do. I've got to know what's happening to me." She took his hand and placed a kiss on the back of it. "This time wasn't as bad as before. I didn't fight it. I knew you were here and wasn't scared." She climbed out of the water and checked out the bag from which Jeanie had taken the meat.

"Ah." She pulled a package of veal from the bag and started munching on the succulent meat.

Several minutes had gone by when Jeanie came back into the room. She placed the x-rays on the lighted board and started writing down more notes.

"Sis, I know that puzzled frown and the tapping of the pencil from college. You do that when there is something bothering you that you can't figure out. What gives?"

She started to answer and then stopped. "Is that *another* package of meat?"

"I was still hungry." Taneika responded with her mouth full.

Jeanie shook her head as she watched the last of the veal steaks disappear. She picked up the wrapper and wrote the weight down on a sheet.

"You can get dressed now."

Taneika ignored the suggestion and padded over to where the x-rays were hanging. Rivulets of water trickled from her hair to puddle around her feet.

"If all of these are of me, why are they different?" Her brows drew down into a frown as she intently studied the pictures.

"I don't know."

Taren heard the uncertainty, the frustration in her voice. He looked at the pictures but they all looked the same.

"How are they different, Sis?"

"Let me show you." She walked over and took two of the films down. "I took this one," she tapped it with her pencil, "before she started the test." She placed the second one over the top of the first. "This is the one I took during the test. Notice the shape of the lung in the second. It appears to be a little narrower and longer than the first. Her blood pressure at this point is not any higher than for an athlete who runs all the time."

"What about the last one you took, Sis?"

She placed the third film directly over the first and the difference was dramatic. The lungs were now several inches longer than in the first x-ray. His eyes riveted on the heart.

"My God!"

"The increase of the heart is proportional to that of the lungs. This is right after you went through what you call 'the pain barrier.' Taneika, at this point your blood pressure jumped to 210 over 125, and your body temp went up to a hundred and four. That would explain the need for a cold shower."

"My God!"

"Taren, you're repeating yourself," Jeanie admonished. "Relax, I would already be calling an ambulance for a normal person."

"That means I'm not...normal."

"Taneika, I'm not sure how I would put this...condition you have. But you are definitely not normal. Your body appears somehow to have the ability to...for lack of a better word, change to meet the increased demands you place on it."

"What about the bleeding and the hunger?"

"Without more advanced tests which would mean a lab or research center somewhere, I can only guess at those. Possibly, because you never did sweat the whole time this is your body's way of cooling down. Again, I'm guessing that when your body changes, it takes a great amount of energy. Energy your body has to replace, quickly."

"Oh." Taneika stared at the two x-ray films. *So, I'm a freak.* She looked into Taren's face expecting to see revulsion, or pity, maybe disgust. What she saw was concern and the molten heat of desire that flared like a torch in the depths of his eyes. How long would he continue to want her if every time they made love, her skin bled? Unless she could control her body, their relationship was doomed. *Yesterday was different, that was pure lust. Maybe…*

"I have an idea for another test."

"I don't think that is advisable," Jeanie cautioned. "At least not so soon after this one."

"Besides, you ate most of the meat," Taren added.

"You haven't heard what it is. Besides, it would depend on how serious Taren is about helping me."

"Just what is that supposed to mean?" Taren blustered.

"The test would involve you."

"What's the test, Taneika?" Jeanie asked.

"Well…last night when we had sex on the kitchen table it…"

"You didn't!" Jeanie interrupted with laughter.

"Until the table broke, then we ended up on the floor."

"Oh, my," Jeanie doubled over, holding her stomach. "That is too much." She looked up at Taren and wiped the tears from her eyes. "Any splinters you need removed?"

"Very funny, Sis."

"Anyway," Taneika continued. "I thought maybe we could hook up the monitors again and we could make love in a…"

"We do *what*?" Taren wasn't sure if he'd heard her right or not. She couldn't be suggesting this. "Leave me out of your impromptu research."

"If that is the way you feel about it, fine." She stomped across the room and got dressed. "I can't stay around and wonder when this will happen to me again. If you don't care enough about our relationship to help me learn how to control it, then I guess this is goodbye."

"Taneika, wait." He stood there with his hand outstretched as she closed the door behind her.

"Don't just stand there like an idiot," Jeanie scolded. "Go after her."

Taren looked for her in the front of the building and then outside. Feeling like the idiot that his sister had called him, he went back inside.

"She's gone."

"I figured that from the look on your face. You know, sometimes I wonder how with all your knowledge of the opposite sex you could be so callous with her feelings. And then I remember you're a man and that explains it. Dammit, Taren, this wasn't some joke on her part. How do you think she feels, afraid that every time you two make love this," she held up the printouts from the monitors, "is going to happen?"

He sat on the chair and dropped his head in his hands. "I blew it."

"Don't sit there feeling sorry for yourself. Go find her, and when you do, try a little groveling and begging. Might be good experience for you."

Chapter 16

She welcomed the pain and embraced it. It swept over her and she felt the renewed power that flowed within her veins.

Tears that streamed from her eyes became frozen in her hair as she ran through the trees. Her clothes, torn and ripped, hung like rags from her body. She clawed her way up steep inclines, sometimes on all fours, using her hands as much as her feet to propel her upward and then down the other side. The avalanches she had caused rumbled behind her with the promise of certain death at the slightest slip or falter.

She stood on top of the ridge looking into a valley. Some inner guidance had directed her path here. She raised her head and howled out a greeting to any wolves in the area. She smiled at the returned voices that were carried on the wind.

She was home.

* * * * *

Jeanie watched as Taren's car turned the corner and disappeared from view. She locked the door to the clinic, got in her car and headed in the opposite direction. On the outskirts of Red Rock, she pulled into a parking lot, hesitated and got out. Ol' Doc Gregger had been her inspiration for going into the medical field. Only she had gone into nursing instead of becoming a veterinarian. She trusted him, but was she about to push the limits of trust too far?

"Hi, Doc."

"Hi, Jeanie. What brings you to this end of town?"

"I wouldn't normally ask this, Doc, but I need a lab test done and was wondering if you would do it."

"Jeanie, I've known you since you brought in here the first stray puppy you ever found. Something is bothering you with possible results of this test or you would send it to the regular lab in Billings."

"It has to kept strictly confidential, no records."

Doc Gregger looked her in the eye. Determined and unflinching, she met his narrow-eyed, penetrating gaze.

"This is highly irregular, Jeanie."

"I know." Holding her ground, she didn't back down from his scowl.

"Come on back to the lab. My assistant went to lunch. We won't be disturbed."

They entered the lab and she handed him the blood samples. She watched as he placed them under a microscope. He stopped once, looked at her as he took off his glasses, cleaned them, and again concentrated on the blood samples.

Doc picked up the gauze she had used to collect the sample and turned toward her.

"What are these, Jeanie?"

"Blood samples."

"*Really!* I didn't know that." He turned and with a sarcastic glance at her, held a tube in front of her face. "Would you mind telling me where you got these?"

"Why?" Jeanie's wariness increased as she saw the puzzled frown on his face.

"So I can better understand what I am looking at, or for. This first tube is human, no mistake about that. This sample from the gauze, my rough guess, is the antigens from the blood of a wolf. This other vial." He held it up before his eyes, wonder and amazement spread across his face. "I have no idea." He continued to rotate the vial in his fingers as if seeing a rare diamond for the first time. "I have *never* seen anything like it before.

"Jeanie, are you feeling all right?" He reached out to her, touching her arm. "You need to sit down? You're awfully pale."

"No, I...I'll be fine, thank you. Please, I beg you!" She picked up the samples. "Forget you ever saw these. I have to be going."

"Jeanie, if you need to talk..."

"Thanks." She turned and left.

Her hand trembled as she tried to put the key in the ignition. Jeanie laid her head on the steering wheel and cried.

* * * * *

Taren paced the floor. Take-out food containers littered the kitchen table and spilled onto the floor. He had checked and rechecked all the hospitals in the area, spent countless hours searching the woods of the park. Nothing. Every wolf pack that was known to exist within the area had been checked and not a sign of Taneika, not even a footprint. Days had turned into weeks and she hadn't been home.

Where are you hiding, my love? Another thought crept into his mind and twisted his heart with fear. *Where is Harold?*

Thanksgiving had come and gone. He had spent it with her mother and the rest of the family on the reservation, hoping that she would return home for the holidays. They had been reluctant to speak of Taneika. The brothers seemed ashamed of her existence. The private conversation he had with Songbird revealed little that he didn't already know. Her warning, to let her adopted daughter live her own life, only strengthened his resolve to find her.

The howling of a wolf shattered the stillness of the night and caused him to jump.

"Taneika!" Taren ran to the door and stepped out into the cold winter wind that blew down off the mountains.

The wolf's eyes glowed in the light that spilled from the open door.

Startled, Taren started to back towards the door when a whine from the wolf stopped him. The wolf approached, head down, ears lowered and tail tucked between its legs.

"Lobo? Is that you? Come here, girl, am I glad to see you." Taren sat on the porch step.

She came to him, placed her head in his lap and then licked his face. "Where have you been, girl? Have you seen Taneika?"

Lobo perked up her ears and barked. She spun around and ran to where Taren's truck was parked and jumped in the back.

"What is it girl? What do you..." He turned and ran into the house, grabbing the backpacks that he had been living out of for weeks. Turning out the lights and locking the door, he ran across the snow to his truck.

"Sorry, girl, I know you must be hungry. This is all I have right now." He tossed a box of cold pizza in the back of the truck and was gratified when Lobo began tearing off large chunks of a dinner he had never touched.

Taren pulled into his sister's driveway in the predawn hours. Lobo hopped out and squatted. "Sorry girl, I'm so concerned about Taneika, I forgot you were back there."

He beat on the door, rattling it on its hinges. A light came on and Bill opened the door. With an exasperated look on his face, he motioned him in.

"Taren, this has got to stop. You look like shit. When was the last time you had a decent meal or a full night's sleep?"

"I know where she is, Bill."

"Where?" Jeanie came down the hall, tying the belt of her robe around her waist.

"At the cabin. Lobo showed up at my place and jumped into my truck. She has to be there."

"Please, Taren. Forget about it and go home. After this much time she obviously doesn't want to be found." Jeanie poured water into the coffeepot and flipped the switch.

"Sis, we've had this conversation before. My answer is still the same. I can't."

He turned in desperation to Bill. "I need to borrow the snowmobile again."

"Taren, I...ah, *hell*." Frustrated, he ran his fingers through his hair, shook his head and let out a long sigh. "Go ahead and take it. Nothing I say is going to convince you otherwise."

"Taren Carpenter, I *forbid* you to go after her!"

He turned towards her, his laughter cut short. She stood in the kitchen exactly like their mother. Hands on the hips and feet planted firmly on the floor. A stern look but one filled with love was on her face. His mother's love had always been the deciding catalyst for obedience. *That was yesterday before you were gone, yesterday when we were young...* He shook off the words that ran through his mind like the melody of an old song. *...and left so very much alone.*

Picking up the key that Bill had tossed on the table, he turned his back on the past and headed towards the future, whatever that might be.

Bill came out the door as he finished hooking up the trailer to his truck and handed him a thermos of coffee and a plastic shopping bag filled with food. "Jeanie didn't figure you had eaten anything so she threw this together."

Taren plugged the trailer's wiring harness into the truck's electrical system and inspected the lights.

"We have never had any secrets until now," Bill continued. "I mention Taneika's name and Jeanie gets all nervous and clams up. She refuses to tell me about the test results. If I can help, for God's sake, Taren, let me."

Bill was pleading for understanding, something Taren had never heard him do. "You already have." He patted the nose cowling of the snowmobile. "Tell Sis I appreciate the coffee and food."

Lobo stood at his side sniffing the bag.

"Okay, you can ride up front, I'm sure there's enough for you, too." He opened the door and Lobo hopped in.

"Be careful." Bill stuck his hand out and Taren gripped it firmly with his. "There's a storm front moving in."

They stood there for several seconds, their hands clasped as they peered steadfast into each other's eyes.

"I will." Taren slid behind the wheel and closed the door. As he pulled out of the driveway, he glanced in the side mirror and saw Jeanie step out of the house. In the glow of the porch light, he saw her wipe her face. *Sis, what is it you're not telling me?*

* * * * *

Taren pulled into the parking lot where just weeks before they had taken their attackers' vehicle. The light snow that had started falling as he left his sister's place was now landing heavily on his windshield. During the last couple miles the visibility had been minimal. Stepping out of the truck the silence engulfed him. It was nearly impossible to distinguish any difference between the ground and sky. Twenty feet from the truck and he would be lost in a world of eerie white.

Taking the heavy snowsuit from behind the seat, he slipped it on and zipped up the legs. Lowering the ramp, he uncovered the snowmobile and climbed on. The engine cranked over with the first try. Backing the unit off the trailer, he took his packs and secured them to the seat.

"Lobo, come here girl." He squatted down and rubbed the wolf behind her ears. "I hope you can understand me. I won't be able to see anything out there. You've got to stay close so I can see you." Taren stared into big soft brown eyes, hoping she understood, "I have to follow you, or I won't make it."

Throwing a leg over the seat, he pulled the helmet over his head and slid his hands into the insulated covers of the controls. Taren opened the throttle and the snowmobile's wide belt dug into the snow, moving him through the all-encompassing shroud of white. Lobo struggled through the deepening snow, sinking to her belly with every leap. Trees appeared in front of him without warning as if cast there by magic, leaving precious seconds for him to maneuver out of the way. He ducked tree limbs bent under the weight of the snow. The slightest movement of a branch would send its precariously balanced load crashing down on top of him.

Taren's helmet hit a large branch and he was covered with the snow that fell. He shook it off and looked around. Lobo had disappeared from view. Calculating his position was impossible with no landmarks to go by. Glancing at the compass, he knew he was headed in the right direction, but he could be anywhere in the valley. The speed had been slowed down considerably as he blindly followed behind the wolf. He pulled up, shut the engine off and removed his helmet. Once again, he was amazed at the silence that surrounded him. Taking the thermos of coffee he poured a cup and sat with one leg propped on the cowling as he sipped the steaming liquid.

"Lobo!" he yelled. "Lobo, come here girl!"

From up ahead came a muffled cry of pain.

Panic surged through him as he listened to the whimper.

Starting the engine, Taren headed in the direction of Lobo's cries. He stopped, turned off the engine and listened. "Lobo," he called out again.

The cry of the wolf was close.

He spotted the wolf's tracks in the snow and followed them on foot. Struggling through the deep snow he came to where the wolf lay, her front leg caught in the steel-toothed jaws of a trap. Anger surged through him. This type of trap had been outlawed for years. Their massive teeth chewed flesh and broke bones, causing cruel torture and eventually, a slow agonizing death.

"Easy girl...easy there, let me take a look at you." He lowered his voice and tried to make it soothing to calm the frightened, hurt animal. Cautiously he approached and Lobo quit thrashing about. Blood flowed from around the jagged steel mouth of the trap turning the snow bright burgundy. "I know it hurts, Lobo. Just a minute and I'll have this nasty trap off."

Taren pried the trap open as gently as he could, hoping that with the sudden pain caused by the moving steel, she wouldn't attack him. Lobo yelped and spun her head around but kept her mouth closed.

As her leg was released, Lobo yelped again and scrambled away. Unable to walk on her injured front leg, she limped, leaving a trail of fresh blood with every step.

"No, Lobo!" He tossed the trap aside and went to her. "Let me look at you, girl. You're in no shape to be walking around now. Lie down, girl, that's the way." Being careful with the injured leg he checked to see the extent of damage done by the outlawed trap.

"You were lucky, girl. Yes, you were. Your leg is cut real bad but I don't think there are any bones broken." He found a handkerchief and bound the torn flesh. "Lobo, stay. I'll be back." He started to walk away and Lobo raised her head. "No, Lobo, *stay.*"

When Lobo laid her head back in the snow, Taren turned and followed his footsteps back to the snowmobile. Climbing on the seat, he stared the engine and drove to where Lobo lay.

"Good girl." Taren pulled an artic tent from a pack and quickly set it up. Lobo watched his every move. Taking the backpack from the snowmobile, he crawled inside. He turned around and Lobo had her head stuck through the opening.

"Come here, Lobo." He patted the tent floor beside him.

Lobo limped over, lay down and placed her head on Taren's leg.

He gently stroked the wolf's head. "I know it hurts. Soon as it quits snowing I'll take you to Taneika." Taking the remains of the sack lunch that Jeanie had given him, he fed Lobo. When it was all gone, Lobo licked his hand.

He was reminded of another time when he had fed Lobo, and Taneika had licked the juice from his fingers and the passion that followed. That seemed such a long time ago with all that had happened since.

The wind picked up, howling through the trees, buffeting the tent. Taren looked outside. The snow was swirling through the trees and had drifted over the snowmobile leaving only a small portion of the nose cowling exposed.

"Well girl, it looks like we are going to spend the night here." He rolled out the sleeping bag, covered Lobo with his coat and settled down to wait the dawn and hopefully the end of the storm.

He wasn't sure what woke him, the lack of wind and the calm that follows a storm, Lobo's movement or the sound from the tent door being slowly unzipped. Taren inched his hand out and secured his revolver. After his near-death brush with the mob, it was never far from his reach.

The tent was illuminated with the soft glow of a full moon. The sight of tangled matted hair filling the door caused him to gasp. With the eyes of a half-crazed beast and lips pulled back into a vicious snarl, she stared at him.

"Taneika!"

Chapter 17

Her eyes flashed to Lobo and then riveted on him.

"What are you doing *here*?" she hissed. "Lobo, come."

Lobo scooted over, nudged Taren's hand up with her nose and slid her head under his arm.

Taneika's eyes widened and her nostrils flared as she looked at Lobo and then back to him. Her eyes narrowed at Lobo's seeming betrayal.

"Same thing I've been doing ever since you left. Looking for you."

She stayed on her knees in the low tent; her firm breasts rose and fell with each breath. She was within reach of his other hand but he resisted the desire to pull her to him.

"Why all the concern? Surely you can find someone else to fill your bed. You can always go back to Linda."

"If I'd wanted Linda, I'd never have broken up with her. I was a rung on the ladder, a stopping place until she could find a more influential partner." He ran his fingers slowly through the wolf's thick winter coat.

There was a nervous tension in the air. Almost like an electric current, it flowed and swept around them.

"Is that what I am to you, a rung on your ladder, another notch in your belt? You've taken my virginity and it appears the loyalty of Lobo. What else do you want?"

"No, not a single rung...you're the whole ladder, and I have no desire for any more notches in my belt. Why did you run out before we could do that test you wanted?"

"I found the trap. How's Lobo's leg?"

Taren smiled at her avoidance of the question. "No bones were broken but the skin and muscles are badly damaged. It could have been worse. With proper care, she should be fine. Now, answer my question."

Why did you bring Taren here? The wolf raised her head. *You were lonely and unhappy. You needed your mate.*

I've told you, Taren is not my mate.

'Woof.'

"Quiet." Taneika ordered.

She turned her attention back to Taren. "Why did I run? I thought you wanted to help, that you cared. When you didn't agree, I realized you didn't. No…let me finish. How long would you want me around if I couldn't control what happens inside? I would rather end our…relationship now, my way, than see your pity and scorn later."

"Taneika…"

She shifted on her knees leaning forward and held up her hand. "I'm not finished."

Lobo edged away from him and crept around the edge of the tent towards the door. Taren thought she was going outside. Lobo turned and jumped on Taneika's back, sending her sprawling across his sleeping bag and into his arms.

"Seems like Lobo knows where you belong better than you do." He took her mouth in a hot, explosive kiss. She pushed against him and struggled to get free. He felt the moment she gave in and he changed his kiss to a tender caress as he ran his hands slowly up and down the curve of her back.

"I do care about you," he said between kisses. "You surprised me at the clinic." He kissed the side of her face and down her neck. "If you would've stuck around for another minute I'd have told you that I'd do whatever it took to help." He kissed the tip of her nose. "I think you were scared at the thought of not being able to control this changing that happens. So you panicked, took the easy way out and ran back to what was known and comfortable.

"I'm sorry you thought I didn't care. Forgive me for giving that impression. I do care, very much. I haven't slept much since you left. I've been worried, thinking about you out in the mountains during the winter." He rolled over, pinning Taneika with his arm across her waist. "What would happen to you, if you were hurt, alone and no way to get help?"

Lowering his head, he took the nipple of her left breast with his mouth. She gasped and arched beneath him. He felt her body quiver as he circled the hardened nipple with his tongue. His hand slid down her waist, his fingers sought the warm silky folds of her womanhood and she opened her legs to give him access. Her hands took hold of his hair, pulling him from her breast. The kiss was explosive.

The moment his lips met hers she knew resistance was futile. This is where she wanted to be. Here was the passion, the excitement that she craved. She felt the tenderness with which he caressed her body and the explosive thrill when his fingers delved into her moist womanly folds of sensitive flesh.

She felt her heart rate increase and the pounding at her temples grew. Control, she must maintain control. Taneika focused on her breathing, taking slow, deep breaths to slow her heart rate down. Her hands worked quickly to remove the clothes that Taren was wearing. Her hand brushed his hardness and she wrapped her fingers around his hot length.

With a quick shove, Taren was on his back and she was sitting astride his hips. A sensuous gleam and a wicked smile was all the warning she received before he grabbed her legs and pulled her forward. As his mouth covered her, his tongue found entrance to the burning core of her passion. A cry of joy and need filled her soul and spilled out to fill the small tent.

Higher and higher she flew as his tongue stroked her sensitive inner flesh. She was floating on a wild erotic cloud. Her back touched the sleeping bag and she opened her eyes. Taren was on top of her. As he smiled, she felt the velvet tip of his hardness slowly slide deep within her.

With his throbbing length fully sheathed inside her, he took her mouth in a tender kiss. At the contact of his chest against her sensitive breasts, she wrapped her legs around his hips. The muscles surrounding her vagina constricted, locking him inside her.

"Ahh," he groaned. "I love it when you do that."

"You mean this?" She flexed the muscles surrounding him and sent a rippling wave of motion along his hard shaft.

He gasped. "*Yes.*"

She pulled his head down and sought his mouth. Tenderness was gone, replaced by wanton desire. But even in the heat of passion came the warning. *Stay in control.*

Ever so slowly at first, he withdrew and then began the exotic pleasure of filling her again. The pace he set was torture, keeping her on the threshold of release but not taking her beyond. Using her legs she pulled him deeper inside her, meeting each thrust with a need that threatened to unleash the wolf from within.

She felt the hot explosion of his seed deep within her. Her body responded with a shattering climax that sent supercharged signals to every part of her being. The cry of release from pent-up frustration, fueled by the power of their union and its joy ripped from her chest, filled the tent and echoed in the valley. Lobo howled.

"Quiet." They both spoke at once.

Lobo lay down and covered her nose with her one good front paw.

Taren and Taneika laughed at Lobo.

He reached down, grabbed the flap of the sleeping bag, and covered them, zipping them both inside a cocoon of warmth. "Are you okay, my love?" Taren whispered.

"Yes." Her heart swelled. *My love.* She snuggled closer, fitting her body to his. "Perfectly okay."

Taneika: Daughter of the Wolf

"I've missed you, Little Wolf." Taren said drowsily and then fell into the first peaceful sleep he had had in weeks.

"And I you, my dearest." Taneika kissed his cheek and ran her fingers lightly down his back. She would savor his nearness while she could. For the moment, it was enough to know she was loved and wanted.

She had been doing a lot of inner searching. As she attempted to put the pieces of her life's puzzle in place, the picture that was forming frightened her. Growing up in a world of superstition and fables, she was afraid to voice her fear out loud lest its very mention cause it to be a nightmarish reality.

A whine at the tent flap announced the arrival of Lobo's mate. She reached out, unzipped the door and let the wolf in.

* * * * *

The sun was shining brightly the next morning when Taren opened his eyes. Lying there alone in his sleeping bag, he thought at first he might have dreamed Taneika's presence beside him in the night. But no dream could be that real.

Wood smoke drifted through the open tent flap and with it the aroma of meat cooking on an open fire. Rising up on his elbow, he watched her as she sat naked, cross-legged before the fire. He shivered at the thought of her hot little love box buried in the snow. She had bathed and her hair sparkled from the ice crystals that had formed. The wildness was gone from her eyes and there was a happy contented smile on her face.

"Morning, Little Wolf."

"Morning?" she laughed. "I think you need to check the time again. This isn't breakfast."

He glanced up momentarily at the sun shining directly overhead. "No, I guess it isn't. How's Lobo doing?"

"With proper medical care she could be all right. But the way it is now," sadness crept in her voice and she shook her head, "she won't be able to use it very much in the future."

"That settles it then," he started getting dressed, "I'll take her into town to the vet's office."

"We'll both go," Taneika stated. "I'll hold Lobo while you drive the snowmobile to the truck."

"Aren't you forgetting something?" He ran his eyes appreciatively over her opulent nakedness.

"What?" She took the meat from the fire and carried him a plate.

"Oh, nothing too major, really." He grinned. "Unless you don't have any clothes to wear."

Once we get to the truck I'll put your snowsuit on."

Taren laughed as he ate the hot flavorful meat.

"What's so funny?"

"The thought of you wearing a size large snowsuit. Don't forget to roll the pant legs up or you will trip and fall."

Taneika laughed with him. "You have a better solution?"

"No, not right now I don't." He finished eating, set the plate aside and stood to his feet. "Let's break camp and head back to Red Rock. We should be able to catch the doc before he closes."

With the fire out and the bags packed, Taneika climbed on the snowmobile and took Lobo from Taren's arms. "Come here," she called to Lobo's mate.

"You stay near the cabin." She looked into the male's bright inquisitive eyes. "As soon as Lobo's able to travel, she'll come back."

The wolf licked Lobo's face and whined.

"Ready?" Taren asked. He climbed on, started the engine and headed back towards the truck.

They arrived at the truck to find a snowplow had been through and he suspected Bill had something to do with the cleared path to his truck. He loaded the trailer and gave Taneika his snowsuit. Giving Lobo a helping hand into the truck, he cleared the windows and hood of snow.

"All set," he said as he climbed in and started the engine. He patted Lobo's head. "Hang in there, girl, we'll get you sewed up good as new." He backed out and headed to town.

Taren pulled into the parking lot and hopped out. Before he could open the passenger door Taneika was out of truck and helping Lobo. "Want me to carry her in?"

"I offered," she shrugged her shoulders. "She doesn't want to be carried." Taneika sat Lobo on the ground and watched as she limped towards the door.

Inside the doc's clinic, Lobo received some frightened looks from customers waiting to have their pets seen. Taren laughed at one woman who scooped her little Pug off the floor and held it securely between her ample breasts. A large tabby cat arched its back and hissed. Its hair stood straight up like it had just gotten a charge of static electricity.

Lobo growled a warning, *Back off, pussy, I'm hungry.*

At her warning growl the cat changed its mind about acting so ferocious, went clawing its way up the man's leg, and didn't stop climbing until it was sitting on his shoulders.

"Hey, lady, control that damn pet wolf or take it outside." The irate man swore, rubbing his leg where the cat had been efficient in the use of its claws.

"An animal like that shouldn't be allowed out of a cage." The lady with the dog's head sticking out from between her breasts added.

"I assure you, she is quite safe as long as I am with her." Taneika tried to reassure them. She sat as far away from the other people in the room as she could. Lobo limped over and stretched out on the floor in front of her.

The little Pug was squirming and barking trying to get loose.

Lobo let out a couple little woofs, *Hey kid, you want to get loose? Try peeing on her.*

"Lobo, enough," Taneika scolded.

The front of the woman's flowery dress turned dark and she screamed. "Fifi, how dare you wee-wee on Mommy!" She sat the dog on the chair beside her, took a paper towel and blotted the material, trying in vain to wipe away the strong odor of urine.

Taneika covered her face with her hand, smothering a laugh.

The Pug danced in a circle on the chair barking for joy, *it worked, it worked. I'm free!* She jumped off the chair and ran over to Lobo, licking the wolf's face, kissing her. *Thank you, I hate it when she does that.*

"Fifi! Come back!" The woman turned white, her eyes rolled to the top of her head and she fainted.

The receptionist took one look from behind the counter and picked up the phone. As she dialed, she called out, "Doc, we have an emergency in the lobby."

Doc Gregger stuck his head through the door and quickly assessed the situation. "Taren, I think you might want to bring the wolf on back."

"Come on, Lobo," Taneika called. "You've created enough excitement for one day."

Lobo got up and limped through the door into the office.

A few minutes later, the front door opened and Jeanie came in carrying a small black satchel.

"Hi, Sis. Taneika took Lobo into the back. I think your patient fainted at the thought of her pet being eaten."

Chapter 18

Taneika followed the doctor back to a small exam room. There was a pedestal table in the center of the room. Several cabinets with glass doors lined one wall, a deep sink, bookcase and a desk sat against the other.

"Hello, Lobo. What happened to you?"

"She got caught in a trap," Taneika explained.

"I'm going out and talk with Sis." Taren stated from the doorway. "She might need help when her patient comes around."

She waved him away and knelt down beside Lobo.

"Go ahead and put her on the table so I can get a better look," Doc Gregger instructed.

Taneika gently picked her up and sat her on the table. "Lie down, girl."

Carefully, Doc cut away the soiled bandage that covered the upper front leg. Seeing the extent of the damage, he filled a syringe. "This will deaden the pain and allow me to get in there and try to repair the damage. But I must warn you. She must not be allowed to use the leg for a while. She could still lose the use it." He slipped the needle under the skin above the jagged, torn flesh, working his way around the leg.

Doc took another syringe and drew a vial of blood, marking it with the date and Lobo's name.

Taneika raised an eyebrow as he placed the vial on a tray. "What's that for, Doc?"

"I work with the authorities on keeping track of the wolves in the area. Any time a wolf is brought in, I take a sample and send it off. Most of the time, the wolves have been killed. Those that have been captured and released in the area are all marked and I record everything I can about them. It gives us a better understanding of the health of the wolf population in and around the park as well as where they're from. If the wolf is alive, and if it doesn't have an identification number already, then one is assigned to it."

Taneika walked to Lobo's head and gently pulled her lip away. There was a tattoo already there. "When did you do this?" She felt violated somehow. This having been done, without her knowledge, upset her.

"Sorry, Taneika, but it's the only way to keep track of the wild wolves. Some of them have been fitted with radio collars and are tracked almost continually."

Doc started prying in the open wound, digging out torn flesh, hair and bits of rust from the trap. "The tattoo is almost painless. I did it while she was here with her mate. I did him too. Listed them as a pair in the records."

He reached for a needle and thread. "How you doing, girl? This is going to take some time to get everything put back. Just lie real still now."

Slowly, he began to sort all the muscles and tendons that had been severed. Starting next to the bone, he painstakingly reconstructed the leg. "You know, Taneika," Doc spoke as he worked. "This has been a busier than normal winter for sending in blood samples of wolves. Jeanie brought in a sample a month ago but wouldn't tell me where she got it. I had a test done on it and the DNA matched Lobo's blood. I wonder where she came in contact with your wolf."

Panic gripped her like the steel trap that had held Lobo's leg. She knew instantly where the sample had come from. Legs that had carried her up and down mountains became weak and she gripped the table with both hands as the doc's words bounced around within the distraught walls of her mind. The classes at college on ancestry and DNA came back to her and tightened around her heart like a steel band. She tried to speak but no sound came from her mouth. It was suddenly difficult to breathe and she tried to swallow the fear that choked her.

Doc Gregger looked up from his work. "Taneika...Taneika, what's wrong? You're white as a sheet and trembling like a leaf." He got up and took hold of her. "Come over her and sit down. Sorry, I forgot that sometimes operations like this can be difficult for someone who isn't use to the blood and what's required in surgery."

He helped her to the chair and she sank into it, thankful she no longer had to stand. A glass of water was placed in her hand and mechanically she drank. She tried to focus on his words.

"Are you going to be all right? Should I have Jeanie come back?"

"I...I'm...fine." She looked around the room, her eyes stopping on the table. "Take care of...Lobo." *Who am I? What...am I?*

The childhood taunts of *The Freak* and *Wolf Girl*, that had followed her around the reservation came back to haunt her like a ghost from the past. She closed her eyes trying to block out the tune of "Mary had a little lamb," cruelly adapted by the other children to torment her. Her parents had known, yet they had remained silent all these years.

Taneika had sought for years to find the missing pieces of her life and now, with the picture was almost complete, she regretted it. Her eyes focused on the back door.

Standing, her legs threatened to buckle under her. She waited for the room to quit moving and walked hesitantly to the door.

"Are you feeling better, Taneika?" Doc Gregger inquired.

"I'm going to...step outside..." Her mind strained to find a reason.

"With the snow suit on and as warm as it is in here," he turned back to the delicate task of sewing a tendon sheath, "I imagine you are a little warm. When Taren returns, I'll tell him you stepped out."

Taren! She'd forgotten about him.

She shivered, not from the cold of being outdoors but from fear. Lobo, lying inside on the table stopped her from running. She leaned her back against the building, slid down the rough bricks, and sat in the snow. Silent tears coursed their way down her cheeks. She couldn't leave Lobo, not now.

A cold nose brushed her face and a long pink tongue licked the tears from her cheek. She blinked and Lobo's mate came into focus. "I thought I told you to stay around the cabin?" she scolded. Wrapping her arms around the muscular neck of the wolf, she pulled him to her and buried her face in his thick winter pelt.

The wolf whined, *I couldn't leave Lobo here alone. She stayed with me when I was hurt. The man here is good and kind, for a human.*

The door opened, Taren stepped outside and closed the door. "Doc said you weren't feeling good." He knelt down beside her and rubbed the wolf's head. "Hi, boy, couldn't stay away?"

"I'm feeling better," she lied.

Taneika started to stand and Taren offered her a hand. Ignoring his help, she moved away from him and reached for the doorknob.

Placing his hand against the door, he prevented her from opening it. "I want to know what is going on. No more lies. You've been out here crying and don't try to tell me differently, your eyes are red and puffy."

"Move, please. I want to go in."

Taren kept his hand flat against the door. "Not until I have some answers."

"Fine, have it your way. Stand there all *damn* night, see if I care." Taneika turned away and started to walk around the building.

His hand lashed out and grabbed her arm. "You are not running away this time."

A menacing growl came from behind him and Taren turned his head toward the wolf. Lobo's mate was posed ready to spring. His lips were pulled back in a vicious snarl revealing long, razor-sharp teeth. The wolf's hackles were raised as a signal. No other warning would be given.

Taren expected a rebuke or command from Taneika to calm the wolf.

"I think you should let go."

Her words, spoken in a slow, deliberate frosty tone shocked him. Something was definitely wrong here. He removed his hand and stared at her retreating back as she walked away, the male wolf following at her heels.

What the hell is going on? He slapped his open hand hard against the brick wall. *Jeanie won't talk to me, and now you walk away.* "Shit."

He went inside and Lobo raised her head and let out a short woof. "Hey, girl, are you feeling better?" Reaching out he scratched the wolf's nose.

'Woof.' *Better than you're doing right now. The stuff the doc gave me is great, man. Can I have some more?* Lobo licked his hand and panted. *It's better than those mushrooms I ate one time on the reservation.*

"I wish I could understand you," Taren spoke in a soft whisper. "You might be able to tell me what to do. Something is bothering Taneika and she won't talk to me."

Take me home with you, Lobo whined. *She'll show up eventually.*

Doc Gregger walked in. "Ah, there you are. I'm all done with Lobo. She will need to stay off that leg as much as possible. Any strenuous use could separate the internal stitches. Where's Taneika?"

"She went for a walk. I'll pay the bill and come back for Lobo."

A few minutes later, he returned and Lobo sat up.

Hey, Taren, Lobo whined. *How come I see three of you and the table is turning around?*

"Easy girl," he cautioned. "I'll help you down. We don't want to undo all the work the doc has done."

He scooped Lobo up in his arms and carried her out to the truck, placing her on the front seat. "You want to go home with me, girl?"

She licked his face. *There's hope for you yet. Let's go.*

Taren paused with the truck door open, one foot on the step as he looked up and down the street. Taneika was nowhere to be seen. He got in, started the engine and left the parking lot. Lobo lay down in the seat, resting her head on his leg. Driving with his left hand, his right hand slowly stroked Lobo's side.

* * * * *

The door opened and Taneika entered the waiting room of the clinic.

"Hi, I thought you were gone." The receptionist smiled at her. "Taren left with Lobo an hour ago."

"He what!" The shock of her earlier discovery gave way to rage. She forced her breathing to slow down. *Control, maintain control.*

"He paid the bill and left. I saw his truck pull out and figured you were in it."

"Damn him!" *Control.* She turned and went back outside, slamming the door behind her. She could picture the grin on his face as he left. The sanctimonious, conceited, conniving bastard knew she wouldn't stay away if he had Lobo.

Taneika stood on the sidewalk with her hands on her hips. She scowled as she stared down the street.

'Woof...Woof.' *Where's Lobo? I want to see how she is.*

"Gone, Taren took her."

A low growl came from the wolf and his canine teeth showed stark white against his dark pink gums.

"Those are my thoughts too, but stand in line."

What are we waiting for, he whined. *Let's go.*

She turned from the clinic's entrance. It was closer through the woods but with the snow, her speed would be reduced. Taneika started jogging down the road, the wolf easily running beside her.

As the early winter night approached, she increased her speed. The first tell-tail signs of pain arrived and she leveled off, staying below the threshold that would change her. Lowering the zippers on Taren's snowsuit, she let the wind cool her body. The added wind drag caused her to labor harder in order to maintain her speed and the pain came back.

Screw this.

She lengthened her stride, pushed the pain and burning aside. Each time going through, it became easier. Coming back was always the same. The power of the wolfs' blood flowed in a vortex of renewed energy through her body.

* * * * *

Taren pulled into his drive and turned off the engine. Lobo sat up and looked around.

"We're home girl. I don't know what's in the fridge but there's bound to be something to eat." He got out and stopped Lobo from jumping down.

"Not so fast. The doc said you were to take it easy." He gathered the wolf in his arms and lifted her from the seat. Setting her down, he waited 'til she had turned the snow a bright yellow and then carried her to the house.

Once inside with three feet firmly on the floor Lobo followed her nose to the kitchen. Standing on her hind legs, she sniffed the boxes on the table before making her choice. Clamping her jaws around the selected box, she pulled it to the floor. The lid popped open and Lobo was rewarded with half of a large sausage and pepperoni pizza.

Taren laughed at the cheese hanging in rubbery strings from Lobo's mouth. "You like that, girl?"

'Woof...Woof.'

"Help yourself, there's more up there somewhere." Taren walked over to the fridge and peered inside. He glanced back at Lobo as she pulled another box from the table. *Looks like Lobo will be the only one getting fed tonight.* Reaching in he pulled out a can of beer and popped the tab. Lobo's ears stood up and her head snapped around.

"What is it, girl? What's the matter?" Her eyes were locked onto his hand, shifting with each movement he made. "Is this what you want?"

Lobo barked, her tongue dangling from the side of her open mouth. Saliva dripped onto the floor.

Taren laughed, took a bowl from the cupboard and poured out a small amount of beer. He leaned down and sat the bowl on the floor but before he could straighten up again the bowl was empty. "Sorry, girl, I don't think you need to be drinking very much. I'm not sure you're of age."

Leaning against the counter, he held his beer loosely in his hand.

Lobo struck without warning. Her movement was a blur as her jaws clamped around the can and took it from him. Metal crunched and gave way. Liquid spewed from the holes made by her razor-sharp teeth. She dropped the can and quickly lapped up the foaming liquid.

"Okay, you win. You can have the beer." He checked his fingers to make sure that none of them were damaged. Pulling another beer from the fridge, he went to the living room, sat on the couch and propped his feet on the old table. He supposed it was an antique; it had been sitting in the back of a second-hand furniture store covered with dust. It went with the couch he had bought, not that it matched, but both were old with battle scars left over from previous owners. Too tired to remove his boots, he looked at the marred table and closed his eyes. *What's one more scratch?*

The couch sagged as Lobo lay beside him, her head resting in his lap.

Taren was awakened the next morning by a rough wet tongue on his face. Lobo whined and limped to the door.

"I'm coming, girl." He lowered his feet to the floor and stood. Lobo was sitting patiently at the door, her injured leg resting lightly on the floor.

"Remember, the doc said no weight on the leg." Opening the door, he found his snowsuit wadded up in front of the door, where its irate wearer had apparently flung it. The snow in the front yard was covered in blood, with a scattering of rabbit fur. Bloody footsteps led off in the direction of Taneika's place.

Lobo stepped outside and whined.

Taren knelt down and placed his arm around the wolf's neck. "Well, girl, it looks like she showed up. Go on, do your business and come back in."

She limped off the porch and squatted. Taren caught movement from the corner of his eye and turned to see another wolf approaching. The low growls coming from the wolf gave him a feeling this was not a welcome home social call. He sniffed as he circled Lobo, and then turned his head towards Taren. With canine teeth bared, he stepped between them. Using his body as a shield, he tried to push Lobo away from the house.

Lobo turned and barked, trying to get back to the house but her path was blocked.

"Go on, girl. Go with your mate and find Taneika."

He watched as Lobo limped across the snow, her mate following close behind, preventing her from returning.

Taren stepped back into the house. It wouldn't be long before Taneika showed up. He hoped she was in a better mood than Lobo's mate.

Chapter 19

Taneika opened one eye and groaned. From her position on the floor, everything looked different and it took her a minute to realize where she was. Weak from lack of food—she couldn't count the two rabbits earlier as they were so small—she struggled to rise. Wondering why dried blood covered her in huge smears, she remembered rolling in the snow. The shower door was open and she stumbled in.

Hunger drove her out of the shower before all the blood was gone. Dripping wet, Taneika left a trail of water through the house to the kitchen. Going to the freezer she found a roast she had purchased for emergencies. Placing it in the microwave, she set the timer and leaned heavily against the counter.

Peering out the window she spotted Lobo limping to the house. Taren was standing on his porch and then went inside. "Damn you, Taren. Lobo was supposed to stay off that leg."

Going to the front door, Taneika let the wolves in. "You're supposed to stay off that leg. Taren knows better than let you walk over here on your own."

'Woof, woof...woof.' Lobo turned her head back towards her mate.

"This was *your* idea?" She turned on the male. "Have all the males in my life gone loco? It was bad enough, Taren leaving like he did and taking Lobo, but you had to make her walk all the way over here. What did you do, get between them and growl?"

The wolf lowered his head and stuck his tail between his legs.

"Figures."

Walking over to Lobo, she examined her leg. "There's no fresh bleeding. I hope you didn't tear anything inside."

The buzzer sounded for the microwave. "You," she addressed Lobo's mate, "can go find some food." Letting the wolf out, she headed for the kitchen.

Bringing the roast to the living room, she sat on the couch and offered some to Lobo.

You need it worse than I do. I already ate. Lobo lay down and rested her nose on her leg.

"Taren stopped and got you some meat on the way?" Licking the juice from her fingers, she was reminded of when she'd done the same thing to Taren and the passion the simple act had ignited between them.

No, he had food on the table and the floor. I love cheese. What I had this morning made me thirsty. I couldn't get into the box where he keeps the beer but I found the one he didn't finish last night.

She hung her head. "He fed you pizza and beer?"

Can I go back? I didn't finish it all. You can have some too, Lobo licked her face. *Taren won't care.*

Taneika laughed at the puppy that still came out in Lobo. "No, you are not going back over. You are to lie down and stay off that leg."

Lobo laid her head down in Taneika's lap and looked up at her with big sad eyes.

"And don't look at me like that. It won't do you any good." She grabbed Lobo by the ears and shook her head.

Lobo whined, *Would you go over and get it?*

"I'm going over there all right but I'm not bringing you back any pizza. I sent your mate out for some food."

Lobo sniffed between Taneika's legs.

"I am not going over there for *that*. Taren had no right to take you. Feeding you leftover pizza and beer proves he has no business having a pet."

Lobo barked and sat back on her hind legs. *Take?* She cocked her head to one side. *What's this about taking me? I told him to bring me here.*

Taneika laid her head against the back of the couch and laughed. "And I suppose he understood you and said that was a great idea."

No...but he did bring me.

There was a noise at the door and Taneika went to check on it. Lobo's mate stood at the threshold with a rabbit in his mouth and two more at his feet.

"Lobo, if you're hungry, there's a rabbit here for you."

Lobo got off the couch, limped to the door and sniffed the rabbit. *Rather have pizza*, she grumbled.

"Outside," she commanded. "But stay on the porch."

Refreshed from her meal, she went back to the shower to clean up. It was time to confront Taren.

Taneika dried off and grabbed a pair of jeans. As she slipped them on, she noticed that they were tight around the waist. Strange, she didn't feel any heavier and living at the cabin for a month should have caused her to lose a little weight, not gain it. She pulled a shirt over her head as she left the bedroom and headed for the door.

Lobo stood with an expectant grin on her face as she stepped outside.

"No, I'm not taking you over to Taren's and I'm not bringing you any pizza."

Lobo whined.

"And no beer either. Damn my brothers for giving it to you to begin with."

Taneika stepped off the porch, turned and headed towards Taren's house.

'Woof.' Lobo's mate barked. *What's wrong with her?*

Lobo looked at Taneika, now halfway across the yard. *Nothing, all humans act funny when carrying little ones inside.*

'Woof?'

Yes, she lowered her head on her paw. *I'm sure.*

* * * * *

Taneika stopped, her shoulders slumped as the confusing emotions swirled inside her head. The month she'd spent tying to sort out her feelings, her life and the relationship with Taren, had been fruitless. Well almost. In that month she had realized one thing.

She loved Taren.

An impossible love. Especially now with this new knowledge given her by the vet, her hopes for a normal future with a husband and children were doomed.

Taneika sat in the snow, driven to the ground by the weight she must now bear alone, for no man would want a wife who was part wolf. The children in her village had been right.

I am a freak.

Tears for crushed dreams and lost hope trickled slowly down her cheek.

Standing at the window, Taren saw her start toward the house. He had been expecting her visit since Lobo had limped over. It still upset him that the other wolf had interfered but he wasn't about to challenge her mate.

Why is she stopping?

Concerned alarm propelled him out the door and he ran to where Taneika, head bowed resting in her hands, sat in the snow. Kneeling in front of her, Taren lifted her head and was shocked to see the tears streaming unchecked down her face.

"Hon…what's the matter?" His voice broke. "Don't cry love, it'll be alright."

Pulling away before he could put his arms around her, she looked at him through tear-blurred eyes. "Go away, Taren."

"If I thought you meant it..." Lowering his head he brushed his lips across her eyes, tasted the salty tears and came to rest on her mouth. "I would."

"You're...not making...this any... easier." She said between kisses.

"I don't intend to."

"Taren," she pleaded. "Stop!"

At the desperation in her voice, he sat back on his heels and looked into her eyes. His heart wrenched at the pain radiating prismatically from what appeared as cracked glass. Beyond the tears, behind the pain, was a soul that had been shattered.

"We have to talk," she continued. "Let's go inside. Your shivering is making me cold."

Getting up, she turned back to her place, trusting that Taren would follow.

He wasn't sure where the old Taneika was, the one full of life and a bright smile with passion flowing through her veins, but he wanted her back. This Taneika walked with the weight of the world on her shoulders. Dejected, wearing the shroud of defeat, she trudged through the snow ahead of him.

Taneika stepped onto the porch and both wolves moved away from her. It was impossible to blame them. Right now she wished she could do the same. Leaving the door open for Taren, she went to stand by the window. If she could keep her distance, if he didn't touch or kiss her, there was a chance, however slim, she could survive.

Standing in her living room, Taren shook his head in aggravation. Two could play this waiting game as easily as one. Sitting on the couch, he propped his feet up and waited.

"I suppose you deserve an...explanation."

Her voice was broken, raspy and a little more than a whisper. Taren didn't answer.

"You deserve someone who can give you a home, children, a family. Things that I can't give anyone, not...."

"That's nonsense," he interrupted.

"Please," she held her hand up. "Let me finish. Remember the blood sample Jeanie took from my skin? Seems she took it to the vet who sent it to the lab. The blood matched a sample taken from Lobo earlier."

Taren felt a strong desire to laugh but saw that she was serious. "What are you trying to tell me?"

"We...have the same DNA."

Unable to control himself, Taren chuckled. "Would you for a moment listen to what you said?"

"Doc Gregger said..."

"Doc Gregger," he shook his head, "is a veterinarian. Besides, labs make mistakes and what you are saying is medically impossible."

"Don't you think I realize that?" She turned from the window and stomped across the room to stand in front of the couch. "Everything you know about me is a medical impossibility. Why should being related to a wolf be any different?"

"Related to a wolf, you mean as in *blood relative*?" He leaned his head back and laughed.

In aggravation, she stomped out. Going into her bedroom, she slammed the door closed behind her.

He got up and followed her, opened the door and found her lying on the bed. Sitting beside her, he gently stroked her hair. "Hon, it doesn't change the way I feel about you. Forget what Doc Gregger said. You are a healthy, vibrant and beautiful woman. You've learned to live with your differences and I will too. Don't add to the lab's mistake by throwing away what we have together."

"I care for you, but," she brushed her hand along the side of his face. "There could never be children. I couldn't bear to have them humiliated the way I was growing up. Suppose they were deformed or something, could you look at them and not blame me?"

"Nobody can guarantee a child will be perfect. Whatever happens, our love will see us through." Taren kissed the palm of her hand. "The important thing right now, we're together. Things have been rather hectic lately. When we put all this behind us, get back into a daily routine of school and work, we'll both have a better perspective."

Brushing the hair from the side of her face, he leaned over and tenderly kissed her. As her arms snaked around his neck, he deepened the kiss, searching out the sweet cavern of her mouth. He trailed his fingers teasingly down her side and back up to cup her breast. The nipple hardened against his palm. Inhaling her sensuous moan, the coals of his desire were stirred. Finding the bottom of her shirt, his hand slid along bare skin 'til he once more cupped her breast.

Taren sat up and looked into her eyes. A light was shining where only darkness had been. The dark clouds had a silver lining. Visible was a thread of hope, be it ever so fragile. Together they could dispel the clouds and build the thread into a chain of steel that couldn't be broken.

Looking into a face that radiated love and compassion, she felt her heart swell with tenderness. *Maybe I overreacted.* Reaching down she grasped the T-shirt and slowly tugged it over her head as Taren unsnapped her jeans and drew them down over her hips.

Taren lay beside her, his mouth gravitated towards her breasts which stood like golden luscious melons, topped with dark, sun-ripened cherries. Tasting their sweetness, he felt her body tremble and a deep sigh rushed from her chest. Smiling against her skin, Taren drew her hardened flesh into his mouth. As he trailed his fingers lightly down her side and across her hip, she spread her legs to give him access to the smooth satiny skin of her inner thigh. Moist heat filled his palm as he cupped the essence of her femininity.

His fingers stroked the flowery petals of her inner flesh. Writhing on the bed, she arched her back and moaned. Her breasts vibrated with the wild pounding of her heart. As Taren moved a leg across hers, she tried to roll away. Pinning her face down on the bed, he heard her husky laugh.

Leaning forward, he nibbled teasingly at her neck. "On your knees," he whispered.

"No." She laughed and wiggled her butt against his hard length.

"On your knees before I spank you."

"You wouldn't da..." She gasped as he moved and his open hand made contact with her flesh. His playful slap surprised her and at the same time stimulated her.

Spreading her legs, she raised herself off the bed and felt the tip of his shaft enter the soft folds of her inner flesh. Pushing backward she impaled herself on his full length. "Ahh!"

His fingers sensuously moved up her legs, across her hips and stroked her sides. Slowly he withdrew, sending erotic impulses along sensitive nerves. Rocking against his legs, she felt his movement inside and her body demanded more. Pulling away, she began moving. With each backward thrust of her hips, his hands held her still. Frustration mounted as she sought the release that stayed so close but out of reach.

Panting for breath, she voiced what her flesh craved. "Faster, don't stop."

"Like this." His words were heated, filled with promise.

As he increased the speed, his flesh pounded harder against hers. "Yes," she moaned. "Oh, yes." Her body, balanced on the edge, slipped over. She felt the hot flow of his release fill her. Gasping to suck air into her starved lungs, the mating howl of the wolf was muffled as she collapsed into the pillow.

Taren, his body slick with sweat, slumped over her. As the shockwaves that rolled across them receded, she released him and he moved to lie beside her. She snuggled up and laid her head on his shoulder, content with the knowledge she was where she belonged and she was loved.

For now.

Chapter 20

Taneika sat in front of Dean Watkins' desk waiting for the decision on whether she would be spending Christmas vacation studying or waiting until the spring semester and starting over.

Taren had smoothed over several of the dean's ruffled feathers by explaining the events following her leaving school. Her composure, however, had been shaken upon learning of Taneika's involvement with the gun battle at the cabin.

"Taneika," she said. "I have looked over your records and believe with hard work you can catch up on most of your studies. What concerns me," she paused and took her glasses off, "as it will the Board of Directors, is the safety of the school and the other students."

"Dean Watkins," Taren interrupted. "The DEA and the Justice Department have shut down Harold Fallings' contacts who were threatening her life. Fallings is a fugitive and was last seen in Canada. Although the department doesn't think any further attempt on her life will be taken, they are prepared to place an agent within the school for added protection."

"Mr. Carpenter, having a policeman or a bodyguard would cause her to be noticed and very obvious," she refuted.

"The agent would be, as far as the school faculty or the other students are concerned, a transfer from another school. She'll be assigned the same classes and schedule as Taneika, doing the assignments and blending into school life."

The dean sat for several moments, her eyes traveling from the records in front of her to Taneika. "I'll have to inform the President and the Board. The final decision will be up to them." She wrote a memo and signed it. "This will allow you to get the work you need to do over the vacation. Catching up won't be easy and how much you accomplish over the next couple weeks may very well determine if you stay in school. The library will remain open during the vacation. I strongly suggest you make use of it during this time."

Taneika stood and took the memo. "Thank you, Dean Watkins. I appreciate your willingness to let me try."

"And you, Mr. Carpenter." The dean turned her attention to Taren. "Will you have your agent here ready to check in the first day class resumes? No agent...and Taneika doesn't continue as long as there is the possibility of a threat to her or any anyone else at the college."

"An agent is already here, Dean Watkins. She is waiting for word to check in."

"Very well." The dean raised an eyebrow and a small grin appeared.

"Young lady, you have work to do," she said dismissing them.

"Mr. Carpenter, may I have a word with you? In private."

Taren closed the door as the dean stood.

"You presumed the outcome of this meeting before you came in here. I'm not an unreasonable woman, although some of the students might disagree. I don't like to have my actions second-guessed so easily. What would you've done if I had said no?"

Taren smiled, "That question is after all, irrelevant...for now. If you will excuse me." Giving her a mock salute, he opened the door and left.

As they left the administration building, Taren smiled and waved to a woman on walking on the sidewalk.

"Do you know her?" Taneika asked.

"Nope, never seen her before." He laughed overly loud and lowered his voice. "Jealous? Don't be, the other agent is watching us. That was a signal for her."

Several cars away the driver's door opened of an old Chevy Impala. Agent Paula Myers took one last sip of her Irish Cream Cappuccino before getting out.

* * * * *

Taneika sat in the almost deserted library. A young Korean girl with short black hair sat between her and the door. As Taneika studied, she had the feeling of being watched. Looking up, she noticed that although the Korean girl had a book open, her eyes never stayed in one place but shifted continually around the room. She reminded Taneika of a hawk, seemingly relaxed but watchful, ready to pounce on an unsuspecting prey.

She allowed a slight smile to lift the corners of her lips. The hawk's eyes returned the smile and then resumed their relentless vigil.

The muscles in her back began protesting the long hours she had spent bent over her books. Standing, she stretched and walked between the tall rows of shelves. A title caught her eye and she stopped. Taking the book down, she was reminded of She Who Walks Ahead and the confusing words about her destiny being written in the stars.

Taking it back to her seat, she entered the world of astrology, planet orbits and phases, whether they were stable or neutral, ascending or descending. The more Taneika looked at the book, the more confusing it became. With so many equations that could be figured in, no wonder predictions varied drastically.

"Damn!" She slammed the book down in frustration, forgetting for the moment she was in the library. Looking up, she caught the disapproving glare of the librarian and the suppressed laughter from the hawk.

The Korean girl stood and walked towards her with graceful, fluid strides, as if walking on air. "Pardon me, but I couldn't help noticing the title of the book. I've dabbled in astrology for several years, maybe I can help."

"That would be wonderful. I'm Taneika, please have a seat."

"I'm Paula. I'm new here. I transferred in from back east." Paula sat where she could see the rest of the library and took the book Taneika had been reading. "Okay, first thing, when were you born?"

"I don't know for sure." She couldn't keep the sadness from creeping into her voice. "I'm adopted and have always celebrated my birthday on the fifth of April, nineteen seventy-nine."

Paula turned to the computer and in a few minutes had Taneika's information typed in for a natal chart. "See this," she pointed to the screen. "As an Aries, your controlling planet Mars, is linked to Jupiter through Uranus. Is there anything special you are looking for?"

"I'm not real sure," Taneika answered. "I was told that Jupiter would affect Saturn and the rings would align with Orion's belt."

"Now, going forward from today we find a date where the chart shows the greatest possibility." Paula studied the chart. "Wow!"

"What is it?" Taneika leaned forward, butterflies fluttered in her stomach as she anxiously waited for the answer.

"With Mars in conjuncture with Uranus in the house of Aquarius, it places Jupiter in your house of Aries, making a significant impact on your life. With the close proximity of Jupiter, Saturn could be affected, as it is weaker being in the house of Taurus. Once Jupiter and Saturn both enter the house of Aries then their powers of influence will be the same. The Moon, which also has a considerable role in your birth chart, will then be ascending and be dominant."

She wanted to know and yet she didn't. The apprehension of not knowing overruled. "When will the planets be aligned like this?"

"If you knew the fifth was the right date, I'd say the second of January." Paula shrugged, "Otherwise, anytime between now and then."

"The library is closing." The loudspeaker crackled. "Please bring library books to the front for filing."

"Don't look so glum," Paula laughed as they walked to the front desk. "Everything will work out."

They walked outside and she gave Paula a wave. "Thanks again for the help."

"No big deal." Paula unlocked her car. "See ya. Merry Christmas."

"Merry Christmas to you." Taneika opened the door and sat down. Her first Christmas away from home and she hadn't sent a thing to her family. She would give them a call tomorrow when they'd be together on Christmas. Checking her purse, she frowned. With finances being low, she was limited in what she could get Taren for Christmas.

Stopping at the mall, Taneika joined the crowd of last-minute shoppers crowding the stores. In desperation to get something for him, she picked up a heavy flannel shirt in earthen green and brown colors. As she left the mall with her purchase, she recognized a car in the next row. *Paula must be the other agent.*

As Taneika backed out and left, she caught the sight of Paula's lights being turned on. She felt better knowing that the hawk was still watching. The lights trailed behind her all the way to her own driveway.

Pulling up in front of her house, Taren's door opened and he stepped out. "I've got dinner ready if you want to eat. I made spaghetti if that's all right?"

"Sounds great," she waved back. "I'll be right over. I want to check on Lobo."

"She's over here. I think she was lonely." Taren went back into the house and scratched Lobo's ears.

"Easy, girl. She'll be here in a minute." The door opened and Lobo sat up, her tail wagging and almost a smile on her face.

Taren was about to turn around when she stuck her tail between her legs, lowered her ears and lay back on the couch.

"Did you walk over here?" Taneika asked.

The wolf looked away and covered her nose with her good paw.

Taneika walked over to the couch and gave Taren a kiss. Shaking her head, she knelt beside the couch and ran her hands along Lobo's back. "I swear I don't know what to do with you. Have you eaten today?" she asked Lobo.

"The other wolf has been bringing a steady supply of food for her all day." He turned back toward the kitchen. "Probably enough to feed both of you."

Getting to her feet, she followed Taren into the kitchen. "Mmm, smells good. I'm starved."

Walking over to the stove, she wrapped her arms around Taren and laid her head on his shoulder. *Ten short days, maybe less.* She sighed.

Taren stirred the sauce and offered her a taste.

"It's good," she smiled, licking her lips. Turning her head, she kissed him. "I could get used to this. If you do laundry too, I might keep you around for a while." A smile played on her lips as he gave her a light squeeze.

"I hope for a long time," he kissed her forehead.

Ten days…

"Anything I can do?" she asked.

"Grab a couple plates, dinner is ready." Taren drained the spaghetti and rinsed it with fresh water. "Let's eat."

As Taneika twirled the spaghetti on her fork, she spoke. "I met a new student at the library today."

"Oh?" Taren paused with the fork full of dangling pasta.

"A young Korean girl, Paula Myers." There was the slightest hint of recognition as Taren took another bite of food.

"She followed me to the mall and all the way home." She laughed at the look of displeasure on Taren's face. "I appreciate the thoughtfulness, but is being watched all the time necessary?"

"Yes." Taren got up and grabbed a beer from the fridge.

"We talked for a few minutes. Paula seems real nice. Are you sure she is up to the task?"

Taren popped the tab on the beer and Lobo stuck her head around the corner.

"No," Taneika scolded. "Go back and lay down."

Lobo's ears lowered and she ducked her head out of sight.

Taren laughed. "She has been begging me for one all day."

"Figures. Thanks to my brothers she's a beer-alcoholic. When she was too young to go with me in the mountains, they would get her drunk and then laugh at her when she couldn't walk straight."

He sat back down at the table. "Don't worry about Paula. From what I've heard she can hold her own. She's supposed to have a black belt and an uncanny knack for getting out of bad situations."

Lobo limped to the back door, scratched at the threshold and whined.

Taneika went to the door to let her out. "Don't go running off."

* * * * *

Curled up on the couch with the warmth of Taren's chest against her cheek and the steady rhythm of his heart pounding beneath her ear, she sighed. Tomorrow was Christmas Eve.

Taneika woke in the night disorientated at being in bed. The last thing she remembered was being on the couch. Taren was asleep with one arm draped across her waist. She snuggled closer, fitting herself against his solid length. *If only we had more time.*

A lone sad tear slid down the soft contours of her face and disappeared into the pillow. Of all the times to fall in love. *Why now?*

* * * * *

Sounds in the kitchen woke her the next morning. Light streamed through the crack of the open door. She rolled to her side and received a hot, wet good morning kiss.

"Morning, girl. Have you had eaten?"

Lobo barked. *Tired of rabbit, want pizza.*

"Ohh," She groaned. Flopping back on the bed, she covered her head with Taren's pillow.

Lobo grabbed a mouth full of blankets and pulled.

Taneika managed to snag the sheet before it was pulled completely to the floor. Unprepared for the sudden jerk to her arm, she found herself half-off the bed.

Taren's laughter at Lobo's antics caused her to look up. Taren was holding the sheet in his hand and Lobo had a silly grin on her face. "You two are impossible. Okay, I'm up. See, I'm out of bed."

"I'll be in the kitchen." Taren chuckled as he turned toward the door.

She slipped her jeans on and reached for her shirt. Unable to fasten the jeans she sat on the edge of the bed. *What is going on with my clothes? They're getting smaller.*

Lobo came up, stood between her legs and licked her stomach. 'Woof.'

"Yes, I know. I'm getting fat."

'Woof.' *Not fat, growing inside.* 'Woof, Woof.'

"What do you mean grow…"

As the concept of what Lobo said registered, she felt a hopeless sinking sensation in the pit of her stomach. *I can't be…* She had no other explanation for the added tightness to her clothes.

Zipping up the front of her jeans, Taneika went in search of Taren.

"Morning." She kissed him quickly on the lips. "I've got to run over to the house. I may have to go to the store first thing this morning."

The door banged closed and Taren watched her run through the snow. "What brought that on?"

'Woof.'

"Come here, girl," Taren opened the fridge and handed Lobo a skinned rabbit.

"Go on, take it outside." He held the door open.

As Lobo went through the door, her mate met her with yelps and kisses.

A car engine started close by. Taren looked around the corner of the house and saw Taneika's car go down the drive.

Taneika stopped at the first pharmacy she came to and went inside. Making her purchase, she went to the bathroom. In horror, she watched the indicator turn positive. "Great." She laid her head back against the wall and closed her eyes. *This is all I fucking need.*

Washing her face, she finger-combed her hair and went out to her car. Finding a department store, she used what money she had on a couple pair of stretch-top pants. Still in a state of disbelief and shock, she headed home.

Suppose her baby was like her. There was no way to hide it from society the way she had been. Not unless she went back to the reservation. Maybe that was the sanest answer she had. Pack a suitcase and go home. As she remembered her own childhood, she realized going home wasn't a viable answer either. How long could she hide it from Taren? She wouldn't trap him into a marriage, even if she did love him.

The problem was still unresolved when she pulled into the driveway. She felt her world being slowly torn apart at the seams. Laying her head on the steering wheel, she groaned. "Why, God? Why now, O Great Spirit? If this is my destiny, I don't want it! Must my baby suffer too?"

Chapter 21

Taneika had avoided any prolonged conversations with Taren, using her studies as a shield through the long afternoon. Watching him out of the corner of her eye, she felt he appeared edgy, nervous, like a caged animal, never sitting still for any length of time. And when he was sitting, his fingers and hands were moving.

Taren's fingers tapped out an almost silent, rhythmic beat on the arm of the couch. She had lost track of the number of times he had finger-combed his hair. His hot sultry glances had already caused a wet spot between her legs. Several times he had stopped and given her a kiss, or gently run his fingers sensuously through her hair.

Her stomach growled, reminding her of her meager lunch.

'Woof.' Lobo's soft bark came from beside her. *Me too.*

"How could you be hungry, girl, after all those rabbits?" Her fingers lightly stroked the wolf's neck.

Lobo whimpered. *They were small rabbits.*

'Woof, Woof,' Lobo's mate lifted his head. *Give me a break, they were all I could find.*

"Enough, you two," she scolded.

"Hey, it's Christmas Eve," Taren announced. "Why don't I try to find someplace open?"

"The only place open tonight would be a…" She spelled out the word, "P-I-Z-Z-A."

"So, what's wrong with pizza and why spell the word?"

Lobo's head came up. 'Woof, Woof.' She sat up, her tongue hanging from her mouth, her ears alert. Limping over to Taren, she licked his face. 'Woof.' Her tail beat against the side of the couch like a snare drum.

"That's why I spelled it," she laughed. "Okay, you win. Pizza it is."

"I better order several." Taren held Lobo's head trying to stem the bath he was receiving from the wolf's tongue. "I've seen the way you like pizza, girl. Yes I have."

'Woof?'

"No." Taneika laughed and rolled her eyes toward the ceiling. "No *beer* for you."

Taren placed the order and walked over to the table where she sat.

"How are the studies going?" Taren reached around her, gently cupping her breasts. He inhaled the scent of her hair and felt its silky softness against his face. "Are you catching up?"

"I should be caught up with most of it in time. The lab work for biology will be the hardest one to make up."

"Take a break for a while. You have been hitting the books all afternoon." Taren saw the hesitation. "A few minutes to relax. After you've eaten, if you still want to study, you will be refreshed."

"Okay." She closed her eyes and enjoyed his soft massaging touch. Sensitive nerves in her nipples were sending "get ready" announcements throughout her body. Taneika laid her book aside. Reluctantly breaking contact with Taren, stood and stretched.

Taren immediately stepped back in, sliding his arms around her waist. "I've missed you." He whispered in her ear.

Her arms rested gently on his shoulders, sensuous laughter caressed his neck. "I've been right here most of the day."

"Not really." Leaning back, he looked into her eyes. "You've been miles away and it hasn't been your books you've been lost in. What's troubling you, my Little Wolf?"

Lowering her eyes, Taneika rested her head against his chest. "Nothing." She flinched at the lie that came so easily to her lips.

"Christmas without family is difficult," he continued. "Maybe we can drive up to your mother's tomorrow and visit. Would you like that?"

"I suppose. If it's no bother."

"Good, then that's settled. We leave first thing in the morning." Taren reached into his pocket. "Before we go, I have something for you. Merry Christmas, my Little Wolf." He gave her a kiss and placed the gift in her hand.

Opening the small package, she gasped. "Oh, Taren." Tears sprang to her eyes like the morning dew.

"Taneika, will you be my wife?"

The diamond ring she held in the palm of her hand was the essence of her childhood dreams. To be loved by one person so much that their lives would be forever intertwined. But those dreams lay shrouded in the past, in a time of innocence, before she knew the truth. Would it be fair to Taren? Would he grow to hate what she was and what she feared she was yet to become?

Taren place a finger on her lips. "Before you start making lame excuses for saying no, listen to me. I love you, just the way you are. When your skin bleeds, I'll bathe you. When you're weak, I'll feed you. When you're frightened, I'll be there to hold you and when you bring our children into the world I'll be beside you."

"Children like me? Are you sure you know what you want, Taren?" Tears stained her face as she felt her resistance start to crumble.

"Yes, I would be happy to have carbon copies of you crawling across the floor or bouncing on my knee. But we don't have to be concerned about babies right now." Taren cupped her chin and raised her head up, gazing steadfast into her eyes. "Or do we?"

Better to hold a dream even for a little while, than not hold it at all. Her mind grasped at the thread of hope dangling before her.

"Yes, Taren my love. I will be your wife and I will have your children…"

He picked her up and twirled her around.

"In about eight months."

"Eight months! You're pregnant! Whoopee!" Taren crushed her to him and kissed her. "When did you find out?"

"This morning. That's why I went to town," she confessed. She felt her smile stretch, beaming at him as she took hold of his excitement. Like a warm summer rain, it washed over her, cleansing her of any remaining doubts.

"Why didn't you tell me earlier?" he admonished.

"I…I didn't want you to feel you had to marry me. I didn't want you to feel…trapped."

"My Little Wolf," he gently kissed away the sheepish expression on her face. "Don't you know by now how much I love you? The month you were gone was a nightmare. I feared I would never find you again and my reason for living would be reduced to only a memory of you."

Both wolves stood, their ears slicked back and their teeth showing as they growled.

"We have company," she announced.

"Probably the pizzas." Taren opened the door and stepped out. A truck with a lighted delivery sign pulled up and stopped.

The driver got out and started toward the house. "You the one that ordered six large pizzas?"

"Right place." He waved at the driver. "Stay there. I'll come and get 'em."

Taren walked out to the truck. "Where are the ones with double meat?"

The driver indicated which red insulated box they were in. Taren took two boxes out and tossed them in the snow. "Don't ask." Taren laughed at the comical expression on the driver's face. He paid the bill and carried the others inside.

Both wolves smelled the food and met him at the door. With excited yelps and darting heads, they sniffed out the contents of the boxes.

"These are too hot for you." Taren held the boxes out of their reach. Taren looked from the wolves to the boxes. *This is stupid. If they really wanted these, there's nothing I could do to prevent it.* "Yours are outside cooling down."

"Outside, you two." Taneika pointed towards the door.

In a blur of brown, black and white, both wolves disappeared outside.

"Dinner is served, my sweet love." Taren opened the carton and sat it on the table. "It's not fresh meat but it will kill the hunger."

"Hey, I eat other food besides meat." Picking up a slice loaded with veggies she bit into it. "See?"

Taren laughed at the strings of cheese dangling from her lips. "Hold still." Leaning forward, he licked the cheese away. "Hmm, delicious. Why don't you go ahead and eat, I'll lick up what you spill."

She thrilled at the husky tone of his soft words as they ignited coals of passion deep within. "You think I'm going to spill some more?" she breathed heavily.

"Oh, I'm sure of it."

"Then I insist you have a clean plate." Taking hold of her shirt, she pulled it over her head. She pulled the pizza away after taking a partial bite. Long strings of cheese floated down to lie tantalizingly over her breast. "I see what you mean. Pizza can be very messy."

"Very." Lowering his head, he used the tip of his tongue to lift the cheese from her body.

Her breasts rose under each ragged breath, reaching out, begging to be caressed by the light feathery touch of his tongue.

"Umm, it appears that the plate is again spotlessly clean. Am I not to be fed from my lovely's exquisite table?"

Want and need surfaced to mix with the swirling fog of passion. Looking into his desire-filled eyes, she smeared her breasts with the pizza in her hand.

"Come, my love, satisfy your hunger."

"Though I feast for as long as I live, I shall never be satisfied." He took her mouth in a hot, devouring kiss.

His mouth left a trail of fire down her neck. The flames danced around her breast, sending barbs of heat radiating with each burning touch.

A deep gasping moan came unbidden from her lips as his teeth grazed her sensitive nipple.

With agonizing slowness his mouth left a searing path down her body. She raised her hips as he pulled her pants off and dropped them on the floor. Languid kisses heated her legs and inner thighs. His breath on her hot heated core drove her over the edge of patience.

Grasping his hair, she pulled him to her wet flesh. She bucked against him as his tongue darted like a bee on a flower, searching for pollen. Releasing her grip on his hair, she turned around.

She heard his zipper lower and felt his hard length against her. "Yes." She panted in anticipation.

Her hands clutched at the cushion as he drove deep into her. With each mounting thrust, she rocked harder against him. With the shudder of physical release came a veil of darkness before her eyes. Even as the cry of passion filled her lungs, she knew she had crossed over.

Releasing him, she turned and kissed him hard, her tongue filling his mouth, tasting the musk of their union. "I need a shower." She picked up a pizza. "You can join me."

Taren held her as her body changed back. She devoured the pizza even as the blood was washed away. "You still want to marry me, knowing this could happen whenever we make love?"

"With every breath I take, my answer's still the same. Yes, my love. I want you for my wife and the mother of our children."

* * * * *

Late in the afternoon, Taren pulled up outside of a low-roofed adobe hut. Wood smoke rose in sky from the chimney. Sheep, brought down from the higher elevation for winter, filled a large pen that surrounded an old rickety barn.

As Taren turned the key and the engine died, the door opened and two dogs came running out. Following them was Taneika's oldest brother. Taren had felt the hostility directed towards him before, when he had been searching for Taneika. He saw the hostility turn to anger as brother and sister looked at each other through the windshield of his truck.

"That's John Bear," Taneika said. "I always called him Grouchy Bear."

"We've met. His attitude hasn't improved."

Bear walked around to the driver's door, standing close enough to prevent him from opening it and getting out. Taren rolled down the window and stared at the broad scowling face.

"Hello, John Bear. Merry Christmas!" Taren greeted.

"You found her, why bring her here? Do you tire of her so soon? Does she no longer please you when you lie between her legs?"

Taren's hand closed into a steel fist as Bear spoke.

"You do not like what I say, then leave, and take this *Punta* with you."

"No, Taren." Taneika's hand on his arm stayed the blood rage that pounded at his temple.

"John, I came to see Mother." Her voice was taut but steady as she defied him.

John Bear spit in the snow and said in a short, clipped aggressive snarl, "She is not your mother."

"Songbird is the only mother I've ever known. Surly you would not deny me a few moments with her. I am to be married and have come to seek her blessing."

"Humph." John snorted and shifted his eyes to glare at Taren.

"You will marry this wolf *Punta*? You are a *fool*. You will stay in the truck. If Songbird wishes to see you, then she will come here." John Bear turned and without a backward glance stomped back toward the house.

Taren was boiling at the treatment she had received. Although he'd kept quiet and held Taneika's hand, his mind churned with thoughts of verbal and bodily abuse to be handed out as befitting presents to John Bear.

After all the hurtful words, she sat with her back straight in the seat. A single tear languorously slid down her face, the only outward sign of the inner turmoil and despair she had to feel.

The door opened and Songbird stepped outside into the bitter cold. She seemed to have aged since he had seen her last. Her face was drawn and she walked stooped as if she carried a heavy weight upon her shoulders.

Taneika opened her door and ran to meet her. The two stood embracing as a window curtain moved. Taren caught sight of the hate that filled John Bear's eyes as the curtain fell back into place.

With her arms around the woman who had cared for her all her life, Taneika walked with Songbird back to the truck. Helping her mother up, Taneika climbed in and shut the door.

"My son tells me you wish to take Taneika for a wife. Is this true?" Songbird asked. "First you come to me, telling me she is missing. Now you show up with her and I am forbidden to let her into my home. It is a sad day for this old woman, but my son lives in fear of the path ahead. Tell me, my son, do you not live in fear of what lies before you?"

"Mother Songbird, you have seen many years and are full of wisdom. I would be lying if I said I wasn't concerned. The fear in my heart is of losing Taneika and the love we share."

She turned to face her only daughter. "My dear, you are with child."

It wasn't a question but a statement of fact, born from years of insight and a heart full of love.

"Yes, Mother."

Songbird shook her head. "You have been as my own flesh. Blame a selfish old woman for wanting to protect her daughter. I have hidden secrets that should have been told."

Taneika gathered Songbird within her arms. "The spirit world has revealed many things to me. I know what I am and may soon become. Whatever or whoever brought me into this world is not important. You will always be my mother."

The door of the small house opened and John Bear stuck his head outside. His eyes blazed with anger, his face etched in hatred of Taneika. Taren suspected much of John's anger was directed towards him for bringing Taneika to see Songbird.

"You must go now, Mother, before my brother's anger is turned away from me and you receive his wrath and scorn." Taneika opened the door and started to climb out.

"Wait, child." Songbird turned towards Taren.

"You, my son, have my blessing. The journey before you will be hard. May the spirits of the ancients guide you and protect you." Songbird held up her hands and chanted a prayer. "Go, my children. Go in peace."

Taneika helped Songbird out of the truck and walked with her towards the house.

"My child, I…"

Taneika watched her struggle with her emotions. Tears filled her eyes and her lower lip trembled.

"I must tell you this before I too go to be with the ancients. Your mother…"

Her voice broke, her eyes pleaded with Taneika for forgiveness and understanding.

"Your mother was a wolf."

"I *know*." Taneika embraced Songbird one last time. With a heavy heart, Taneika watched as she walked with slow, measured steps back to the house.

Taren drove home in silence with an arm around her shoulders, her tear-stained face a mute testimony of the grief within. He suspected the tears were for a mother she never knew and for the one she needed now.

He parked the truck and carried Taneika inside. Lobo and her mate followed at his heels. Setting her on the bed, he removed her clothes and tucked her in.

'Woof?'

"Quiet, girl," Taren whispered. "She's tired. It's been a long day."

The wolves lay down beside the bed as the shadowy gray of pre-dawn crept across the sky.

Chapter 22

Taneika closed the book with a loud smack that echoed through the library. The grouchy librarian's head popped up like she had been shot. Her smile was sinister as her eyes searched for the guilty offender.

At this point Taneika didn't care if she got tossed out of the library or not. Her eyes hurt, back ached and she was hungry. Every day since her emotional return home, she had been the first one in and the last one out of the building.

With the exception of the first day, Paula had kept her distance as well as her vigil. Her constant presence and the fact that Taren always kept his revolver close was a reminder of why she was sitting here during vacation. Trying to catch up on a mountain-high pile of work from her missed classes was the least of her problems.

Harold Fallings was still free and considered a threat.

Glancing over at her shadow, she caught the twinkle of her eye and the grin partially hidden by her hand. Following the deliberate shift of Paula's eyes to where the librarian sat, she giggled.

The woman's neck was stretched to its limit as she looked over the top of the books on her desk. With her grayish hair done up in a tight bun and her glasses on the tip of her nose she looked like a nanny out of Mary Poppins.

Taneika's stomach growled and in the silence was easily heard. Covered laughter came from several tables further infuriating the woman.

"Quiet, this is a library! There will be no *growling* allowed."

Unable to hide her laughter, Taneika earned the full rebuke of the woman who saw it as her duty to rid the library of riffraff and insufferable youth.

Striding across the room in all her righteous indignation, she stopped in front of Taneika's table. A wicked gleam shown from her eyes, and her tight-lipped frown disfigured her already stern face.

"Out!" She forcibly pointed toward the exit. "Get out and don't come back 'til you can learn some manners."

Taneika stood, picked up her books and walked away from the table.

"Miss, get back here and put these library books where they belong."

She turned around and stared at the librarian, who was standing with her feet spread, hands on her hips like a drill sergeant. Taneika's arm rose in the air with a clinched fist. Slowly the middle finger pointed to the sky.

Laughter and clapping broke out from the other students as Taneika turned back towards the door.

Once outside Paula joined her and they hugged in laughter. "I will probably be banned from the library for life," Taneika managed. "But damn if it wasn't worth it."

"Congratulations on your engagement," Paula grabbed her hand and gushed happily. "The ring is gorgeous. Are you and Taren going out to celebrate the New Year and New Millennium?"

"No, Taren wants to, but I feel I should stay close to home for the next few nights. Listen, I have to go. Take care."

"Taneika, wait!" Paula ran to catch her. "You're not worried about that astrology prediction are you? You can change a lot of things in your life but not *your* destiny. Don't resist Orion's power."

"The woman who gave me the prediction said the same thing." Taneika thoughtfully pondered the similarity of words. "If it does or doesn't happen, I won't be going out tonight.

Besides, I'm not much of a party animal." She continued on to her car, and as she got in, gave Paula a half-hearted wave.

* * * * *

Taren was waiting for her as she pulled up. She got out of the car and ran to the house, giving him a kiss.

"Short day?" He wrapped his arms around her, nuzzling her neck.

"I got tired of sandwiches and my idea of fast food is something I have to chase. I'm starved." Even though it was daylight, she started shedding clothes as she walked through the house.

"It won't be dark for another hour," he advised.

"I'll be careful." Picking up her knife as she went out the door, Taneika sprinted across the opening to the trees. Half an hour later, she found the tracks of an elk, driven from the high country by the harsh winter snow.

The young bull was feeding on the lower branches of a tree as Taneika drew closer. Hunkering down in the snow, she mentally prepared herself to attack the huge animal by herself. The burning in her chest and the momentary veil across her eyes surprised her. She had crossed over. Leaping to her feet, she ran with the full power of the wolf.

The startled elk turned to flee but was too late as Taneika plunged the knife deep into his side. Nine hundred pounds of frightened, whirling flesh slammed into her and sent her flying through the air. Quickness and pure instinct saved her from the pounding hooves as the elk charged.

In a flurry of snow, deadly feet and slashing horns, a gray blur joined the battle, attacking the animal's hindquarters. The elk turned to defend against the attack and Taneika leaped, plunging her knife into its neck and slicing through the jugular vein. As she and the wolf circled, staying clear of the flailing hooves, which even in the last throes of death had the power to break bones and even kill, the elk collapsed.

After the first fresh meat she had had in days, Taneika sat back against the elk and sighed. Lobo's mate lay down beside her. A dull pain caused her to gasp as her blood began to mix with the blood from the elk. Rolling in the snow for several minutes she was amazed. Although she still bled, it was over and the pain had vanished. The bleeding and the hunger afterward remained, and apparently, weren't going to change. She turned back to the carcass and buried her face in the hot meat.

Taneika used her knife to cut away a large portion of meat. With a full moon brightly shining in the eastern sky, she threw the bloody slab over her shoulder and headed home.

* * * * *

Lobo lifted her head, her ears erect and alert. Leaping to her feet, she turned in mid-air. Using all four paws to propel her across the hardwood floor, she slid to a crashing halt at the back door.

'Woof.' She scratched at the door trying to open it.

Taren turned the knob and laughed at Lobo's sudden use of her leg. *The little faker.*

Lobo hit the door, forcing it open and ran towards the trees.

Taren waited at the window for the assurance Taneika was home safe. He should be with her but knew she wanted to be alone and remove the gore from the hunt.

Since saying goodbye to Songbird, Taneika had been distant. Several times he had found her sitting in a trance, seeking guidance from the spirit world.

Damn. I could use some of her spirit guide's help myself.

The lights came on in her kitchen and a few minutes later, the bathroom. Going into the living room, Taren sat down and turned on the television. Fireworks lit the sky over New York City ushering in the New Year.

Taren leaned his head against the back of the couch and closed his eyes. His mind went over the events of the past couple of months. Their paths had crossed, joined and were now detoured on an uncharted road.

Where does this path go? It doesn't matter; I'm committed to follow it to the end...

* * * * *

Taneika stepped out of the shower and wrapped a towel around her hair. Walking into the living room, she found both wolves staring at the couch. Their ears were laid back and their tails were lowered and slightly curled to the side in full alert.

They can sense I am here, but they can't see me. Taneika heard the words in her mind. *You have discovered many things in your journey, my child. Do not be afraid of the night, for it is your friend.*

Go now, my child; use the truths that you have discovered to prepare yourself, for the hour approaches quickly and even now stands at the door.

The wolves relaxed and she knew her spirit guide was gone. Looking at the clock, she was surprised to find what had seemed like only minutes had been almost three hours. *What truths have I found?*

Taneika ran to the kitchen and grabbed the slab of elk meat. Sinking to the floor she began to greedily devour it.

It started as always. The burning in her lungs, her heart felt as if it were going to be torn from her chest and a veil of darkness over her eyes. Only this time, the darkness blinded her as she doubled over on the floor.

In the midst of the darkness, through the veil of agony, she heard the words. *Accept this change; do not resist the power of the Hunter.*

Black searing pain erased all further thought as she rode it to its crest. Every joint was being ripped apart. Her legs became as rubber, unable to rise and flee from the living nightmare. The air in her lungs sent a scream bursting from her lips.

Responding to her scream, Lobo and her mate gave a low wavering howl. Backing up in fear with hackles raised, their tails tucked tightly between their legs, they stood ready to attack the hideous beast writhing on the floor.

The pain died away and she turned back to the elk. As she ate, Taneika snarled and snapped viciously at the lesser wolves in her pack, warning them to keep their distance.

Bolting up from the couch where he had fallen asleep, Taren's heart was gripped in fear at the scream that woke him. It couldn't be classified as human.

Taneika!

Taren ran to the door, nearly tearing it off the hinges as he threw it open. Missing the last step, he rolled in the snow. Finding his footing again, he started towards her house. His foot broke through the top crust of hard snow and he fell. Clawing and fighting his way forward it seemed the snow was alive, fighting against him to prevent his reaching her side.

Why did I leave her alone? Why didn't I insist to be with her?

"I'm coming, love. Don't worry, I'm coming!"

The door exploded open and the glass shattered. Taren came to an abrupt halt, face to face with a snarling wolf. With lips curled exposing long gleaming teeth, the wolf crouched. Two other wolves stood in the archway between the kitchen and living room. They were submissive, acting like rebuked children, a typical reaction of a wolf pack beta member.

Taren jumped off to the side as the wolf sprang past him and through the open door. The other wolves moved across the room and followed.

Horrified, Taren stood in Taneika's kitchen. There was a small portion of meat on the floor and a pool of blood. A white bath towel lay on the floor. The dark crimson stain slowly spread across the cotton material. Picking up the towel his eyes caught the sparkle of something shiny in the blood at his feet. Reaching down, he picked up Taneika's engagement ring.

Taren blindly groped for a chair before his legs, which threatened to buckle, no longer held him. Staggering into the chair, his mind tried to grasp the evidence before him, and couldn't.

Yet, it had happened.

Why, my love, why? Resting his head on his crossed arms, he held the ring tightly locked in his closed fist.

Taren wept.

A wispy transparent form of a woman stood in the door. She watched as great racking sobs shook his body. *Weep not, my son. You have accepted her, stood by her and loved her. Do not, I pray thee, falter now.*

Taren raised his head and searched the empty room. His eyes locked on the ghost-like figure in the doorway.

You are the only one she has to give her the comfort, acceptance and the love she desperately needs.

Heartbroken and defeated, her sudden appearance gave him an avenue of release for his anger. "This is your fault, you meddling *witch*."

Amused laughter filled his head.

I assure you, I'm no witch. I have no power to change the future.

"You could've warned her earlier to prevent it," he clamped his jaws tight. Taneika's ring cut into the palm of his hand. "Why didn't you? What's going to happen to her, to our child?"

I cannot interfere with destiny in matters of the heart. I have no power over life and death.

"You hypocrite. Aren't you interfering now?

Your heart has already decided. Take the time to listen.

"Damn you! Answer my question!" Taren jumped up and slammed his fist against the cabinet.

Silence greeted his tortured mind.

"Please. Don't leave!"

Listen to your heart.

The words were but a fading whisper on the wind.

Taren slid slowly down the face of the cabinet and rested his head on his bent knees. *A wolf. I made love to a fucking wolf. Of all the normal women in the world, I not only pick one that turns into a damn wolf, I get her knocked up and ask her to be my wife.*

"Why?" His tortured cry pleaded for an answer.

In the midst of all the turmoil within his mind came a still, small persistent voice, which refused to be silent. The answer was from the heart, sent out with every beat.

You love her.

* * * * *

A cold wet nose nudged his arm. Taren raised his head and stared into the eyes of a wolf. "Lobo?"

She whined and licked his face.

Taren lightly stroked the wolf's head. "Taneika, where is she, girl?"

'Woof.' Lobo barked in his face and started for the door. She stopped, turned her head around and barked again. 'Woof, woof.'

Taren climbed stiffly to his feet and shivered in the cold.

"Okay, girl, let me get my coat." Taren jogged to his house, grabbed his coat, flashlight, strapped on a pair of snowshoes and followed Lobo into the forest.

Lobo's mate rose out of the snow as he approached the remains of an elk. Taneika lay on her side in a fetal ball. Dried blood was smeared over her body, the snow red-streaked where she had rolled, trying to cool her skin. Dropping to his knees beside her, Taren checked for a pulse at her wrist. It appeared strong and normal.

Taneika moaned, "Go away."

"Is it over? Are you back to normal?"

"Normal," she turned onto her back. "When have I ever been normal?"

"Come on, love, time to get you back to the house. If I have to, I'll carry you."

"Leave me alone." She swatted his hand away. "Better that I'd died, than to have it happen again."

"Dear, open your eyes. Look at me."

Slowly, she opened her eyes. Concern, compassion and most of all, love radiated from his face. "How can you stand to look at me after last night? Why even bother finding me?"

His hand smoothed her matted hair, his touch gentle and loving. Taren lowered his head and touched his lips to hers.

"Because, my dear, I listened to my heart, and with each and every beat, it says your lovely name. Although my mind still rejects what happened, in my heart, I love you and have accepted what and who you are. We must be going, love; it will soon be light."

"I'm hungry. Let me gain my strength and we can go."

With her body replenished, she walked beside Taren back to the house. The wolves followed several steps behind.

Taneika stepped out of the shower and dried her hair. Her womb felt heavier today. Feeling movement from the baby surprised her. It should be several more weeks before that happened.

Looking up, she found Taren watching her with tempered desire.

"Are you afraid to make love to me, worried I might change completely? No need to lie, my love, I can see it in your eyes."

Going to him, she wrapped her arms around his waist and laid her head on his chest. "I'm worried too. I see the desire in your eyes and my own comes alive. But, until I can control the wolf and learn to keep it at bay…" She sobbed against his chest.

"Shh, don't cry, love." Picking her up he carried her to her bed and gently rocked her to sleep. "We'll work it out." *Somehow.*

Chapter 23

Taneika pulled into the parking lot and got out. The first day back after winter break found students running to make it to class on time or standing in small groups catching up on the latest gossip and news. Looking around the campus, she didn't see Paula. As she walked across the pavement, a hawk landed in the tree above her and let out a screech. She had the ridiculous feeling that the hawk was watching her.

As the day wore on and still no Paula, Taneika began to get worried. The last class was over and as she stepped outside, the hawk she had seen that morning glided from the tree and circled the parking lot.

Taneika drove home and found Taren, his face white and his hands shaking. "Taren, what's wrong?" She ran to him and wrapped her arms around him. "What's happened? Is it Jeanie? Bill?"

"It's Agent Myers. Two ice-fishermen found her body down by the lake."

"Oh, God! No!" She began to sob. "I talked with her Friday afternoon."

"Dear, you couldn't have. The coroner said she had been dead almost two weeks."

She moved away from him and sat on the low table. "Paula has been at the library every day for the past two weeks. Medium height, dark complexion, black hair just below the collar and almond-shaped black eyes."

"That fits her description perfectly. Must be someone else you saw. They swear it's her body at the morgue." Taren shook his head and with a heavy sigh continued. "I'm the only agent in the area that knew her. Although she had all of her identification on her, they want me to come down and make sure it's her."

"I'm going with you. I'm telling you, I talked with her on Friday in the college library."

Taren drove to town and pulled up at the county morgue.

Taren paused and turned to face her. "If this is the same girl you saw at the college for the last two weeks, don't say a word, look at me and nod your head."

Taren got out and Taneika slid out his door. Walking with their hands clasped in fear and confusion they entered the building. They followed the coroner down an empty hallway and into a room of stainless steel and florescent lighting. In the middle of the room a table stood, draped with a sheet.

The coroner lifted the sheet.

Taren took one look at Taneika's white face and knew that the woman she had seen at the library was the same one that now lay lifeless and naked on the table.

"That's Paula Myers." Taren suddenly felt very tired. Nothing about this case had been normal. Every lead was turning up with dead bodies blocking the way forward. "You're positive as to the time of death?"

"Positive as I can be, within plus or minus a few hours." The coroner covered the face of Agent Myers. "Sorry to have you come in, but we had to be sure."

They left the building in silence.

The screech of a hawk caused Taneika to look up. *You show up at school and now here.*

Raising her right arm level with her shoulder she patted her arm with her other hand.

"What are you doing?" Taren looked up at the hawk.

"If I'm right, that hawk will land on my arm." Even as she spoke, the hawk swooped down and landed.

"Well, I'll be damned." Taren gawked at the bird of prey.

"Taren, dear," she smiled knowingly. "I would like for you to meet an old acquaintance. May I present my spirit guide, in yet a different body?"

You, my child, must learn to control the wolf within, as you control those around you.

The hawk flew off and they watched it 'til it could no longer be seen.

* * * * *

"Are you sure you won't reconsider?" Taren watched as she removed the last of her clothes and dropped them by the bed. "There has to be another way. What if something happens and you can't control it?"

"Don't you see, this is the only way that's safe for both of us?" She stepped closer and lovingly stroked the side of his cheek. "I have to be out there in case I don't have control. There has to be a supply of meat if the wolf is released. I see the smoldering fire in your eyes when you look at me. For your information, I want you just as badly, maybe more. But if the wolf overpowers me and turns on you…"

"Go." He took her in his arms and kissed her. "Take control of the wolf as you have taken my heart. Hurry back to me, love, and be careful. Our enemy is still lurking in the shadows."

The night was clear and bright as Taneika and the wolves traveled through the trees. They found the herd of elk bedded down and slowly circled it. A yearling on the edge of the sleeping herd was singled out and they moved in for the kill.

She felt the wolf begin to stir. *So, you want to come out and play. I am the alpha. You will obey me. I will use your power from within.* The transition was mild as her body adjusted and she felt the new power released throughout her body.

The herd bolted from their beds as the wolves attacked. Startled in the confusion, a late season yearling hesitated a moment too long and was overtaken. Taneika found the tender throat and clamped her teeth around the pulsing jugular vein. The elk's hot sweet blood sent a burst of renewed energy and strength surging through her arms and legs as she wrestled the elk to the ground.

Her body changed as she ate and she rolled in the snow. The other wolves joined her in the romp turning it into a time of play instead of pain.

Peeling back the hide, Taneika ripped off the remainder of the elk's front shoulder and carried it home.

From its perch high in the top of a tree, a hawk let out a screech, swooped down and helped itself to the remains of the fresh kill.

Taneika dropped the meat in the snow outside Taren's back door and turned to the two wolves. "This is mine. You want more, you know where the kill is, go get your own. I plan on being hungry again before the night is over."

Lobo turned on her mate. *Get your nose out of there. That's not me you're smelling.*

He turned away and curled up in the snow. 'Woof.'

Taren watched her walk through the door. Did the sight of her body covered in blood turn him on? Was it the sultry look in her eyes? Or the way she walked towards him, as if stalking her next meal? Whatever the stimulus, it was working.

"Tell me you kept the big bad wolf at bay and now it's our turn to play." He had been waiting in the nude, anticipating her return.

She watched him stand, her eyes riveting on his erection as he walked toward her. "Promise me, my love, if I tell you to go...you will run and not look back." She saw the hesitation. "Damn it, Taren. I've controlled the beast one time. I think I can control it again but I'm not willing to bet your life on it. The first few seconds after the change could be deadly."

"My darling Taneika, I'll go but I won't go far."

Wetting her lips, which had suddenly gone dry, she heard him groan. Placing her arms around his neck, she sprang up and locked her feet behind his waist. Lips met and parted, tongues dueled for access as the heat of passion grew to a fevered pitch.

"Take me...to...the shower." She felt his hard shaft against her and shifted to allow him entrance.

Taren chuckled, "Is my Little Wolf in heat?"

"No!" Taneika moaned as she lowered herself around his length and tightened around him. "Little Wolf is past heat. She's on fire for her mate."

Stepping into the shower, Taren adjusted the water 'til it was warm.

Taneika released him and swung her feet to the floor. "Wash my hair, love." She slid to the floor as Taren reached for the shampoo. With her face resting in the tightly curled hair below his waist, she began kissing his hardened shaft.

"You expect me to wash your hair...ahh...while you're...doing that?" He looked down and saw her wicked little grin as she licked him with her tongue.

"Is Little Wolf's mate not *up* to the task?" she teased.

Taren poured the shampoo onto her hair and began to work up a lather of thick suds. *The only way to wash his woman's hair.*

Unwilling to have him finish before her own need was filled, Taneika worked her way up his body with little love bites and kisses. "Wash the rest of me," she begged.

His hands moved sensuously over her body, slowly working down her back, then her arms. When fingers touched her sensitive breasts, she moaned and arched her back. A whimper of regret came from her as his fingers moved on. Spreading her legs, inviting him to touch and invade her body, her desire was heightened when his fingers lightly skimmed across her.

Taren turned the water off. "All done."

"Done? We haven't even started." Taking his hand, she led the way to his bed.

Bound emotionally together by the chains of desire, the union of their souls was complete with Taren's hardness fully sheathed inside her. At the telltale burning pain beneath her breast, Taneika knew the wolf was awake and had raised her ferocious head.

If the power of Orion set you free, by his power you shall be in submission to me. Lie down, now! She commanded the inner-wolf. *Another time and place I'll let you run free.*

Carried on the wings of passion as autumn leaves caught in a whirlwind, she rose with each driving thrust of his body. His mouth captured hers and drank in her moans of exquisite pleasure. Warmth flooded her as his body stiffened and his eyes flashed open. Their wild smoky gaze revealed the pinnacle of his satisfaction and pleasure at filling her with the essence and power of his desire.

Taneika gasped, the breath in her lungs spilling forth in a low sensual howl as her body responded to his release. Her climax took her over the crest and she felt herself floating in love's sweet embrace.

* * * * *

Early the next morning Taren made his decision. "I don't think Paula's death was a random act. I think she was removed to get close to you. Pack whatever you need, we're going back to the cabin."

"Good, maybe we can stop and have Jeanie check me over."

"Is something wrong? Aren't you feeling okay?"

She heard the concern in his voice and laughed. "Relax, love. I'm fine. I want her to check the baby."

* * * * *

Taren pulled up in front of the clinic. He had received several curious stares at the sight of the two wolves riding in back. For most of the trip, they had their faces to the wind and seemed to take great delight in watching the other cars from his side of the truck.

"Taren, there's no need for you to come in. Why don't you go load the snowmobile and meet me back here?" She stepped out of the truck and told the wolves, "Stay."

"You sure you don't need me to come in?" Taren had his hand on the door.

"Go, I'll be fine." She walked around the truck and gave him a kiss.

'Woof.' *I've got to pee.*

'Woof.' Lobo barked. *Me too.*

Taneika's shoulders sagged. "When Taren stops again you can get out. But you must get back in when he does. No running off."

She went into the clinic as Taren drove away.

"Hello, Taneika," the receptionist smiled. "Taren's not shot again, is he?"

"No," she laughed. "I need to see Jeanie about a natal checkup."

"Congratulations, dear." Her eyes got big with excitement. "Have a seat. Jeanie should be with you shortly."

"Jeanie," the receptionist said as she entered the front office. "Taneika is here for a natal exam. I told her to wait and that you would see her."

"Great. I know she's excited." The joy faded as reality hit her. "*Damn you*, Taren."

"Is something wrong? You look troubled."

"I'm sorry, I can't discuss it."

A few minutes later, another patient left and Jeanie came out to the waiting room. Taneika could tell by the expression on her face that she wasn't entirely overjoyed to see her. *I guess if I was in her shoes, I wouldn't be overjoyed either.*

"Taneika, you can come back now." They walked back to the room in silence and Jeanie closed the door behind them. The apprehension showed in the little worry lines on her face and Taneika felt sympathy towards her.

"So, you're pregnant. Does Taren know?" Jeanie took her blood pressure.

"Yes. He knows everything." Taneika paused. "He's asked me to marry him."

Jeanie gave her a penetrating stare, exhaled tiredly and took the pressure cuff from around her arm.

"I see." Jeanie turned away. "I am having a difficult time with this, Taneika. Knowing that my brother is getting married to a…"

"Wolf," she finished for her. "I don't understand why I am this way…but if Taren can accept me and we can be happy, isn't that enough?"

Jeanie turned back with tears in her eyes. "I hope so…for both of you." She put her arms around Taneika and gave her a hug. "Welcome to the family. I'll help all I can."

Jeanie finished the exam and rolled the sonogram away. She sat on the edge of the table. "The baby appears healthy. Are you sure it's Taren's?"

"Why would you ask that?" She couldn't keep the hurt or the anger from her voice. "I was a virgin. Taren is the only person I've ever slept with."

"By the size of the baby, you're at least four months along." Taneika didn't have to count the months she had known Taren, or the time from her last cycle. "That's impossible, no way!"

"With you, it could very well be possible. Taneika, how many times have you…changed since you became pregnant?"

She sat back stunned, thinking. "I don't know, several times. Only once since I..."

"Since you what?" Jeanie sat up straighter and leaned closer.

"Completed the change." Taneika's voice was low, barely above a whisper.

"Sorry, I didn't hear you."

"Since the wolf inside came out." Taren stood in the doorway. "Is the baby all right?"

"Yes, the baby... Oh God! You mean, she...she..." She whipped her head towards Taren.

"Yes." He watched the color drain from his sister's face and her eyes got large.

"I've got to sit down."

"Sis, you are sitting."

"Oh." She looked down as if seeing the table for the first time. "Right."

"Jeanie," Taren walked over to the table and put his hand on her arm. "You must realize she can't go to anyone else for medical help."

Taren felt sorry for his sister. Placing her in this situation wasn't fair, but what was family for if they couldn't pull together in times of difficulty?

"If you will excuse me a moment." Jeanie walked in a daze to her desk and opened the bottom drawer. Pulling out a pint of whiskey, she unscrewed the cap and drank from the bottle.

"Sis?"

She buzzed the front desk. "Cancel my appointments for this afternoon, and reschedule please. Oh, and take the rest of the day off."

"Are you all right, Mrs. Yates?" The speaker amplified the confusion and sudden worry in her voice.

"Yes...I'm fine. Please lock the door on the way out." She took another swallow from the bottle and recapped it.

Her hand shook as she replaced the bottle in the drawer. "I...I was afraid this could eventually happen but I couldn't bring myself to believe it from a medical standpoint. Of course, I realize the ramifications if she went somewhere else. I'll help you any way I can and I know I can speak for Bill too. Do you two want to spend the night or do you have other plans?"

"We're going up to the cabin for a few days. Not sure how long we'll be there. I stopped by the house and grabbed a snowmobile and trailer."

"Fine."

Jeanie got up and made her way across the floor. "Taneika, at this point the baby has a healthy, strong heartbeat. It appears that when you...when you change it speeds up your metabolism, and the baby's. How much, I don't know. When you come back, I need to know if it has happened again. Now, if you don't want to get caught in the dark, you two had better leave." She gave them a hug and returned to her desk.

As Taren walked out the door behind Taneika, he saw Jeanie reach toward the bottom drawer. Her face was wet with the tears she was unable to hold back any longer.

Chapter 24

While still some distance from the cabin, Taneika spotted a deer. "We need fresh meat." She pointed to the deer as it bounded away.

Taren pulled up and she stripped off the snowsuit. "You go on ahead. I'll meet you at the cabin."

He sat there watching her naked backside running through the woods. Her image stirred his loins and he hoped she wouldn't be long in reaching the cabin. Taren drove on, his thoughts on an evening of pleasure on an old bear rug.

As he pulled up to the cabin, he noticed the tracks but it was too late. Harold Fallings stepped out of the shadows. *Son-of-a-bitch!* Taren took off his helmet and slammed it on the ground.

"Well, well, well...look what we have here. 'Welcome to my parlor, said the spider to the fly.' Figured you'd show up here when the bitch agent didn't show up. Don't try anything, Taren. At this range I don't miss. Turn the engine off and stay awhile."

Harold was standing there with a pistol aimed at his chest. His own weapon was deep inside the snowsuit, hopelessly out of reach. Taren slowly reached over and turned the key, shutting off the engine. A deadly calm surrounded the house. Pure hatred for this man and fear for Taneika caused his heart to pound wildly. Every muscle tensed, waiting for the slightest change to overtake Fallings and get control of his weapon.

"Where's the little wolf-loving bitch? I want to see her face when I shoot your ass. After that, just to let you know, we're going to have a good time before I slit her throat."

Taren forced his features to remain calm against the rage he was feeling. With his last dying breath, he would somehow kill this bastard before that happened.

"What, don't you have anything to say?" Harold laughed. "You cost me a small fortune and I expect to have my pay in flesh. Maybe I'll tie you up and let you watch. Tell me, is she a good fuck?"

Harold's smile was evil as he rubbed his crotch. *Please, God, if I'm going to die, let it be with my hands locked around his neck,* Taren prayed.

Movement in the trees caught his eye. *Stay hidden, my love. Please, stay in the trees.* Without taking his eyes off Harold, he watched as blurs of gray and white filtered through the trees. *I know what you're thinking of doing. Please, don't try it. For God's sake, think of our baby.*

"Go ahead, Taren." He sneered. "Try it. I know you want to." Harold stepped off the porch, the sound of crunching show loud in the deadly silence. "What's the bitch's name, Taren? Teakie, Tanaka, I know it's an Indian name. Taneika, that's it. I think I'll call her *FUCKaneika*." He laughed at his crude joke. "Shame you're not a man, Taren. Then you would know how to treat a whore like her."

Harold's words traveled the distance to where she was hidden. Having worked her way behind him, she summoned the wolf. *My mate's life is in danger. By the power of Orion, be swift in your coming.*

She bolted from the trees.

His heart sank and then leapt to his throat in fear. He wanted to scream for her to go back, that her life and the baby's life were more important. The fear in his eyes must have given him away. Harold smiled and turned his head.

"Time to say goodbye, Taren." Harold raised his pistol.

"No!" Taneika screamed.

Her scream became that of an anguished animal.

Taren watched as thick dark gray hair appeared over her body. Like soft sculptures, clay on a pottery wheel, she collapsed in a billowing cloud of snow, blocking out his view. A snarling wolf exploded from out of the cloud as Taneika continued toward the unsuspecting Fallings.

Taren saw Harold's finger on the trigger tighten.

A terrifying screech sounded from overhead and Harold looked up. Sharp talons ripped into Harold's face and he dropped the gun, trying in vain to dislodge the hawk. His screams became terrifying as the hawk sank a talon into one of his eyes.

Taneika leapt from the ground catching Harold in the chest, her solid weight and speed knocking him down. Instantly her jaws snapped shut, sending her canine teeth deep into Harold's throat.

A blur of gray went past Taren as Lobo joined the battle. She struck, her teeth sinking into the soft flesh between the legs. *Grrrrrr. You have an itch there? Let me scratch it for you.*

Taren stood there in shock. The attack had been so sudden and fierce there was nothing he could do.

Harold's hellish screams faded as Taneika's powerful jaws closed off his windpipe.

Taren watched as blood sprayed from a severed artery, turning the snow around Harold's head bright red. Both wolves shook their quarry 'til there was no more movement. Only the slowing trickle of blood from torn flesh remained of an evil life of greed.

The two wolves released their hold and backed away, blood dripping from their snarling lips. Lobo's mate walked up, sniffing Harold as the last of his life's blood was pumped from his body. Seeing there was nothing else to do, he hiked his leg and pissed.

'Woof!' Lobo barked. *Why did you do that?*

'Woof!' *It beats walking back to a tree.*

Recovering from the vicious attack, Taren squatted in the snow. "Taneika, come here."

She walked over, laid her head lovingly on Taren's leg and licked his hand.

"I don't know if you can understand me, but I hope so. You need to go find your food. I'll be right behind you. Go quickly."

She looked up at him with big amber eyes and whined.

"Go, before you change back and don't have the food you need."

Taren started the snowmobile as the three wolves headed toward the trees.

He had gone several hundred yards from the cabin when he spotted a gray form lying in the snow. Pulling up he jumped off and ran to the still wolf.

"Taneika!"

As he reached the wolf, it sprang from the snow and knocked him over.

"Lobo? You scared the life out of me. I thought you were Taneika. I haven't got time to play games. I've got to get to Taneika."

He started to get up and Lobo pounced on him, rolling him in the snow.

"Damn it, Lobo! Enough." Taren brushed the snow off and climbed back on the snowmobile.

A hard tug at his pant leg and a low growl caused him to look down. Lobo had a mouth full of material and was trying to pull him off the seat. "What the hell has gotten into you?"

Lobo let go of his pants leg and stood in front of the Artic Cat. Putting her front paws on the cowling, she tilted her head from side to side. As if asking, *'Now what you gonna do?'*

Shaking his head in utter frustration, Taren dropped his hands away from the controls and turned off the motor. "All right, you win. I'll stay here."

Time seemed to stand still in the woods. His impatience grew with each passing minute. *Damn, this is ridiculous.*

"Are you laughing at me, Lobo?"

Her ears went up and she turned, running through the woods.

"Finally." Taren started the engine and followed.

He found Taneika, her skin still bleeding, lying next to the deer.

Lobo went up to her and she wrapped her arms around her neck. "Good girl."

Taren trotted over and fell in the snow beside her. "Are you okay, love?"

"Relax, dear. I'm fine." She tore off another chunk of meat and chewed it.

"I suppose it was your idea to have Lobo keep me away?" Taren smoothed her blood-matted hair from her face.

"Yes, I...I wanted to spare you from seeing me change."

"Do you remember what happened?" Taren questioned softly.

"Yes. I was afraid he was going to shoot you. I couldn't let that happen again."

Taking her in his arms, he held her close, rocking her much like he would a child. "Promise me you won't do anything like that again. I couldn't stand it if something were to happen to you."

"I'm fine. Quit worrying."

Taren sat back and looked at her. Something was different but he couldn't place what it was.

Until she stood up.

"My God, dear. You've gained considerably around with waist."

His eyes were large and frightened and she looked down. She felt a distinctive kick in her womb. "I was afraid that would happen."

Taking her breasts in his hands, he felt the increased fullness and weight. "You need to explain it to me then."

"A wolf's pregnancy lasts about two months. Every time I make the switch, even partially, it speeds up my metabolism and the baby's growth."

"Promise you won't do any more changing 'til after you deliver." Taren held her close with his arms around her ample waist. "Sit on the seat while I cut some more meat. Soon as you get cleaned up, we'll head back and let Bill know what's happened."

As they pulled up to the cabin, Taneika looked away from Harold's body.

"Put it behind you, dear. It was him or us and thanks to the hawk's attack, neither of us was hurt." Taren carried the meat in and stirred the coals in the fireplace. While Taneika washed away the blood, he sliced a piece of meat for his supper.

Their meal was eaten in silence and then they extinguished the fire. Taren threw a tarp over Harold and they headed back to his truck.

With the trailer loaded and lashed down, Taneika wrapped her arms around Lobo's neck. "Hey girl, its time you started your own family. This is a good place with plenty of food. You and your mate stay here and I will come back to visit you."

Lobo looked up with sad eyes. *I'll miss you,* she whined.

"I'll miss you too, but you and your mate need to start your own pack."

Will you bring me a pizza when you come back? Lobo wagged her tail expectantly.

"All right, I'll bring you a pizza," she promised.

And a beer? Lobo sat up begging.

Taneika laughed. "Okay, one beer."

Lobo jumped forward on her hind legs and with both front paws on Taneika's shoulders began licking her face. *Oh, thank you*, she barked.

As they pulled out, Taren looked in the mirror. The two wolves were standing side by side, watching them leave.

Taneika curled up beside him and was soon fast asleep. Gently he stroked her hair as the events of the day played out in his mind. *We were lucky today.* He looked at her sweet lovely face.

A hawk flew low over the truck and disappeared into the night.

Thank you for watching over us.

Taren backed the trailer into Bill's drive and got out. The porch light came on and the door opened. "Jeanie said you were going to be up there for a while. What changed your mind?"

"Fallings was waiting for us. You might want to send somebody to get the body. It's next to the house."

"Are you both okay?" Jeanie asked as she came out and stood beside Bill.

"We're fine but I'd appreciate it if you'd check Taneika again. She had a stressful day."

"Sure, come inside. You can spend the night here," Jeanie offered.

Jeanie gasped as Taneika got out of the truck. Taren's warning look of, 'Not now, I haven't got time and I'm not in the mood for it,' flashed in the artificial glow of the bright porch light. She closed her mouth and laid her hand on Bill's arm.

Taneika looked exhausted but what concerned her most was the increase in her waistline from a few short hours ago. Only one thing could have caused it. A complete change of her body over a long period.

"Taren, if this keeps up I don't know how the baby will handle it. This has got to stop." Jeanie carried her medical bag to the bedroom.

"Damn, Sis. Don't you think I know that? We went up there to get away from Fallings, not to confront him."

"Come on, Taren." Bill put his arm across Taren's shoulders and walked with him to the kitchen. "Leave Jeanie to look her over and you can tell me what happened."

Jeanie listened to the baby's heartbeat for several minutes and took Taneika's blood pressure. "Taneika, I want you to get a good night's rest, and tomorrow I'm going to do another sonogram. There's a strong heartbeat and you're doing fine, considering what you have been through. Your baby is bigger than it was earlier today and that has me concerned."

"Don't blame Taren. I had to do it to save his life. The baby will be fine." Taneika curled up on the bed and closed her eyes. "I just need some rest."

Jeanie covered her and quietly left the room. She returned to the kitchen. The anger that had been building over a situation out of control had reached the boiling point.

Taren was sitting with his elbows on the table and his head resting on his hands. She walked up and placed both hands flat on the table as he slowly looked up. "Look, Brother, I know you've had one hell of a day. But you *are* going to listen to what I have to say."

Taren sat up and groaned. Sis was livid. Her eyes were narrowed into little slits and the muscles in her face were taut with anger.

"If you two are planning on getting married before the baby is born then I wouldn't count on a long engagement. It appears healthy but I'll know more tomorrow morning. At noon, the baby was about what a normal fetus would be at around four months. Now, I'm just guessing, *your* baby has aged about another month."

She slammed a hand on the table bouncing the coffee ups. "Thirty days Taren! — In the last seven damn hours! Babies need time to develop their little brains and bodies, which I might add are a hell of a lot more complicated than wolves."

"Will the baby be...?" Taren stumbled for the word.

"Healthy, normal or is human the word you want?" Jeanie sat heavily in a chair. "I can't answer any of them."

"Go to bed, Taren." Bill stood and patted him on the back. "Things will look better in the morning."

* * * * *

Clear sky and a brilliant sun announced the morning. Taren woke to find he was sleeping alone. Slipping on one of Bill's robes, he headed for the kitchen. The rich aroma of freshly brewed coffee greeted him halfway down the hall.

"Morning, Taren." Jeanie smiled and reached for an empty cup. "Did you get enough rest?"

"I...think so." Seeing Taneika sitting naked at the table he could appreciate but he was taken back by the near transparent blue pastel gown his sister wore. It had been a number of years since he had seen that much of his sister.

"Bill had an early morning call. There was an accident south of town." Jeanie handed him a cup.

The rising steam sent wake up calls to his dulled senses.

"We were having girl talk and the time slipped away. I've got to get moving, or I will have patients stacked up all day." Jeanie hurried down the hall to change.

"Morning, my Little Wolf," Taren kissed her. "How are you doing? No problems after yesterday?"

"No," she laughed. "You sound like your sister. You both worry too much."

"Jeanie was saying last night that she thought...."

"...that we should get married, and the sooner the better." Taneika smiled and ran her hand up the back of Taren's leg. "I know. I think I got the same lecture this morning."

Taren felt her fingers slide over his butt and between his legs. He leaned down and gave her a warm kiss that turned hot.

"All right, you two," Jeanie scolded good-naturedly. "This isn't a hotel. I don't do laundry every day. The couch is off limits, it has recently been cleaned and I don't want any cum stains on it. Whenever you're ready, stop by the clinic for a few minutes. I want to do another sonogram." Jeanie swallowed the last of her cooling coffee and with a final wave, dashed out the door.

"Have you thought about her suggestion?" Taren threaded his fingers through her hair. Its soft silky strands sent currents of warm pleasure up his arm.

"Which suggestion are you referring to, the one about the sheets or the early marriage?" Her hand stroked his hard length.

Her fingers were sending red-hot sparks of desire through his body, making speech difficult. "Both," he managed. His body shook as she gently squeezed him.

"I want to be married in the dress my mother made for me, if it's okay. Considering my brother's feelings toward me, I doubt she can make it. Wearing the dress will be like having a part of her there. Yesterday the dress might have still fit." She looked down at her tummy. "It won't now."

Opening his robe, she urged him to step closer. "As to the other suggestion…"

He gasped as she kissed the head of his sensitive, inflamed shaft.

Epilogue

In the early morning hours of May fifth, a white-hot searing pain in her womb awakened Taneika. Her sharp gasp woke Taren from his sleep.

"Hon, what is it?"

"Nothing to get excited over," she hissed between clinched teeth. "My water broke."

"Oh." Taren started to lie down again. "*Your water broke!*" He jumped out of bed and picked up the phone while he was trying to put on his pants.

"Why didn't you say so?" Dropping the phone, he bent to pick it up. Off-balance, having one pants leg on and the other halfway, Taren fell to the floor.

Reaching up, he turned the light on, and Taneika screamed.

The bed was soaked in blood.

Taren felt the panic rise like hot acid 'til he nearly gagged. Frantically he dialed Jeanie's number. *Thank God, we rented a house near Sis last month.*

"I need Jeanie, now! There's blood everywhere!" Taren screamed into the phone.

"Calm down, Taren. She's on the way over right now."

"Thank God." Taren breathed a sigh of relief. "There's blood everywhere. I'm afraid she may bleed to death. She's white as a sheet, Bill. I'm scared to death."

"I've radioed for the ambulance in case it's needed."

Bill's calm voice eased some of the tension. He pulled on the phone cord to give some more slack and laughed.

"What's so funny, Taren?"

"I've got the phone cord inside my pants and riding up the crack of my ass."

"I'm not going to ask how that happened," Bill's laughter joined his. "But I'll be sure to remind you about it every birthday the kid has."

The back door opened and he heard Jeanie running through the house. "Sis is here, thanks."

"I'll be over in a few. Try to remain calm. It may not be as bad as you think."

The line went dead as the bedroom door was flung open.

"God, Sis! Am I glad to see you."

"Taren, get the phone cord out of your ass, I'll need some help here." Jeanie went to the bed to check on Taneika.

"Taren, get some clean sheets." Jeanie put her fingers on Taneika's wrist as she listened to her heart rate and then the baby's. "Slightly elevated which is normal at this time. How far apart are the pains?" She put the blood pressure cuff on check Taneika's pressure.

"About three minutes, maybe four," she answered.

Taren had never seen her sweat before, but as another contraction seized her, beads of perspiration popped out on her brow.

"Whatever you do, you have to keep control of the wolf." Jeanie finished stripping the bed and helped Taren spread a clean sheet under Taneika.

"Do you understand me?" She looked into Taneika's pain-glazed eyes. "You have to stay in control."

"Maintain control. Yes...I understand." The contraction passed and she fell back on the bed.

A siren broke the silence of the night and grew louder.

"Tell the ambulance crew to stand by outside for now." Jeanie instructed.

Jeanie slipped on the latex gloves and began a closer inspection. "Well I have some good news. There doesn't appear to be any fresh bleeding."

"Where..." Another contraction gripped her; she latched onto Jeanie's arm with one hand and a fist full of sheet in the other. "Where did all the blood come from?"

"In your case, Taneika. I'd have to say from the baby." Jeanie saw the concern and fear in her eyes.

"I don't think there is any cause to worry. It has never hurt you and I don't think the baby has been affected either. I believe you passed on the wolf genes to the baby. Every time you changed, the baby did too. The only way you have of getting rid of the wolf enzymes is through the skin. It would be the same with the baby."

"So," Taneika said thoughtfully. "The baby is like me."

The pain from another contraction washed over her. The agonizing cry of labor escaped from her throat.

Jeanie checked the time from the last one and checked her progress. "You don't do anything slow, do you?"

"What do you mean?" she hissed through gritted teeth as the wave crashed and she could breathe again.

"Remember try to breathe. Focus through the pain. You're less than two minutes apart and almost fully dilated. You're going to have your baby real soon." She wiped Taneika's brow with a damp cloth.

"Taren, get the hell in here!" Jeanie checked the blood pressure and began to worry. Knowing the baby was due, she had reviewed the charts from the test they had run such a short time earlier. Taneika was near the edge.

"Taneika, control. Focus on your control. I know you can do it."

"*Taren!*"

"I'm right here, Sis. No need to scream." He saw the worry in her face. Jeanie's eyes were large, like a deer's when caught in the headlights of an approaching car. Some of the fear that Bill had displaced outside returned.

"Sis, pull yourself together, 'cause I sure as hell can't do this." Taren picked up Taneika's hand.

"I'm here, love. I won't leave." He felt her plus racing against his fingers. "You have to focus, dear. Be in control of the wolf."

"It wants to…"

Her hand clamped down on his like a vise, grinding bones together.

"*Come out.*"

"Taneika," Jeanie bathed her forehead and the cloth came away with a slight pinkish color. "You are on the edge. Please don't slip over."

"I," she was breathing heavily now. "Won't…just get the…damn thing out of me."

"Squeeze my hand, love, when the pain hits you." Taren took over the wiping of her brow.

"You did this to me. I'll squeeze it all right. I hope I fucking break it."

"What are you going to break?" Jeanie asked in laughter. "His hand or his dick?"

"Bothhhh!"

"The baby's coming. Breathe, Taneika, maintain control. The head is almost there."

Wave after excruciating wave of pain swept through her. She felt the wolf raise its head. "Damn you!" she cried. "Back on your *chain*."

Taren exchanged a worried glance with Jeanie.

"Okay, Taneika, the head is clear." Jeanie rotated the baby's shoulders. "Push! That's it. Just a little more."

With one final push, she screamed and her baby was clear.

"Congratulations, you have a baby girl." Jeanie felt Taneika's brow.

Taneika's smile was brilliant through the pain. Tears of joy ran down her cheeks.

"Taren, grab some wet towels. I'm afraid she crossed over." Even as she spoke, Taneika's skin started oozing blood. Jeanie looked down at the baby in her hands and watched in awe as her skin began to bleed also. There was a difference. The baby didn't feel any warmer than a normal newborn would feel.

Wrapping the baby in a soft damp blanket, she handed her to Taneika.

"Taren, give me those towels. Do you have any fresh meat? Never mind, of course you do. Bring Taneika a roast or something. I won't sever the cord 'til she gets her strength back."

He hurried from the room and ran to the fridge. Bill was in the kitchen helping himself from the pot of coffee he had made. "Well?" he asked.

"It's a girl."

"Congratulations, Taren." Bill slapped him on the back. His smile was wide and genuine, but his eyes held a question.

"She's normal."

"Thank God for that." Bill sighed.

"Well, as normal as her mother is anyway." Taren picked up a couple of large portions of meat and carried them back to the bedroom.

A few minutes later Bill knocked on the door. "What shall I tell the ambulance crew? Do you need them?"

"No," Jeanie answered. "Tell them thanks but the situation is under control."

"Okay. There's a couple here waiting. They *claim* to be the grandparents of the baby."

Taren looked at Taneika and then Jeanie. He received a blank stare from each. Taneika's eyes opened wide. "Oh my...!" Her hand flew to her mouth. "Remember, I'm adopted."

"Yes, but I thought your mother…."

"Yeah, me too." Taneika interrupted Taren and looked towards the door.

"First, I need to cut the cord and clean you up." Jeanie finished the task and helped Taneika into a gown.

"Show them in…please."

Taren walked hesitantly to the door. With his hand on the knob, he looked at her. "You sure?"

Afraid to trust her voice, she nodded. Taren opened the door and motioned the couple to come in.

With their hands clasped in warm affection, they walked towards him.

The woman was beautiful, young, too damn young to be a grandmother of anyone.

With a long face and graceful neck, her skin shone like polished alabaster and her hair was as black as a raven's wing in the sun. Her stride was smooth and confident like that of a queen.

The man claiming to be the grandfather couldn't have been much older than Taren. Strong, broad shouldered with a narrow waist, he would command attention wherever he went. His hair was the color of wet sand and lay like the waves of the ocean. Set inside his rugged face with a solid square cut jaw, penetrating eyes of crystal blue mirrored the happy smile he wore.

Taren stepped cautiously aside and let them enter.

"Taren, Taneika, we just had to stop in and see our granddaughter."

"If you will excuse me." Taren stepped between the couple and the bed. "You seem to have us at a disadvantage. We don't know who you are. What right do you have coming in here and making this claim?"

"If you will allow me the opportunity, I will try to explain. My name is Artemis, this is my beloved Orion. I am Taneika's birth mother."

"I—don't understand." Taneika paused. "I was told my mother was a wolf."

Artemis smiled. "In body, yes. That is true. Tell me, *my child*, did you not encounter an old Indian fortuneteller? Taren, is there a scar on your leg where you were shot? Were you not also aided in your fight against evil by a hawk?"

"Artemis and Orion?" Taneika questioned. "As in Greek mythology?"

Artemis laughed. "My child, it is only a myth as far as Orion dying. Having only wounded my beloved, I acted as if he were dead. Knowing my brother, Apollo would never allow us to be together. Afraid my brother would take matters into his own hands and kill him, I placed Orion out of my evil brother's devious hands and nurtured him back to health."

"But what, I mean that doesn't...I'm confused." Taneika confessed.

"Every twenty years, Orion is allowed to return. We have one day where we are allowed to meet and share each other's love. Fortunately for Orion, today he was allowed to be present for a child's birth. This is the first birth of a child or grandchild he has been able to attend since that tragic day when I was tricked into shooting him.

"Now, my child, if we could but give our daughter a hug and hold the dear child for a moment...? We must be leaving."

"My dear Taneika." Orion moved around the bed. "It does my spirit good to be here today." He leaned over and gave Taneika a kiss on each cheek. "May I? Please?

Taneika felt confused and disoriented as she looked into Orion's face.

"Relax, my daughter. For I would rather be confined to the heavens for eternity than see hurt come to one hair on this precious head."

Hesitantly, she handed the baby to Orion.

"Have you thought of a name for the child, my dear?"

"Let her be named after one of your stars in the heavens," she looked to Taren for approval.

"You do me great honor. Let her be called Mintika.

"Oh, what a beautiful girl you are, Mintika. My heart swells with pride to hold you. I am the mighty hunter and yet, my little one, you have captured my heart. Look, Artemis. Isn't she the most beautiful baby you've ever seen?"

"Yes, dear, and if you don't let me hold her, all I'll get to do is look at her," she scolded good-naturedly.

Artemis took the child and held her to her breast. Kissing the top of her head, she softly spoke. "Mintika, granddaughter of the gods, be filled with wisdom and grace. Let love and mercy rule your life. Kill only what you shall eat. Be careful of life, for it is precious and soon lost." She held the baby close to her face and kissed her on both cheeks before handing her back to Taneika.

"Now, we must leave you." Orion smiled sadly. "You have only to look to the sky at night to know you are loved."

Orion and Artemis kissed them goodbye and left as quietly as they had arrived.

About the author:

Romance Author, R Casteel, retired from the US Navy in 1990. He enjoys the outdoors, loves to Scuba Dive, and is a Search and Rescue Diver. With twenty years of military service, which included experience as flight crewman, search and rescue, and four years as a Military Police Officer, it is of little wonder that his books are filled with suspense and intrigue.

As to his ability to write romance, Gloria for Best Reviews writes "I had thought Leigh Greenwood was the only man who wrote wonderful romance...I was wrong...Rod Casteel is right there too!"

Mr. Casteel lives in his hometown of Lancaster, Missouri and would love to hear from you. You can write to him c/o Ellora's Cave Publishing at 1337 Commerce Drive, Suite 13, Stow OH 44224.

Also by R. Casteel:

The Crimson Rose

Texas Thunder

Mistress of Table Rock

The Toymaker

Ellora's Cavemen: Tales from the Temple II

Why an electronic book?

We live in the Information Age—an exciting time in the history of human civilization in which technology rules supreme and continues to progress in leaps and bounds every minute of every hour of every day. For a multitude of reasons, more and more avid literary fans are opting to purchase e-books instead of paperbacks. The question to those not yet initiated to the world of electronic reading is simply: *why?*

1. *Price.* An electronic title at Ellora's Cave Publishing runs anywhere from 40-75% less than the cover price of the <u>exact same title</u> in paperback format. Why? Cold mathematics. It is less expensive to publish an e-book than it is to publish a paperback, so the savings are passed along to the consumer.

2. *Space.* Running out of room to house your paperback books? That is one worry you will never have with electronic novels. For a low one-time cost, you can purchase a handheld computer designed specifically for e-reading purposes. Many e-readers are larger than the average handheld, giving you plenty of screen room. Better yet, hundreds of titles can be stored within your new library—a single microchip. (Please note that Ellora's Cave does not endorse any specific brands. You can check our website at www.ellorascave.com for customer recommendations we make available to new consumers.)

3. *Mobility.* Because your new library now consists of only a microchip, your entire cache of books can be taken with you wherever you go.
4. *Personal preferences are accounted for.* Are the words you are currently reading too small? Too large? Too...**ANNOYING**? Paperback books cannot be modified according to personal preferences, but e-books can.
5. *Innovation.* The way you read a book is not the only advancement the Information Age has gifted the literary community with. There is also the factor of what you can read. Ellora's Cave Publishing will be introducing a new line of interactive titles that are available in e-book format only.
6. *Instant gratification.* Is it the middle of the night and all the bookstores are closed? Are you tired of waiting days—sometimes weeks—for online and offline bookstores to ship the novels you bought? Ellora's Cave Publishing sells instantaneous downloads 24 hours a day, 7 days a week, 365 days a year. Our e-book delivery system is 100% automated, meaning your order is filled as soon as you pay for it.

Those are a few of the top reasons why electronic novels are displacing paperbacks for many an avid reader. As always, Ellora's Cave Publishing welcomes your questions and comments. We invite you to email us at service@elloracave.com or write to us directly at: P.O. Box 787, Hudson, Ohio 44236-0787.

Printed in the United States
25312LVS00003B/61-363